THROUGH TITAN'S TRAIL

The Fabled Quest Chronicles

Book One

AUSTIN DRAGON

Well-Tailored Books

Copyright © 2018 by Austin Dragon

All rights reserved. No part of this publication may be reproduced, distributed, or transmitted in any form or by any means, or stored in a database or retrieval system, without the prior written permission of the publisher.

Published by Well-Tailored Books, California

Through Titan's Trail
(Fabled Quest Chronicles, Book 1)

978-1-946590-81-7 (paperback)
978-1-946590-80-0 (ebook)

http://www.austindragon.com

Book cover design by Humbert Glaffo

Printed in the United States of America

This is a work of fiction. Names, characters, places, and incidents are the product of the author's imagination or are used fictitiously. Any resemblance to actual persons, living or dead, events, or locales is entirely coincidental.

CONTENTS

Chapter One 4
Chapter Two 10
Chapter Three 15
Chapter Four 23
Chapter Five 37
Chapter Six 42
Chapter Seven 47
Chapter Eight 61
Chapter Nine 82
Chapter Ten 103
Chapter Eleven 129
Chapter Twelve 143
Chapter Thirteen 148
Chapter Fourteen 184
Chapter Fifteen 191
Chapter Sixteen 220
Chapter Seventeen 247
Chapter Eighteen 253
Chapter Nineteen 258
Chapter Twenty 270

Once upon a time...

The known world of Pan-Earth, or the Lands of Man, was divided into the major continental regions of Larentia, Gondwana, Oceania, Laurasia, Baltica, Avalonia, and the uninhabited Borea. Of all the Seven Empires, however, it was only Avalonia, at its northernmost tip, that possessed the sole legendary gateway to the realm of the Magical Lands. Men had passed through the gateway in the millennia since its discovery in search of adventure and, later, riches—a gateway created by the ancient Titans themselves.

Long ago, before the dawn of man, fae, and beasts of light and darkness, was the Age of the Titans. They were gigantic humanoid beings of such size that their heads reached high above the clouds into the heavens. According to myth, a Titan known as the Maker of All Mountains was so devastated by the death of his beloved, he walked the entire circumference of Pan-Earth, dragging his fabled weapon, the Star Slayer, upon the earth. He inadvertently carved a massive valley, before he killed himself by leaping off the world to disappear into the void of space. This valley, cut through not only the known world, but every other realm, was known as Titan's Trail, and the Avalonia gateway was its entrance.

Every three years, the northwestern lands of Avalonia became the starting point of the Kings' Caravan—or simply the Caravan. Some twenty years ago, the Kings of Xenhelm began their royal ritual journey attracting men—royal, noble, and commoner alike, farmer and knight, apprentice and warrior—from every corner of the Lands of Man. It was a year-long journey like no other through unimaginable dangers, mortal and magical, by day and night, all for one reason—to obtain the limitless riches of its final destination—the magical kingdom of Atlantea. Most brave men would never risk such a venture filled with danger and death, even with the protection of the Caravan. However, there were plenty of men who would and gladly did so under the auspices of the Four Kings.

Caravan's Row was the name given to that final road to the gateway, which wound through four main settlements. The journey even here was long and lonely. Many would die along the way, never to fulfill their dreams of beholding the Magical Lands, victims of robbers and marauders. So much sacrificed before even leaving the Lands of Man, possibly forever, as those that left on Caravan were never heard from again. The rural town of Hopeshire was the first of the settlements of Caravan Row.

The Fabled Quest Chronicles begin.

PART ONE

THE LANDS OF MAN

CHAPTER ONE

Hobbs

"The Caravan shall give me a new life beyond my most fantastic daydreams!"

That was what the boy had declared a mere two days ago. Now, his lifeless body lay off the side of the road, his throat slit and his eyes empty. Hobbs stood for a while, quietly, sadly looking at a life that would never be. The boy was no more than sixteen and, despite his eagerness to join the Caravan, would never become a man. His barefoot body was stripped of all clothing, save his tattered leggings. It was a fate that could have befallen any road traveler without a weapon or armed escort. Hobbs came out of his contemplation and began to walk again. No man should be denied a proper burial, but the Row was too dangerous for such courtesies.

The settlement was called a town, but it was only a market. Merchants came from near and far to take advantage of the triennial pilgrimage of the Caravan to Goodmound's Castle. The dirt road that stretched from Hopeshire to Goodmound was called Caravan's Row and catered to the influx of men who hoped to be hired and join the Kings' Caravan out of the Lands of Man for the treasures of the fabled land of Atlantea. It was those riches that drew men, like the boy, from all corners of Avalonia and beyond. Many would die, like the boy, before the Caravan even began its royal journey from Goodmound.

Hopeshire was the official first point of Caravan Row, but unnamed settlements had been hastily erected all around it and grew in size every year. The food, supplies, and services sold were cheaper than Hopeshire but lacked the quality. Most Caravan seekers simply ignored these settlements with their gaggle of bossy road merchants until they arrived at Hopeshire proper; some would wait until they reached Ironwood or even Goodmound's Castle before purchasing a single item. However, the market would make plenty of money and trade from the desperate, foolhardy, and uninformed. As the boy had found out with his life, thieves and killers were also attracted to these settlements and towns, looking for easy prey to rob of their money, food, supplies, and clothes—even if it meant murder.

Much of the settlements were filthy. Well-worn tents and rickety wagons lined the road on either side, with people and livestock everywhere. Hobbs had found a spot next to one of the larger and more presentable tents, which offered good protection as its merchant employed a few guards to watch both the tent and goods inside. It was here that Hobbs had first met the boy, who was curious, helpful, and good-natured—virtuous traits anywhere else but here. They had shared a friendly conversation as they ate their meager food, nothing more than days-old slices of bread, as they watched newcomers pass through for Hopeshire.

He was here for the same reason—to find a party to join. Ordinarily, there would be no settlements, but three months prior to the Caravan's arrival, the first settlements appeared, expanded, and would remain until a month after the Caravan had passed through to fully capitalize on late-comers. The anticipation and excitement were palpable in the air. As the time of the real Caravan neared, the crowds would grow. Some, who would never join the Caravan, came simply to watch great warriors pass by in their splendid armor, men on fearsome warhorses, or maybe even catch a glimpse of a sorcerer, or at least a pretender draped in a dark hooded cloak. Who and what was seen by day would become the stories at night around the fire or candlelight while enjoying supper, for those fortunate enough to have it.

As he took a bite of his bread, Hobbs remembered warning the boy to be cautious as to who he approached for work and never go anywhere alone. It was advice that, sadly, the boy had not heeded. Many risked all they had for the Caravan, but even the most optimistic of men knew that most of them would never make it, and they accepted the fact that many would die along the way. But even the small chance of success to possess unimaginable treasures, to travel through the mythical Titan's Trail to see the Magical Lands beyond man, made it a risk worth taking for Hobbs and the thousands of men who arrived every three years to try. The only way possible for the average man to undertake such an incredible journey was to join the Caravan.

Hobbs lifted his head to gaze at the sky; the sun was setting. His middle-aged body became more intolerant of the cold every passing year. He shifted his backside upon the ground where he sat for his daily vigil. The passersby were fewer as the night approached, and soon he would have to rise to seek shelter someplace, anyplace he could find, until he returned early the following morning. Settlements such as these were known for thieves, bandits, and marauders, who took advantage of the lack of security, leaving behind a wake of corpses.

The day was not particularly productive as the men who had passed through were not especially remarkable, good or bad, in any way. None of them were well-equipped, possessing anything of value, or worthy of battle. None of them inspired the loyalty that true leaders did. He had to wait until such men did pass because only through them could he ever hope to join the Caravan.

His mind recalled the dead boy again. Hobbs saw himself in the lad, how he could have ended up if life had taken a different path when he was starting out at that age. He remembered a time when his bare feet would never touch the open soil. Those were the days when he was in service to the Theogar Royal Family as master of the household and counsel to King Theogar. Hobbs had charge of the entire palace household of servants. His once high status was long gone, replaced by the bleakness of hunger, loneliness, uncertainty, and despair. A fortnight ago, he traded his last trinkets of value for the money to sustain himself with the food and water he could find and afford, but his last pieces of coin would be gone soon. Now, every day was spent huddled on the dirty roads, waiting. There were many others in the settlements outside Hopeshire with neither house, nor master. However, he would not allow his dignity to sink any further than it had. He never sought out handouts and never resorted to thievery as many around him had. In his heart, he was still a man of nobility, even if his king's house was stripped from him many moons ago. Though hunger and cold were his only constant companions, he would rather starve—rather die—than lose his dignity. All was far from lost, though.

Avalonia was governed by many kingdoms and ruled by many royal families. As with the nature of men, those kings and queens could be like an angel, demon, or all in between. To survive, people often had to affiliate themselves with a kingdom, whether they desired it or not. Hobbs had found a good king, but that good king and his territory was no more. The people of Theodor would become part of new kingdoms, but the nobles, like Hobbs, who served a defeated royal family, could not. They had to escape far away to where none knew them, and becoming a noble again was unlikely.

However, while his former nobility to a defeated king and lost kingdom—despite his years of loyalty and service—were a black mark to other kingdoms within Avalonia and beyond, it was a clear advantage here. Royals of kingdoms chose their nobles based on familiarity; they steadfastly mistrusted outsiders, regardless of their breeding. For a royal or noblemen assembling a party for the Caravan, his qualifications would be highly sought after. He simply had to find the right party before danger could find him. It was the chief reason Hobbs wanted to venture beyond Avalonia. The Lands of Man had lost their appeal to him. Why confine oneself to a single realm in the world, when there were so many others?

◆◆◆

In real towns and cities, the setting of the sun meant that the drinking and rollicking would soon commence at the local taverns. In the settlements, merchants would quickly pack up their tents, goods, and livestock to head back into town for the night. Very few, if any, would remain outside the towns. It was at night that most of the evil in these parts occurred. In Avalonia, the only creatures to fear were men.

Hobbs decided to wait another few moments, careful not to walk back to town alone.

"What is your name, sir?" a passerby asked.

"My name is Hobbs, sir," he replied, looking up. His frayed blanket doubling as a hooded cloak slipped from his head. He grabbed and situated it back in its place as he watched the inquirer. A man's dress, more so than any facial expression or stance, would tell if his purpose had good or ill intentions.

The hooded stranger was dressed commonly but cleanly, with two covered, sheathed swords strapped to his cloaked back. His dark hair was groomed short, and he had no other hair on his face that Hobbs could see. The man's boots were clean but well-worn. Then Hobbs saw the man had his own watchful companion—a large gray wolf dog that watched him intensely. The regal animal was slender in form with a smooth coat, uncharacteristic of other wolf dogs.

"I have seen you here on this road for the last few days," the man said. Hobbs lowered his head. "I say it not to criticize, only as an observation. Are you hungry?"

"I do not need any charity, sir. I seek only honest pay for honest work."

"I do not offer charity. I seek information and can pay for your time." Hobbs looked up again. "If you are hungry, I can pay for a meal and we can talk a while."

"Yes, I am agreeable to that, sir."

"Good. You know the town better than I do. My dog and I shall follow."

Hobbs rose from the ground and wrapped himself in his blanket, more to hide his dirty clothes from himself than the stranger. He hoped he did not appear too shabby with his thinning graying hair, and unkempt facial hair, but the stranger had sought him out. His nearly fifty-year-old frame remained stout, despite the many days of existing with little food. However, for the moment, it seemed this was about to change. He led the way to town.

CHAPTER TWO

Traveler

"What do you know of Kings' Caravan?" the stranger asked. "There are many eager to join, however, I would wager I could barely find a half-dozen men who have any true grasp of the danger involved."

Hobbs had not had a full meal in a long time, and was thoroughly enjoying his hot bowl of soup filled with chunks of meat. He had almost forgotten what it felt like not to be hungry. "You are absolutely correct, sir. If you are asking why any man would undertake such a journey, the answers range from greed to foolishness. If you are asking why I would, the answer is simple: As a former noble, it is the only possible chance for me to regain my status. Status and purpose are of more value to me than any wealth. For that, I would risk all."

"All that you possess and more may be the price, though."

"I would be content with that outcome, sir, as I would have tried. If I remain here, as I am, I die here as I am. I go on the Caravan and there is a chance of more—just a chance." Hobbs took another large spoonful of his bowl of soup; he hadn't yet touched his cup of ale.

Within the tavern, Hobbs could see the stranger's face clearly—dark brown eyes, sharp features, and carried himself with confidence. To

Hobbs, the man seemed more a just noble than a warrior in search of a royal quest.

"How long have you been in this place?" he asked Hobbs.

"I arrived a fortnight ago. Then I stationed myself along the Row's road. I hear it is no different than any of the settlements that sprout up for the visitors the Caravan brings—and all will disappear afterwards until the next three years. Men come from all across Avalonia, and I have heard some come from as far as Baltica and Larentia, every one of them flocking for the lure of untold riches."

"Or unspeakable death," the stranger added.

Hobbs had employed many men when he was a noble of Theogar Castle. The stranger was questioning him in the same manner as he had done so back then. Hiring men for a royal household was a matter of honor—the honor of the king. Hiring men for the Caravan would be a matter of life and death.

"I have seen unspeakable death before, sir. It took everything from me, except my own life. I do not fear it, so I can risk seeing it again, if it may mean a better life. Even a life not as good as what once was is better than what I have now. In this world, most die only a short distance from where they were born. I chose a path different than most. I chose to embark on a journey, no matter how far, no matter how dangerous, that will be no more than a dream to most men."

"Do you feel you know enough about the dangers of this journey?"

Hobbs managed to smile. "I need not, sir. *You* possess that knowledge and that is not what you need. You need men. Men you can trust. Men who are capable."

"Men who can govern such men."

"I once governed the entire household of a royal family."

"I suspected as much."

"How so, sir?"

"I am an observer of the nature of men. You have a noble bearing that you try to conceal, but it is apparent nonetheless."

"I doubt I will ever appear as a commoner, though I was born as one."

The stranger took his cup of ale in his hand. "Tell me of your life as a nobleman."

"I was the steward to the Theogar Royal Family for nearly thirty years," Hobbs answered. "I started when I was a young man. I oversaw the internal palace affairs of both the king and queen. I governed the entire household of servants, nearly fifty, and had a personal staff of a dozen reporting to me."

"What happened?"

Sadness returned to Hobbs's face. "They were killed. King Theogar's so-called allies decided they wanted his land more than his alliance. The king was exceedingly old and had no male heirs. His only daughter was married to one of his hated enemies of the region. The king's allies, his lifelong friends, made war against him. I, by chance, was on errands in the surrounding cities when they attacked. I returned to see the castle in flames. They slaughtered everyone, including the king and queen, and all of the army. There was no one left alive except for me and a few others also fortunate to be elsewhere at the time. As the highest member of the king's staff to remain alive, I had to escape, or they would have also killed me. I had nothing more than the clothes on my back and had to quickly sell my horse for money. They would be looking for anyone fleeing on horseback not by foot. I escaped...but I escaped to a life less than any commoner in my former kingdom."

The stranger saw the emotions were still raw for Hobbs. The dog watched Hobbs too, sitting on all fours, stationary but alert. The stranger took another sip from his cup.

"Tell me about any caravans you commissioned."

"My duties as steward of Theogar included assembling and equipping all the king's expeditions and travels, throughout Avalonia. Also, I personally commissioned and commanded the servants and bearers of our only expedition, some five thousand men, to the farthest ends of Baltica. I may not know the particulars of the Kings' Caravan firsthand, but I do know of the management and morale of caravans through unknown lands."

"The journey, even with the power of the Kings' Caravan in the lead, will be, again, extremely perilous. I can offer food, shelter, clothing, protection, and supplies. Money will also be offered at any stop we make, whether it's these last cities of Avalonia, or any along Titan's Trail once we cross over into the Magical Lands. The final city of Caravan's Row is Last Keep and will be the only opportunity for those of the party to decide if they wish to continue forward with the journey, including yourself. Many do not. However, I will follow the Caravan and not stop until my foot touches Atlantean sand."

"Do you seek treasure, sir?"

The stranger hesitated. "Of a kind. But wealth is not my motivation, though I do not fault any man who does. How does this prospect strike you?"

"I am extremely interested, sir. For me, it would be equal parts wealth and adventure that are my motivations. That, and I have nothing left here for me. My king and his family are gone. I have no other roots to keep me here. I have always dreamed of what lies beyond Avalonia. To see an elf, other fairy-folk, flying horses, giant birds, the fantastic fowl and fauna of magical lands, sea and air. I have heard of them in stories all my life. My life has been one of routine, privilege, and safety—nothing more. I wish it to be much more, though I do firmly recognize the danger of which you caution."

"Good. Those chosen for my party must be mindful of the honest facts of the journey and what the Caravan is and is not," the stranger emphasized. "We may see lands no man in Avalonia, or anywhere in the Lands of Man, will ever see; we may have a chance for great treasures at the end, but so many join the Caravan with notions more fanciful than the lands we will cross. This is a long, back-breaking journey with only occasional comfort and more frequent danger, sometimes terror. The Caravan through the Titan's Trail is more hope than reality. A hope of a life of bounty. Our real chances of success will be marginal, and that is generous talk on my part. There are far safer dangers on Pan-Earth to confront than these."

"I am not concerned, sir. Your sword hand and your dog will protect us."

The stranger laughed. "I like you, Hobbs. I know enough to be willing to take the chance. It is a gamble for each of us, which is often the way of life. If your mind is set, there's no need to delay. I hire you as my first. There's much to accomplish before the Caravan arrives. Are you ready?"

"I am, sir, save one thing."

"What would that be?"

"Your name, sir. I don't know your name."

"Call me Traveler. That name suits me better than any other in this world."

CHAPTER THREE
The Dog

Hobbs realized he was smiling; he had not done so in ages. Deep within him was the emotion of hope again. Traveler finished the last of his meal, a quick gulp of the last of his ale, and stood from their small table. Hobbs followed him out of the tavern into the night; the dog took up a position right alongside his master. Hobbs had to almost double-time to keep up with them.

"Are we not going to find shelter for the night, sir?"

"Yes, but not in town."

Hobbs followed Traveler and his dog back the way they had come. It was nice to have a warm meal in his belly, but as they walked, Hobbs had to tighten his blanket cloak around his body as the chilly night wind blew. It was nearly dark, but carefully placed pole torches fixed along the sides of the roads lit up the main dwellings throughout the town. Outside, men loitered in groups, conversing and drinking, some singing, others engaging in horseplay. They continued past them deeper into the night where the settlements used to stand only a couple of hours before.

Hobbs glanced back at the townsmen, who watched them disappear into the night with surprise. He felt the apprehension grow within himself as they moved further from town. Traveler continued to move quickly. Hobbs glanced at the dog; the only light was now from the moon above. The dog glanced back at him periodically, his gaze locked on Hobbs's eyes. There was a strange intelligence to the animal that Hobbs had never seen before.

"Here," Traveler called out.

Hobbs could not see a thing but heard a sharp sound, then a small ball of fire appeared near the ground. The dog was standing across from him, watching closely. Hobbs could see the fireball diminishing as a fire grew on a torch in Traveler's hand. His new master walked to him and handed Hobbs the torch.

"Build a larger fire while I erect our shelters."

It was something Hobbs had done many times before. There were many rocks about, and plenty of hay and kindling from the daily back-and-forth of merchants and their livestock. By the time Hobbs finished the campfire, Traveler had erected two small tents, each with the front open and close enough to the heat of the flames.

"You take this one and the dog and I shall be in the other," Traveler said.

Traveler then gave him a wool mat for the ground and a thick fur hide for his blanket. Hobbs moved into his tent to settle in and, with the heat of the campfire, was able to get comfortable quickly. However, they were but two men and a dog. If robbers were about, their flame could draw them from many miles away.

"You do not have to be concerned, Mr. Hobbs," Traveler called out from his tent. "The dog will be on guard for any unwelcome visitors, so you can sleep soundly. You have much to do tomorrow."

"Yes, sir."

Hobbs peeked out and saw the dog resting his head on his front paws, but his eyes were alert. With that reassurance, Hobbs lay down and covered his head with the blanket. He knew fire-lighting well, and the campfire would last them until sunrise. He was not a wildly optimistic man, but he had had his share of luck over his lifetime and chose to be optimistic now. Besides, he thought to himself, full stomach, warm sleeping, a dog on guard, and a new employer—today was a good day. And tomorrow, he would find out if they were really a step closer to joining the Kings' Caravan or if the night before was no more than this. There were no other sounds to be heard besides the fire, which made it easy for Hobbs to fall fast asleep.

◆◆◆

Hobbs sat in the chair with his eyes closed, a blade at his throat. A man with a thick mustache and beard deftly moved the blade across Hobbs's neck under his chin.

"There you are, sir," the barber said as he wiped Hobbs's face and neck clean with another warm, wet cloth.

Hobbs opened his eyes and rubbed his face, chin and neck. "A fine shave," he said with a smile. There was no mirror to see himself, but it did not matter.

The barber quickly passed a comb through Hobbs's graying dark hair again. The man wore a dark green tunic with a leather belt over his leggings as was custom for the resident menfolk of Hopeshire. These legitimate tradesmen and merchants came into the settlements before dawn and left for Hopeshire proper just before sunset. "You appear as you should," he said. "Some men carry hair on their face well. You are not one of those men."

Hobbs laughed. "I agree." He gave the man coins for the service.

The barber's shack was near the stables and the bathhouses. Hobbs rubbed his face again as he exited and saw Traveler waiting for him. The dog was crouched beside him and, as always, watched Hobbs's every move. *Will the animal ever warm to me?*

"Much better," Traveler commented.

"It has been some time since I have been able to feel my bare face." Hobbs found his hand still touching his face and neck.

"Get yourself some new clothes." Traveler threw him a pouch of coins. "One set to wear and one set to carry. Most important are the boots. They need to last over many leagues, over different terrain, difficult terrain, dry and wet. What weapons have you handled?"

"I've handled most but have mastered none. I left such tasks to others."

"On Caravan you will have no such privilege. When your clothes and boots are obtained, carefully choose a weapon you can handle well."

"Must it be a blade?"

"There are many weapons in the world, Mr. Hobbs. Choose the one that suits you. If you cannot thrust a blade through a man, then buying a blade would be of no use. There are many alternatives. Make the decision. I do not need to be consulted, but remember there may be many times on the Trail that the only thing between you and the person who wants to kill you will be that weapon you choose."

Hobbs weighed the pouch in his hand. "Sir, where would you like me to go to purchase the items?"

"Mr. Hobbs, go where you must in town. Return to the tavern when you have finished, and I will find you."

Traveler did not wait for him to respond. He walked away with the dog following. Hobbs shook the pouch again, somewhat surprised his new employer would place such trust in him so soon.

Hobbs felt as if he had been reborn in his brand new clothes. He was tempted to purchase the brightest colors he could find, as was common in Theogar, but they were going to lands where conspicuousness, he wagered, could spell death. His appearance was that of a nobleman again in light and dark blues for his new tunic, pants and hooded cloak. He had bought a pair of brown boots that seemed to be made for his feet alone and of the highest quality. He changed out of his rags behind the market area and tossed them in a pile to be forever forgotten. A squalid man of the road pounced on them. The man's face brightened and he laughed, jumping in joy at his fortunate find of new clothes. Hobbs had been so eager to rid himself of the rags, but they brought genuine happiness to this man. He felt a brief pang of shame, but if he had offered the man the old clothes, they would not have been accepted out of suspicion.

The large establishment was outside Hopeshire and guarded by armored knights. It was filled with every manner of weapon one could purchase. They were probably not as good as those to be found in Ironwood or Goodmound, but he needed something immediately.

"I would like a small dagger for my waist," Hobbs said to the proprietor, who had been watching him with arms folded. "Something to keep an opponent at bay, slash them, if need be."

The proprietor turned to lead him to a section of the huge cluttered tent. He, too, was dressed in mostly greens. Hobbs amusingly watched the heavyset man grab a large, flat wooden box and kneel on the ground as he opened it. It was filled with daggers of all shapes, sizes, and metals. He looked up at Hobbs.

Hobbs pointed at one and the man handed it to him. The weight felt good in his hands. He gripped the metal of the curved blade and touched the sharp point. Hobbs nodded at the man. He closed the wooden box, returned it to its place, and stood. The man grabbed a pile of sashes and belts from a corner and threw it on a nearby table. He found the one he wanted and picked up a belt with a small attached sheath. Hobbs took it and the dagger fit in it perfectly.

"I also need a weapon for close combat but not a sword."

"Ax or mace?" the proprietor asked.

Hobbs hesitated.

"Too noble of a man for violence? If you cannot use a weapon, then do not carry one. Let your opponent simply kill you."

"That would not be desirable."

"Crossbow?"

"No. Close quarters."

"Staff?"

Hobbs smiled. "Yes, that may be it. A solid quarterstaff."

He led Hobbs to another part of the tent. What Hobbs saw was a paltry display of sticks. Hobbs turned to the man.

"This is for the Caravan, sir," the man said to Hobbs. "Men come in here for weapons, not walking staffs."

"Fighting staffs do exist."

"But I don't offer any."

"I will simply purchase the dagger and belt."

"Wait, I may have one."

The man walked to the center of the tent. He searched through a small pull-cart filled with swords and pulled out a thick dark-brown staff.

Hobbs smiled. "Yes, that will do."

◆◆◆

Hobbs waited at the same tavern where he first had his meal with Mr. Traveler. He stood with his back to the wall with his hands folded and resting on the top of his staff. Every day more men appeared, those passing through and those who waited on the roads to watch passersby.

"Good morning to you, Your Highness." A swarthy man stood in front of Hobbs with an unsheathed sword gripped in his left hand. Fortunately, from the man's dirty white tunic and dark pants, both either borrowed or stolen, Hobbs surmised the man was not a professional thief. Though that did not matter, as even an amateur with a sword could strike him down.

There was nothing unusual about a nobleman in the settlements but not one completely alone as he was. Thieves and killers took notice of all. It was still early enough in the day that passersby were relatively few, and from a brief glance of the road, Hobbs knew there would be no aid from anyone should his exchange become violent.

"How many coins can you afford to part with this day?" he asked Hobbs. "I am very hungry, and so are my men. Give me all that you have, and I may let you live."

But Hobbs's new clothes and employment had restored his self-confidence. "Sir, I have faced more dangerous men than you will ever be. Go about your business."

The man's face turned red with anger by Hobbs's lack of fear.

"I will kill you then and take it from you," he sneered.

"I doubt that. Go about your business, I say."

The man started breathing more heavily as if he were summoning the courage to attack.

The dog appeared. Hobbs and the man noticed it standing in the road almost at the same time. It was only a few feet away, but neither had seen it approach. It stared at the man with cold black eyes. Hobbs noticed the animal seemed bigger somehow and the nails on its paws were more like claws.

"That is my companion," Hobbs said as he returned his attention to the man. "Shall I give him the command to rip you apart?"

The man did not take his eyes off the dog. "I will kill you, but I am happy to kill it first," he said with false bravado.

The dog snarled, showing its teeth—pure white, long, slender, sharper than any dagger. The man swallowed hard. Hobbs casually turned his head to look again. *The dog was bigger.* It slowly lowered its forelegs to the ground as if it were readying to pounce; the muscles tightened. The man gripped his sword tightly but began to step back with a growing expression of panic. Suddenly, the man's eyes widened, and he screamed, dropping his sword and dashing away.

Hobbs watched the man disappear in the distance, then glanced back at the dog. For a brief moment it seemed as if the dog's head was something else, but it was facing away from him. He blinked, and it seemed that it was in normal form again, as if he had imagined it all—

but he knew he had not. The dog stood fully upright on all fours in front of Hobbs.

He stared at it for a while. The wolf dog did not break his gaze either. Hobbs had seen many dogs in his life of all breeds and dispositions. This animal appeared as a dog, but it was not, and Hobbs would never treat it as one ever again.

CHAPTER FOUR
Lady Aylen

Traveler appeared, approaching from the road. Hobbs remained stationary with his back to the wall; he knew the animal would not be far from his master. The dog ran up to Traveler and followed.

"Good, Mr. Hobbs. You are appropriately dressed for Caravan," Traveler said. "However—"

"However, sir?"

"I see a dagger on your belt, but I see no weapon."

"My staff—"

"Is not a weapon. I have other more important tasks for you, but see to it that when we leave Goodmound's Castle you have a weapon and not a walking staff. If your mind is set on a staff, at least, obtain one of metal that can foil a blade, preferably a spiked one so you can do more than just defend."

"I shall see to it, sir."

"I do recognize, Mr. Hobbs, that you are a noble accustomed to running the household of a royal palace and have never had to deal with issues of personal security. But until we have the luxury of having the additional men to assign as your personal guard, that task falls to you. Besides, any man should at all times be able and ready to defend his own life and shouldn't need to be a trained warrior to do, so as is natural for any living being."

"I shall have the proper weapon, sir."

"Then I shall not mention it again. We leave for Hopeshire. There you shall finally be able to exercise those dormant skills of yours again in assembling our Caravan party. You cannot be my steward without first selecting and retaining able men."

Hobbs smiled and said with a twinkle in his eye, "Sir, I shall only choose those men who possess proper weapons."

"Very good. Perhaps, if we are truly fortunate, they will even be able to help a certain person we know with that matter."

Hopeshire was not far. As Hobbs followed, he studied the two long swords strapped to Traveler's back. They were not only sheathed but their handles were covered so there were no clues of their quality or provenance—only that one was much larger than the other. Hobbs had seen many knights in his day, many swordsmen—from exceptional down to cowardly. Only the gifted ones carried their weapons in such a fashion. The smaller sword he would grab and, because of his skill with the blade, would suffice to defend against most attacks. However, it was the larger sword that was the true weapon.

They would travel the main road of Caravan Row through the settlements to Hopeshire, then Ironwood, and finally Goodmound's Castle. Hopeshire was where parties acquired their men; Ironwood, their best weapons, and sought to officially join the Kings' Caravan. It was here that only the best of the best had a chance to be chosen by the Four Kings to join the Caravan. From Goodmound, the fortunate set out on the perilous, year-long journey to the fabled Lands of Atlantea. The unfortunate returned home to try again to join the Caravan in three years.

Traveler was a man who walked briskly with long strides and seemingly little effort. Hobbs oftentimes had to quicken his pace or be left behind by his new employer and his dog. He viewed them as a duo of fearsome power, while he was a man with nothing more than a stick as a weapon, so his eyes remained vigilant for anyone following or approaching from behind or their flanks. Many others also walked to Hopeshire, but many more from every station of life stood along the sides of the road. They approached the bustle of Hopeshire proper with a population eager for selling and trade.

"Mr. Hobbs," Traveler called as he stopped and turned.

"Yes, sir."

"We part company here until dusk."

"What shall I do, sir?"

"Your task is to hire the needed servants for our party. Remember that the men you hire may one day save your life, or not, depending on your choice here today. Focus your hiring on the servants—bearers, cooks, fire-lighters, laborers. Any fighters we need will find us in Ironwood and more in Goodmound's Castle, but do not turn away any suitable ones you may come across."

"I understand, sir. Where will you be, sir?"

"We will scout the path to Ironwood."

Hobbs raised an eyebrow. "Sir, that is a journey unto itself—"

"We will see you at dusk."

Traveler turned, and the dog followed him down the road.

Hobbs looked around. Danger on the roads of the settlements was plentiful, but at Hopeshire, nonexistent. Thieves and marauders looked for easy prey, but they would find neither here; Hopeshire was an orderly town. With his new clothing, he looked like the nobleman he was, so he would play the role to his advantage, without the pomposity.

Hopeshire was typical of a town on a busy through-way, businesses of every kind were what any visitor would see on either side of the road and as far off into the distance as one could see. Also, like any market, proprietors did not wait for customers to enter their establishment—they came out on the road or sent their employees to aggressively fetch them. Hobbs found himself bombarded by multiple people, young and old, all at once, like every other passerby, for goods and services.

However, Hobbs had his attention focused on those who waited along the roads watching passersby, not to sell goods or services, but to find their next master, as he had done, for Caravan. Already, many men were watching him.

"You there, lad," Hobbs said to a young man.

"Yes, sir," the man acknowledged. He had been sitting on the ground near the road but quickly stood. Hobbs guessed that the boy was around eighteen at most. He was surely one of the biggest and tallest men he had ever seen.

"You eat well."

The young man nodded. "I try not to, sir."

"I want you to walk down the road to that goat tied there, then walk back to me."

He looked at a goat tied by rope to a small cart and looked back at Hobbs. "Why should I do that, sir?"

"Why are you here, young man?"

"To join the Caravan."

"Then do as I ask, and I shall see if I can use you."

The young man was holding up his large trousers with both hands to keep them from falling. He breathed in hard and hobbled down the road to the goat, stopped to look back at Hobbs, then walked back to him. There was clearly something wrong with his feet, and despite his efforts to hide it, he was in pain with every step.

"Was that good, sir?" he asked.

"No, it was not," Hobbs answered. The boy's smile disappeared from his face.

"Where are you from in Avalonia?"

"I am not from Avalonia. I am from Baltica."

"That is a very long way to come."

"It took me three years to get here."

"Alone?"

"I was with others, but…I am alone now."

"I cannot use you, lad. In fact, if you go on Caravan in your state, you will die." The tone in Hobbs's voice was cold.

"I have to go, sir."

"No, you don't. Go find work. Save your money. Buy yourself a rope to hold up your trousers. Train and prepare yourself. In three years' time, you will be ready. You may not want to listen to me. Youth are always reckless, but I tell you this, so you don't end up as another boy I met on this journey. He too was not ready but would not listen. I saw his corpse the morning before today, his throat cut, his clothes and shoes gone. I do not want you to be that boy. You are young, and there is time. There will be another Caravan."

The young man remained quiet as Hobbs began to walk away. Hobbs stopped and said with compassion, "Lad, have a healer see to your feet. I know my words sting, but it is better that you wait until you are ready for this dangerous journey than be cast off at Goodmound's Castle, or worse, be one of the first to die on Caravan." Hobbs turned away to continue his inspection of the men that waited along the Row.

"What do you require, sir?" a scraggly-bearded man asked. He wore a full cloak that completely covered his body to the ground. He could have had armor underneath, or tattered clothes. There was no way to tell.

"What do you offer?" Hobbs asked. "I am in need of men, but I am not a sorcerer who can read minds."

"I have two other men in addition to myself. They are bearers, and I am a fighter."

"What weapon?"

"Swordsman." He pulled his cloak back to reveal he was wearing a knight's armored breastplate. A sword's hilt peeked out from the back.

"Where are your men?"

The swordsman gestured to two men who were standing across the road. Hobbs studied the men and nodded. "You three will do."

"Does your employ include shelter and provisions?"

Hobbs gave him a suspicious look. "You came for Caravan with neither?"

"We did, but let us just say that others deprived us of both in the wee hours of the night."

"Robbed?"

"Not, I promise, due to any lack of fighting prowess on my part. It was simply a matter of inattentive night sentries—they fell asleep. Thieves are very experienced on the Row, as I am sure you have learned."

"Yes, I have. I need many bearers, so your two men are fine, but if you claim to be a swordsman, then you must prove yourself."

"Against who, sir? Yourself?"

Hobbs laughed. "I am no swordsman. My master, of course, who commands our party will decide."

"That is fair enough, but what compensation do you offer now for us to join your party? You would not be the first to hire men from the Row, and then conveniently have no money to offer."

"My master returns at dusk. He will inspect those I have assembled. If he concurs, you shall be compensated. You do not honestly expect me to give you money now for you to run off. You are not the first to pretend to be hired from the Row only to be a clever group of thieves who pocket a naive nobleman's money."

The swordsman laughed. "I hope your master is as honest as you. We will join. All my men."

"All?"

The swordsman gestured, and twenty more men stepped forward.

♦♦♦

There was no place within Hopeshire proper to gather with the growing congestion of passersby and visitors. Hobbs waited with the men—more than a hundred in all—about a mile outside of town in open grassy fields. Hobbs was pleased with his assemblage. Traveler would have solid choices to pick from. Where they waited, they were not alone. Others were doing the same, gathered in groups smaller or much larger than theirs. As he scanned the many groups, Hobbs wondered just how large the Caravan would be when it left Goodmound.

"A woman," Bilfreth, the swordsman, said to Hobbs.

Hobbs turned to see a large party approach. A noblewoman, of a strong and confident demeanor, a headband around her hooded navy cloak, galloped along on a white horse. At her side was a maiden in a black hooded cloak on a brown horse. Behind them rode three armored knights. On foot, followed three columns of knights, many horse-drawn covered wagons, and another three columns of knights at the rear. Hobbs estimated the party numbered well over a thousand.

"Do you know who that is?" Hobbs asked.

"They say her name is Lady Aylen."

"She is known already?"

"Mr. Hobbs, you can count all the women who have attempted to go on Caravan on one hand, so yes, *any* woman would be known," Bilfreth answered with a smirk.

They had been seated around campfires passing the time with casual conversation. Traveler returned before dusk as he had said. Hobbs noticed him first and stood. The other men around him began to stand as well. As Traveler approached, Hobbs observed the condition of his employer's clothes—dirt, dust, even moisture—all signs of a significant trek. Did he really go to Ironwood and back? Impossible. Or was it? His wolf dog companion's gray coat was unblemished.

"Mr. Hobbs," Traveler said, "I see you have assembled men for me to inspect."

"Yes, I have, sir."

"Let us begin with the most important. Where are your fire-lighters?"

Hobbs was not expecting him to ask for such a menial position first. He looked at the men and did not know what to say. Two men stepped forward.

"We can do that task, sir," one of them said.

"While I talk to the rest of the men, I want you to build a roaring bonfire." Traveler turned and pointed across the road. "There."

"There, sir?"

"Yes."

The two men looked at each other and reluctantly started toward the other side of the road.

Traveler's expression turned angry. "Are you going to start the fire by magic? Where are your tools?"

"Sir, we do not know how you want us to do what you ask."

Traveler looked back to Hobbs. "Mr. Hobbs, your task tomorrow is to find a dozen fire-lighters. It may seem trivial, but when we are out there on the Trial, you will realize that a simple fire can be the difference between living to the next day or freezing to death, or worse, being snatched away by some creature of the night. Out on the trail, a campfire will be as welcome a sight as the sun in the heavens."

"I take your last point well, sir, but we have never heard of the magical lands having such extremities of temperature," the swordsman said.

"This is Bilfreth, sir," Hobbs added. "He is a knight by birth."

"Yes, but I work for no king or queen, carry the flag of no kingdom, except by choice. I am my own master, as I am sure is true of most of the noble knights on the Row."

"As for the magical lands, that is true, Mr. Bilfreth, but we must first cross that threshold. Do you know how many miles we must travel from Last Keep in Avalonia to reach the magical lands?" Traveler asked.

Bilfreth thought for a moment. "I do not know, sir."

"Three hundred miles." The revelation surprised the swordsman. "You are a swordsman?" Traveler asked him.

"Yes, sir."

"Mr. Hobbs, give him your staff."

There was a gleam in Bilfreth's eyes as he took the staff. Traveler walked further down the road and turned. Everyone knew what was about to happen, and for the hundreds of men who had spent all day sitting, smoking pipes, and waiting, the coming entertainment was welcome. The men moved in around the giant circle that Traveler was drawing in the dirt with his boot. He unstrapped both swords from his back and placed them on the ground at the foot of his dog then walked to one of the men and touched his quarterstaff.

"May I?"

"By all means, sir." The man gladly parted with it as he grinned, looking at his colleagues around him.

Traveler walked into the circle with his staff and focused his gaze on Bilfreth. "Shall we begin?"

"What are the rules, sir?"

"The man who gets in three clean strikes first."

"Are you sure you wish to do this, sir? I am quite good."

"Show me. Do not tell me."

Traveler held his staff with both hands as a sword. Bilfreth did the same.

Hobbs looked at the gathered men. Competition of any kind elicited smiles and laughter and would contribute to the stories of the night and the next morning.

Bilfreth did not delay and thrust his stick at the center of Traveler for a quick strike. He hit his mark, but Traveler knocked the stick out of his hand with a solid whack, sending it flying through the air, and returned the move, hitting him in the center of his breastplate.

"Good start," Traveler said, "but you lowered your guard. Not all opponents out there will be felled with one thrust."

Bilfreth recovered his staff from one of the men. "I seem to have been cursed by the spirit of my old swordmaster. He, too, would lecture me on form. When I was a child, I would let him defeat me, so I could end the lesson quickly. Later, I would defeat him as quickly as possible, so my ears would not drop to the ground from his incessant nagging."

"Will it be the former or the latter?" Traveler swung so hard at Bilfreth's head that the man barely had time to react, but he did, blocking it. Immediately, Traveler tried to knock the staff out of Bilfreth's hand again, but it remained tightly held. "Good." Traveler sliced at Bilfreth's shoulder causing the swordsman to jump recklessly to the side. Bilfreth struggled to gain his balance as Traveler attacked wildly, but he blocked each blow.

Bilfreth fell to the ground but kept his sword poised. Traveler lunged at an angle Bilfreth could not block, striking him solidly in the stomach. The swordsman leapt from the ground, lunged back, and hit Traveler in the ankle.

"Good," Traveler responded.

"No, sir, that blow does not count."

"If it were a real sword and you struck a man in that manner would it be fatal?" Traveler asked.

"Possibly," Bilfreth replied.

"You are too modest. You would have severed his Achilles tendon and he would no longer have the use of that foot, so if that blow did not end his fighting, you would have certainly struck him again. Like so." Traveler lunged again and struck an unsuspecting Bilfreth in the center of the chest.

The men laughed and clapped. Bilfreth acknowledged defeat with a nod.

"Mr. Hobbs," Traveler said as he handed his staff back to its owner.

"Yes, sir."

"Mr. Bilfreth is a swordsman."

The men laughed.

"Yes, he is, sir."

"What are the positions of the other men?"

"Cooks, sentries, and bearers, sir."

"Take the men into town and find lodgings." Traveler tossed him a bag of coins. "The rest for drink." The men cheered. "Tomorrow, I want men specifically for fire-lighting. Mr. Bilfreth?"

"Yes, sir."

"We may be in Hopeshire and you and the men may be under a solid roof, but that does not mean security for the men should be any different than if we were out there on Caravan. Understand?"

"I do, sir. Not all of us will be drinking tonight."

"Good. Mr. Hobbs, the dog and I will join you tomorrow morning."

"Perhaps you can join the men for drinks," Bilfreth added.

"Perhaps."

Traveler and the dog walked back into the town.

"How long have you been with him, Mr. Hobbs?" Bilfreth asked.

"He hired me only a day ago."

"Where is he from?"

"I do not know. But we do know more about him today than we did yesterday."

"That we do, Mr. Hobbs. He is a swordsman too."

Hobbs smiled. "A good one."

♦♦♦

Lady Aylen and her maidservant came from around the corner on horseback, riding to a stop in front of Hopeshire's largest tavern. It had two levels, its own connected stables, and its own contingent of guards. She dismounted, handed the reins to her maidservant, and brashly walked up the steps into the establishment. Everyone took notice of her as she passed through to the back.

A stout man in a wide-brimmed felt hat stood from his table.

"Lady Aylen."

"Squire. Where are they?"

"Upstairs, m'lady."

He led her up a flight of stairs, where it was quieter, but a crowd of men were gathered. She brushed past a gray wolf dog, glanced down at it, then looked up at its master—a hooded man with two swords strapped to his back. The squire gestured her to a table to sit.

Lady Aylen instead pulled its chair away and leapt onto the center of the table to use it as a platform.

"Good day, men. Many of you know I rode into Hopeshire with a party of fifteen hundred men. We will be joining the Caravan with that force at Ironwood. I have all that I need in men, weapons, and provisions, save one thing—a guide and trailmaster. I have never in my life been comfortable with another knowing the path to my destination, even if it is the noble Kings' Caravan. However, the difficulty in hiring such a person is recognizing whether he truly knows the lands or if he is telling tales."

A man raised his hand. "I know the way to Atlantea, m'lady. I've been there and back many times—or was that my dream?"

The men laughed at him.

"Yes, it may be amusing, but whomever I choose for the position will be richly compensated. I will be downstairs and await all legitimate inquiries."

Lady Aylen jumped down from the table effortlessly and went the way she came with the squire following.

She took a seat at a secluded table by herself with the squire standing guard a few feet ahead. On a stool next to the stairs, her maidservant sat watching the men who came down the stairs talking amongst themselves. Most left the tavern, but one group walked to the back.

Her maidservant watched the men pass the squire and take a seat in front of her princess. Another man descended the stairs, a swordsman, with a gray wolf dog following. He glanced at her, as did his dog, as he passed towards the back.

"You can wait here," the squire said to Traveler.

Traveler listened to the men speak with her. She questioned them and, after a few minutes, smiled and waved them away. They rose from the table. The squire stepped aside to let them pass and gestured for Traveler to go through.

"Sir, please do not waste my time," she said to him without looking him in the eyes.

Traveler sat. "I do not intend to, m'lady." His dog nudged him. She watched him turn to his dog and after a moment turn back. His eyes narrowed as he stared into her crystal-blue eyes.

She looked at both animal and man. "Is something wrong?"

"Why would *you* need a guide?"

"I do for the reasons I stated upstairs."

"A guide through Faë-Land?"

"Yes."

"Faë-Land Minor and Faë-Land Major?"

She did not respond as she looked at him with surprise.

"I am sorry, m'lady. I am unable to assist you after all."
He rose from the chair and left with his dog.

CHAPTER FIVE
Gwyness

Lady Aylen stood from her table and watched them leave. Her maidservant approached.

"M'lady, has something happened?" Gwyness asked.

"I found our guide and trailmaster."

"M'lady, we have five guides."

"No, he is the one."

"But he left, m'lady. Why?"

"Gwyness, find him. When we leave for Ironwood, I expect him to be amongst the men."

"How can I manage that, m'lady? I am not an enchantress."

"I shall leave it in your capable hands." Lady Aylen walked past her maidservant. "We need to return to camp. We have an early start."

Gwyness was agitated but followed.

♦♦♦

It was common for a party to commandeer an entire tavern, and that is what they had done. Sprawled throughout the establishment the men rollicked with mugs of ale, and some had taken to drinking straight from barrels. Hobbs laughed with his meager cup moving through the men.

Outside, Bilfreth and four others maintained a vigil at the front door of the tavern.

A young woman in a black cloak rode up on horseback. She had dark eyes, dark hair, and fair skin. "Good day, sir."

"Good day, mistress," Bilfreth replied.

"Do you know a man who carries two swords on his back and has a large wolf dog as a companion?"

"I do."

"May I speak with him?"

"He is not here but will return tomorrow morning."

The answer distressed her. "Then I have no choice but to return."

"I saw you with Lady Aylen's party."

"Yes, I am her maidservant. Do you continue to Ironwood?"

"We do."

"May I help, mistress?" Hobbs stood at the entrance to the tavern.

"No, sir. I have the information I need. I shall see you at some point in the future. My lady would like your party to join hers."

Hobbs was surprised. "I will relay that offer to our employer."

"There is more, but I will speak with him directly. Good day, sirs."

"Good night, mistress."

The maidservant rode off on her brown steed.

Bilfreth turned to Hobbs. "Mr. Hobbs, she wants us to join their party? They have a thousand men!"

"We have to confer with our employer first. Do not unwrap the gift until we know that it is truly ours."

"Mr. Hobbs, I choose to enjoy the gift now and worry about such things later."

◆◆◆

The sun had barely risen when Lady Aylen, her maidservant, and ten knights arrived in Ironwood.

"Lady Aylen, the Fates either have given us special protection or have a terrible end forthcoming for us ahead to have allowed us to ride through the night without attack or incident," the lead knight said.

"Samac, you worry too much. We are here, before most others, and we will take full advantage."

While Hopeshire was a large rural town, Ironwood was a fully fortified city of metal and stone. It was known all across Avalonia and beyond for forging the best weapons by the best weaponsmiths.

"Wait here for us," Lady Aylen commanded her men. "Ironwood's weaponsmiths keep their shops at the far end of the city's main entrances."

"Should I send at least one man with you, m'lady?" Samac asked.

"Not necessary." She dismounted her white horse. Samac took the reins from her outstretched hands. Another knight did the same when Maiden Gwyness jumped down from her horse.

The shop walls were made of stones identical to that of the city wall. Both women had to push the door to open it; it creaked loudly. A giant of a man appeared at the door and helped by easily closing it behind them. Weapons were neatly placed and stacked on table after table; on the wall hung others.

"How may I help, fine ladies?" a bushy gray-haired man asked, walking to them. He wore a leather apron. His arms were exposed by his short-sleeved tunic showing the cuts, burns, and welts of a lifetime of weapon forging.

"Your shop is known for its exquisite polearms," Lady Aylen said to him. "I hear the Kings' Caravan replenishes its own weapons here."

"That is true, madam."

"I would like to purchase as many as you have. No good party can protect its perimeter without them. I want the best."

"Unfortunately, madam, someone has already beaten you to it. A man came here yesterday and bought all that I had from me."

"Yesterday?"

"Yes, madam."

"Do you know who this man was? Perhaps, I can hire him to join my party."

"Possibly, I have never seen him before. He had two swords strapped over his back."

"Did he have a gray wolf dog with him?"

"No dog, madam. Do you know him?"

"Perhaps," Lady Aylen replied as she glanced at Gwyness. "How many polearms did you have?"

"I had five hundred of them, and he bought them all. I sent my men to deliver them by wagon. I am sorry I do not have more to sell." The giant man opened the door for them. The owner walked them to their horses.

"How did this man travel?"

"He had his own horse, madam. It was very large, with an unusual pelt."

"Unusual, sir?" Lady Aylen asked.

"Unusually remarkable. His horse had a splendid, shiny pelt of gray fur."

"Thank you, sir, for your time. When my full party arrives at Ironwood, I may return, assuming agents from the Kings' Caravan do not purchase your entire weapons stock."

He smiled. "It has happened before, madam."

The two women mounted their horses and galloped away.

◆◆◆

Traveler was the first of the column, marching with his dog at his side. Hobbs led the rest of the men, glancing back as he walked. At the very end was Bilfreth with two of his fighters. They neared Ironwood. The road was still part of Caravan Row, so all along the sides were servants, swordsmen, spies, and thieves. Hobbs noted that, with every step closer to Goodmound, the crowds grew, as did the danger.

A young woman in a black cloak approached. "Good day, sir."

"Good day, madam," Traveler greeted. "I recognize you."

"Yes, I am the maidservant of Lady Aylen of Sirnegate."

"I noticed you when I spoke with your lady at the tavern in Hopeshire."

"Well, sir, my lady still wants to employ you. She apologizes if she did or said anything to offend you."

"She does not need a guide to cross the magical lands."

"I do not know why you believe that, sir, but she does."

Traveler asked, "Will your lady be vexed with you if I do not agree?"

Gwyness inadvertently touched the chain around her neck. Traveler glanced at her amulet, but she quickly covered it.

"A very fascinating amulet you have," he said.

"It is nothing, sir, a trinket from my family."

"Here is my proposition. Since we all will be joining the Caravan and starting out together, when you are about to leave, find us and we will follow."

"Thank you, sir. My lady will be pleased."

"Good. It will be our arrangement between our two parties. It is not an uncommon practice for parties on Caravan to form alliances."

"Then we shall be allies, sir," she said.

"We shall."

"What is your name?" Traveler asked.

"I am Maiden Gwyness of Sirnegate. What is your name, sir?"

"I am Traveler."

CHAPTER SIX
Estus the Forge

The city of metal that was Ironwood was encircled by great stone walls and all the official structures of its government were forged of solid iron. Every other building was made from the same stone quarry that its wall came from. The main gates remained open during the season of Caravan, and the Row extended well inside the city.

In Hopeshire, it was a town of rustic people dressed in green attire, mostly dedicated to farming and livestock. In Ironwood, it was overflowing with outsiders and difficult to pick out its citizens. Residents were a people devoted to the warrior classes with their metal quarries to fashion weapons, armor, war wagons, and the like.

"Sir, will we be resting within the city for the night?" Hobbs asked Traveler as the men marched into the city's environs.

"Yes, but it will be the last time we do so within Avalonia."

"Sir, we will not rest within Goodmound?"

Traveler glanced at him. "We can talk of there when we arrive. Have Bilfreth take charge in getting the men into lodgings. You know your tasks, but in addition, I want you to assume this will be the last time we will be able to secure men or provisions—not even from Last Keep."

"Nothing from Last Keep, sir?" Hobbs was perplexed. Last Keep was the last city in Avalonia before the Caravan left the Lands of Man for the magical lands. "Sir, have you been beyond the Lands of Man? You seem to possess a special knowledge of the Trail," Hobbs whispered.

Traveler put a hand on Hobbs's shoulder. "Mr. Bilfreth."

"Yes, sir," Bilfreth turned to respond. "Assign two men to be Mr. Hobbs's guardsmen."

"Yes, sir." The swordsman moved through the men.

Traveler lowered his voice to speak to Hobbs. "Yes, I have been beyond the Lands of Man. But my personal adventures are not relevant. I was young, and I was not master of a party. The goal is not to get the dog and me to Atlantea; it is to get *us all* to Atlantea."

"Thank you, sir, for confiding in me."

"I will leave you to your tasks as I complete mine."

"Are we sure we will be able to secure the additional swordsmen here, sir?"

"The swordsmen we require for our journey are not sought after. They find us. We must impress them and not the reverse with the caliber of our party."

"Yes, sir. And I will make sure to get a proper weapon for myself," Hobbs said as he raised his quarterstaff. Traveler grinned.

◆◆◆

Bilfreth had sent out a dozen men to find lodgings. One returned, and now they all were walking down a dusty path to an inn near the eastern corner of the city. The roads were thick with strangers—knights, swordsmen, daggermen, axemen, archers, and horsemen. Unlike Hopeshire, there were more men that looked to be nobility or of royal blood. The livestock of goats, cows, and chickens were not of Ironwood but brought in from Caravan-seeking strangers from Hopeshire.

"Mr. Bilfreth," Hobbs called.

"Yes, Mr. Hobbs."

"When the men are settled, assign some to acquire all the livestock we would need. If we wait to do so in Goodmound, there may be nothing left of worth or too expensive to afford."

"Yes, I agree. I do not recommend any large animals. They are nice but will slow down the party. Traveler walks at a pace that most of the men will struggle with."

Hobbs smiled and nodded. "Yes, I am one of them."

A man's scream pierced the air. Everyone looked on at several men battling each other with swords.

"Mr. Hobbs, we must get off the road." Bilfreth pulled Hobbs away and motioned to the men to follow.

In the brief time it took them to turn the corner, another two men were killed as the road battle grew between the two growing factions.

◆◆◆

It was past sundown when Traveler walked into the stone-brick tavern with dim lighting and few patrons. He stood across from where a large, bald man enjoyed his meal and drink at a table furthest to the back.

"Estus, the Forge, I presume," Traveler said.

"I am."

"May I sit?"

Estus gestured for him to do so, then continued to stuff his mouth with his meal. Traveler sat on the bench opposite him. Both the table and benches were made of stone.

"What of your companion?" Estus asked; he had already swallowed the food in his mouth.

Standing near the entrance, in the shadows, was another man. Estus could not make out any of his features other than he was very big, had thick arms and legs, and had a hood obscuring his head.

"He is content where he is," Traveler answered.

"My father told me you call yourself Traveler."

"Yes."

"Are you a commoner, noble, or royal?"

"A commoner."

Estus laughed. "That means you are a noble. You answered too quickly to be a true commoner, and you do not wear the silly dress of a royal. You seemed undeterred by my father informing you that I have already secured a position with the Kings' Caravan."

Traveler placed an item on the center of the table.

"What is this?" Estus touched the metal to pick it up but dropped it. He glanced at Traveler for a moment. Estus tried again but was more careful. The piece of metal was as light as a feather and had a visible glow. He lifted it so it was eye-level and stared. "This is—is this elfin steel? How did you get this?"

Traveler placed another item on the table.

Estus placed the elfin blade fragment back on the table and picked up the other. It was extremely heavy, and it took effort to lift it up to examine it in the torch illumination of the tavern. "This is dwarven steel." He returned it to the table.

Traveler placed another metal fragment on the table. "You know your metal well, Mr. Estus. But you would not know this one. This is goblin steel."

Estus eagerly picked up the dark metal piece to study it. He returned it to the table. "Mr. Traveler, you have my attention."

"I need an expert weaponsmith among my party, one who can both forge and repair any weapon for the men."

"Mr. Traveler, the means to forge and repair a human-forged blade exists in a proper smithy, but that means cannot be transported casually along the road. Wait, a moment. Are you showing me these metal fragments to entice me to join your party or to suggest I would be tasked in forging and repairing non-human metals?"

"Both."

"No campfire can be made hot enough to do either, unless you have a sorcerer amongst your men."

"We will have other means to create the heat needed to forge or mend any blade. We journey into the magical lands, Mr. Estus. One does not need a sorcerer alone to do magical things."

Estus studied the blade fragments on the table again. "How did you get these fragments?"

"I possess the blade that cut them in half."

Estus looked up at him. "You did this?"

"I did."

"There are no elves, dwarves, or goblins in Avalonia, Mr. Traveler, or any place in the Seven Empires."

"I wouldn't go all that far, but there are certainly many in the magical lands, along with many other races."

"If you did what you claim, you would never have escaped alive."

"Very true, but my companion was with me."

Estus glanced at the giant of a man in the shadows.

"Mr. Traveler, I must be mad to be considering abandoning the Kings' Caravan for yours."

"I have one hundred men so far, and we have an alliance with another party of fifteen hundred men under royal leadership that we will be following. Many on Caravan will have blacksmiths, but few will have weaponsmiths, which is worth a king's ransom where we will travel. Though, the position of forge is an essential task, it would not be the primary. That would be as weaponsmaster. As such, you would manage and maintain all the weapons of our party, including any we would acquire along the way to Atlantea, whether they be forged by the hands of men—or not. I doubt the Four Kings would entrust you with such an honor."

"Mr. Traveler, you have hired your weaponsmaster."

CHAPTER SEVEN
The Four Kings

The triennial arrival of the Kings' Caravan was never on a specific day. Everyone who would accompany it, or planned to, had to be ready to depart on whatever day it happened to be. The departure date was whenever the Caravan appeared—whether a day, a week, or a fortnight later. Parties prepared themselves to wait for as long as a month, if need be, but when it did arrive, the Caravan would make its ride to Goodmound's Castle and be gone, not to be seen again for another three years. No one dared venture to Atlantea without the guide and protection of the Four Kings of Xenhelm.

Caravan Row at Ironwood was overflowing with crowds. There were those men whom no party would take on—weaklings and beggars. There were local onlookers and Ironwood citizens. Above all, there were the able men, waiting in their respective camps outside Ironwood's walls, eager to be selected by the Four Kings for the journey.

"Do you think we will wait long, Mr. Hobbs?" a young lad asked. He was one of the cook assistants, tidying up the camp after the men's morning meal.

"I do not believe they will arrive today, but there is no way to know. They arrive when they arrive, but we must remain ready."

Hobbs sat, smoking his pipe and watching the men work. He had risen before sunrise and this was his first chance to relax in the hectic day. Even during the meal, he ran around ensuring duties were being done. He glanced across the open field. There were dozens of other camps stretching as far as the eye could see into the woods. One of those camps was that of Lady Aylen's with its posted sentry knights. He had glimpsed both Lady Aylen and her maidservant a few times since the morning. Women were almost unheard of on Caravan, and the people of Ironwood, as with Hopeshire, kept their womenfolk indoors during Caravan season.

Earlier, Samac, Lady Aylen's master knight, came into camp to meet Bilfreth. They sat with drinks and talked for some time by the campfire. Hobbs encouraged it, as the two men would be in frequent contact along the Caravan journey.

"Mr. Hobbs, he returns," another lad called.

Hobbs turned and Traveler approached with a new man, the dog following.

"Sir," Hobbs greeted as he emptied his pipe and put it away as he stood.

"Mr. Hobbs, this is Mr. Estus, our new weaponsmaster. Mr. Estus, Hobbs is the camp steward."

"Oh, very good, sir." The new man nodded to greet him.

"Introduce him to Mr. Bilfreth and the men, then get him settled." Traveler turned to Estus. "This shall be your one and only day to relax, so take full advantage. Mr. Hobbs, see me afterward."

"Yes, sir."

♦♦♦

Traveler stood at a table staring at a map, with a cup in hand. The dog lay on the thick fur blanket of Traveler's bed. The camp's tents were all three-quartered, one side always open at Traveler's insistence; no privacy here. Hobbs stepped in, paying no heed to the dog. The animal seemed to be more relaxed in his company but remained suspicious of anyone near its master.

"Sir, some of the men are inquiring about why they should not have proper tents as the other camps do."

"Tell them there once was a fearsome camp with fearsome men. One night an undead creature crawled into one and went from tent to tent until every last man asleep was devoured. Because the men insisted on closed tents, not a single sentry outside heard or saw any sign of the evil deed until it was too late."

Hobbs smirked. "Sir, I will simply tell them it is your instructions."

Traveler grinned. "Thank you. How many fire-lighters do we have, Mr. Hobbs?"

Hobbs stepped to the table and looked at the map. "Over a dozen in all, sir. I tested their ability myself."

"Good. We still have a major deficiency. We have no archers."

"They are always the first to be hired in major parties, correct, sir?"

"They are. I attempted to hire a crew before arriving at Hopeshire but was too late. For some strange reason, there seemed to be no unattached ones here in Ironwood. It's unlikely there will be any at Goodmound's Castle, so we will need to acquire them from other parties on Caravan."

"Lady Aylen has many archers, sir."

"Yes, but we cannot rely on that. We must have our own. Ensure that each man who does not carry a sword has a weapon on their person at all times, and their shield. When we set out from Goodmound, we will assign polearms."

"Yes, sir. Will Bilfreth be our master-at-arms, sir? He does want the title."

"At Last Keep I will assign that position, not before. Assess the strength of the camp for me in your estimation."

"Well, sir, we have nearly 150 men. Being generous, 50 of them are able swordsmen. Maybe half are near the caliber of Bilfreth on a good day. The servants are very good and diligent in their duties. You instructed me that you did not want any horses, so rather than wagons, most of the men will have and maintain a pull cart."

"If we are in battle, it will be difficult for the attackers to deprive us of all our food and water with them so widely dispersed among the men."

"Very true, sir. However, horses can help with both transport and battle."

"You do not know this yet, Mr. Hobbs, but horses, sadly, tend to become the food of others in the magical lands."

"Food, sir? Of what others?"

"You will learn, Hobbs. I am fond of the animals personally, but beyond the Lands of Man, they will become a detriment to all who possess them. Something the other parties will find out very dramatically. We must do without them."

"Lady Aylen has many, sir."

"As do most of the major parties that will join Caravan."

"Sir, do the Four Kings know this about the horses?"

"I have no doubt they do, but I also have no doubt they will tell no one. The Kings' Caravan is not done out of benevolence. They do it for the benefit of Xenhelm alone. We must extract the benefit for ourselves on our own."

"Sir, I was told the Four Kings are good men. You imply otherwise."

"I am simply a cautious man."

"Yes, of course. Though, sir, I have a strong feeling of foreboding. You said at our first encounter that most will never make it to the magical lands, but my assumption was that it would be gradual attrition."

"Mr. Hobbs, I am so sorry. You will see the most fantastical things ever in your life, but also the most nightmarish. I apologize because there are no words to prepare you for either, but you must prepare nonetheless. Remember always that there is no guarantee we will reach Atlantea ourselves."

◆◆◆

Night was falling when a knight approached the large command tent of Lady Aylen. The knight wore no helmet but kept a hand on the hilt of his sword at his side. Traveler and the dog followed him. The dog saw the princess standing in wait for them and stopped in its tracks, but Traveler continued forward.

"Your animal does not seem to care for me, Mr. Traveler," she remarked, smiling. Maiden Gwyness stood next to her.

"He does not care for…royalty, m'lady." Traveler returned the smile.

The dog sat on the ground where it stopped, but watched her closely.

"Join us, Mr. Traveler." She turned and led him into the tent, where a large number of knights were already assembled. "Samac, this is Mr. Traveler. His party will be following ours."

"If that is your wish, m'lady," Samac responded. "What is his particular value to us?"

"The Kings' Caravan will be our guide, but we will have our own, if needed."

"But, m'lady, I hear he cannot even purchase proper tents for his men."

The knights broke out in laughter but Traveler ignored them as he moved to the large oval table with a large detailed map, which they encircled.

"No need to commit any of the map to memory. I have a feeling you will not be on the Caravan for long," Samac said to him.

"Strange thing to say when I am the only one in this tent who has been beyond the Lands of Man, traveled across the magical lands, and returned to do so again." The men quieted. "Do you have any sense as to when the Four Kings shall arrive, m'lady?" he asked.

"I am acquainted with some of the larger parties, a few who have paid handsomely to be among their preferred alliance. They say very soon."

"Which could mean tomorrow, m'lady?"

"What is your feeling on the matter, Mr. Traveler?"

"I believe tomorrow, m'lady."

"You seem certain, Mr. Traveler. Do you have your own spies in Hopeshire or beyond that we are unaware of?"

"A little bird whispered in my ear, m'lady." He looked at Lady Aylen with a furrowed brow. "You are not part of the Kings' Caravan's preferred alliance, m'lady?"

"No, why? Why should I pay their extortion? I have an excursion party nearly as large as any of theirs. All the kingdoms know that Xenhelm uses the Caravan to enrich its city's coffers, not for any altruistic reasons. I am not averse to being taken advantage of as long as it is mutual. I am here to gain wealth, not to give mine away needlessly."

"Have you met them before?" Traveler asked.

"My late father, the king of Sirnegate, met them once. Others who I know well have met them. They speak highly of them, despite the normal flaws of men."

"Lady Aylen, now that I have met your inner circle, do you require anything further?"

"No, Mr. Traveler. Be ready to leave when the time comes, and please keep up. We wait for none."

"Nor should you be expected to, m'lady. I bid you all good night."

"See Mr. Traveler back to his tent," she commanded one of the knights. "Good night, Mr. Traveler."

◆◆◆

Hobbs enjoyed his pipe of the morning, sitting in his chair at the campfire. Even if only for a quarter-hour, it was a cherished respite. Estus the Forge was a fine addition to the party. He had a roaring laugh and brought a sense of levity to the camp that it needed. Most were not warriors or fighters of any kind, so even though they had their shields and weapons, they lacked the courage to defend themselves adequately. Hobbs wondered if he would have the courage needed himself when the time came. However, he would never give up and had a strong sense of duty to the men, most of whom were mere boys. He intended to throw himself into the task of building their courage as the Caravan progressed.

He pulled his pipe from his mouth and kept still. The ground was rumbling. He looked around and one of the morning sentries threw him a glance.

"Mr. Hobbs?" the boy asked.

"Yes, lad, I feel the ground too." Hobbs stood from his chair then noticed Traveler walking to him with the dog.

"Mr. Hobbs, break camp immediately, and get the men ready for departure."

"Yes, sir."

Hobbs tucked his pipe away in his cloak pocket and called out orders to the sleeping camp. Bilfreth ran to him.

"Is it time, Mr. Hobbs?" he asked.

"Yes. Prepare to leave."

The swordsman ran back to his section of the camp and yelled at the men to wake. Men jumped up. Everyone was already dressed, as standard, prepared to respond to an attack at any time, day or night. They gathered their things and ran to their designated pull carts, more than one man shared a single cart. Men ran to the edge of the camp to relieve themselves; others ran to the water carts to splash water on their faces and attempt to look presentable.

"Get something warm prepared for the men," Hobbs commanded the cooks.

He surveyed the camp. In quick time, it was broken down, and men were forming up. Traveler always broke down his own tent and bundled it with his sleeping effects for one of the carts. Hobbs watched as Bilfreth and his fighters took their positions in formation. A few stragglers rushed in, but the entire party stood in formation with weapons in hands and the carts lined up.

Traveler nodded as he lifted his hood to cover his head, his two swords strapped to his back. The dog stood at his side.

Every other party was also striking camp but it would be some time before they were ready. Among them, across the way, Lady Aylen waved, and Traveler acknowledged her with a raised hand.

◆◆◆

The sounds were clearer—hooves and marching feet. The silhouette of the Kings' Caravan approached in the distance, flags high. The sound of shrieking hawks also cut the air. Hobbs noticed a delegation ride out of Ironwood and stop at the main gate entrance, three men in all, dressed in royal attire of silver and black—the colors of Ironwood. The center man wore a gold crown.

The first wave of the arriving Kings' Caravan was armored knights, in muted silver armor draped with sashes in the colors of Xenhelm—orange and white. All of them wore helmets and carried spiked polearms that rose at least ten feet in the air. The second wave was the archers with helmets and armored breastplates. They carried longbows and crossbows with quivers on their backs that went from their shoulders to their thighs. The third wave of armored knights carried massive silver shields emblazoned with the symbol of Xenhelm—a majestic griffin. With them was the contingent of standard bearers on horseback, seven on each flank, bearing the Xenhelm flags flying higher than any of their polearms. The fourth, fifth, and sixth waves were the repeats of the first three. The seventh wave was warriors with spiked helmets, chainmail armor, and battle axes, flanged or spiked maces, war hammers, morning stars, or pikes. The eighth wave was armored horsemen with lances, spears, or swords. The ninth wave was the war-wagons with cannons.

The Kings' Caravan was not a caravan; it was an army—beyond what any man or woman had ever seen. It appeared endless.

When the column stopped, they could see the food and supply wagons, three-times the size of any wagon they had ever seen. They all heard the shrieking of hawks again. Then the Kings rode into full view. Awe and shock appeared on every onlookers' face. The first knight was Prince Wuldricar the Savage. He was a huge, brawny man, and his armor was built to suit his frame. His hair was blond, but his beard was dyed orange. The second knight was Prince Renfrey the Wily, revered for his strategic war thinking. Prince Wuldricar could lead an army to destroy any enemy or threat; Prince Renfrey would devise the plan to do so. Prince Gervase the Fair was primarily known for his womanizing. However, he was as clever as his brother, Renfrey, and as gifted a swordsman as his brother, Wuldricar. All three men, in their stunning silver armor, were overshadowed by their steeds—*hippogriffs!* The creatures had the hind half of a horse and the front half of a giant eagle. They shrieked as their front leg claws dug into the ground and their wings flapped. The brothers held their fantastic steeds easily as they lined up, side by side.

King Oughtred of Xenhelm galloped in last, appearing from between the column of knights and warriors. Red-hair, mustache, and beard, an orange cape billowed out from his chest armor and a crown of orange metal sat on his head, but he too was eclipsed by his steed—*a giant griffin.* Its body, tail and hind legs were that of a lion. Its head and forelegs were that of a giant eagle. Its wings were far larger than those of the hippogriffs and its lion fur was golden yellow. The talons of one of its feet were larger than the three hippogriff steeds combined. The griffin let out a guttural roar that echoed through the air, frightening everyone. Even the hippogriffs responded by briefly rising up on their hind legs and shrieking.

The Ironwood royal delegation slowly approached King Oughtred on horseback. Everyone watched as they held their breaths. *Would the griffin eat the men?* The creature was well-behaved as King Oughtred dismounted. The King of Ironwood followed suit, and the men embraced with firm hugs. The conversation between the two went on for some time. No one else moved or said a word. All watched them, but eyes moved back to the magical griffin and hippogriffs. The men laughed, and one of the hippogriffs shrieked again. Finally, King Oughtred gestured to his sons, and they, too, dismounted. Dozens of guardsmen approached the creatures and held their reins as the Kings followed the Ironwood delegation back into the city. When they were no longer visible, the guardsmen slowly led the creatures back between the columns of the Kings' Caravan.

The mood relaxed, and the gossiping began. Most were still in awe.

"Why are they called the Four Kings?" one of the lads asked Hobbs.

"King Oughtred broke with royal tradition and, rather than wait until his death, he elevated all three of his sons to the title of king and gave them each their own lands equal in size to his own. In his presence, they are called prince, but they are true kings in their own right with their own kingdoms," Hobbs responded.

"Did you know they had such beasts as their steeds?" the boy asked.

"No, I did not." Hobbs looked to Traveler. "Sir, have you ever been to the Kingdom of Xenhelm?"

"No, I have not but I have heard many accounts for years."

"You don't seem too taken with their fantastic steeds, sir."

"You have already deduced why, Mr. Hobbs. I have seen their species before. You and the men shall find out why we are fortunate not to have any horses in our party. The beasts are fantastic for their owners alone."

"Why, sir?"

"What do you suppose griffins and hippogriffs like to eat?" Traveler asked.

Hobbs and the men looked at each other.

◆◆◆

"Feast! Feast!"

As the sun began to set, the yelling of the two Xenhelm lads got the attention of everyone in every party in camps outside of Ironwood. The two boys repeated their words continuously from the time they appeared at Ironwood's main gates to the time they passed each camp to the very last camp, miles away.

Hobbs waved as he noticed Lady Aylen and her maidservant in the camp column across from them. They waved back. Lady Aylen's men were as giddy as Traveler's, and those in every other camp.

"Mr. Hobbs, what does it mean—feast?" a man asked, speaking for all others.

"We shall see," he responded, looking back at him with a smile. As he looked back, he noticed Traveler. There was no smile on his face. "Anything to be concerned with, sir?"

Traveler realized his outward expression and smiled. "No, not at all, Mr. Hobbs."

They were not far from the Ironwood gates, and what looked to be a double column of Xenhelm and Ironwood riders galloped out, pulling wagons, followed by torch-carrying men on foot.

"Feast, indeed, Mr. Hobbs," another man in camp said. "Smell that hearty aroma, even from here."

It was as they hoped. A contingent of Xenhelm and Ironwood riders came to each of the Caravan parties that waited. Their wagons were filled with well-cooked pig, deer, lamb, large quails, and geese as the main course, thick but finely sliced breads and cakes, and, more importantly, plenty of wine with the goblets to match, courtesy of Ironwood.

Hobbs already knew it was a hopeless cause as he walked through the men; there would be no order to be had. Men were already gorging themselves on food and gulping down as much wine as they could manage.

"Mr. Hobbs." Traveler appeared beside him, his dog at his side.

"Yes, sir."

"Enjoy yourself. No more duties for the rest of the night, as it would be completely pointless."

"Yes, sir. Very much so."

Hobbs relented and made his way to one of the food wagons, which was almost empty. He ignored his noble upbringing to fight his way in to get his own food and drink.

From the shadows, Traveler stood quietly, watching Lady Aylen's camp. No one else saw the group of dark-cloaked men with only a couple of torches surreptitiously exit the Ironwood gates and march forward into the camps.

"M'lady! M'lady!" Gwyness ran to the princess who rose from her seat on the ground just outside her command tent. She had been eating with Samac and all her senior knights, all of whom also stood. They froze as they saw the men behind her. "M'lady, I present the king of Ironwood—"

The tall silver-haired man with a gold crown nodded.

"M'lord," Lady Aylen said, as she and her men bowed their heads in acknowledgment.

"—and this is King Oughtred of Xenhelm," Gwyness continued.

The man lowered the hood from his head to reveal his bright red hair, mustache, and beard. He was taller than she thought, distinguished, and had the commanding demeanor of a warrior king.

"Princess Aylen of—is it the Kingdom of Sirnegate?"

"It is, my king," Lady Aylen replied. "Properly, I am Lady Aylen, as there is a Princess of Sirnegate." She could see all the men around him in black cloaks were in armor.

"Of course, but you are next in succession. Yes, I have heard of your kingdom—western Avalonia. It is a great pleasure to meet you. There are not many true royals on this Caravan. May I introduce my sons?" Three men stepped forward and pulled the hoods back from their heads. "My son, Prince-King Wuldricar the Savage." The largest of the men, blond with a dyed-orange beard, nodded. "My son, Prince-King Renfrey the Wily." The blond-haired man nodded. "And my son, Prince-King Gervase the Fair."

The brown-haired royal stepped to her. "Lady Aylen, it is my pleasure." He took her empty left hand and slowly kissed the back of it.

"Thank you, King Gervase."

"No one shall ever accuse me of not knowing how to treat a true woman."

"Yes, dear brother, no one will ever make that mistake," King Renfrey quipped.

"Lady Aylen, is this your full contingent of men?" the Ironwood King asked.

"It is, m'lord." Lady Aylen turned. "This is Samac, my master-at-arms, and there is"—they all looked to see Traveler now standing among them—"Mr. Traveler, my trailmaster."

"Mr. Traveler?" King Renfrey asked. "Surely, you could have come up with a better alias than that."

"Sorry, m'lord, I have never been all that creative in those matters."

"I heard a rumor, Mr. Traveler, that you are also a guide," Renfrey continued.

"M'lord, the only guide of note on the Kings' Caravan of Xenhelm are the Four Kings themselves."

King Oughtred had his eyes fixed on Traveler's dog. "An exquisite animal."

"Thank you, m'lord. I raised him from a pup."

King Oughtred turned to Lady Aylen. "You have a very impressive party. We continue on to inspect the other camps, but we shall be very honored to have you amongst us. So many travel so very far to join the Caravan, however, they are so often deficient in both their preparation and their resources."

"Thank you, my king, for your kind words."

King Oughtred nodded and led his sons, the Ironwood King, and his cloaked knights to the next camp. King Gervase hung back a bit to give a final bow to Lady Aylen with a smile, then briskly walked to catch up to his father's side.

"What an impressive man," Lady Aylen said.

"Yes, m'lady. The reputation of the Four Kings precedes them always and we can behold for ourselves that it is well justified," Samac said.

"What are your thoughts of the Kings, Mr. Traveler?" Lady Aylen asked.

"I am a cautious man, m'lady. It takes more than drink and venison in the moonlight to win me over. Ask me when we cross into the magical lands."

"Mr. Traveler, that is a very uncharitable position to take in regard to our noble benefactors. You can at least pretend to be grateful."

"Yes, m'lady. I am grateful—for the potential of good things to come." Traveler bowed. "I bid you goodnight, Lady Aylen. I must see to my men."

Traveler turned and walked back to his camp. His dog flashed a snarl at Lady Aylen and followed.

"Well, I never," Lady Aylen said under her breath.

"An insolent knave, if you ask me, m'lady," Samac added.

CHAPTER EIGHT

Pangolin the Berserker

The next morning brought renewed excitement to all those who waited. The Four Kings would select those to join their ranks and those who were sanctioned to follow. Then would come the travel to Goodmound, Last Keep, and then into the Magical Lands. For many, it was a waking dream years in the making. Lady Aylen stood at her command tent's entrance, every bit as eager as the men. She watched riders from the Kings' Caravan break formation and gallop to specific parties.

"Do you know what they are doing, m'lady?" Gwyness asked.

"I assume the Four Kings of Xenhelm will move all their preferred alliance parties to the head of the pack. It will be the official Kings' Caravan, the preferred alliances, and then the rest of us. But to all who behold us, we will all be the Kings' Caravan."

"M'lady, are you sure we made the right decision not to be part of their preferred alliance?"

"I admit their performance last night and the feast for the men was persuasive; however, it is the principle of the thing, Gwyness. We will be fine as we are following without paying their ridiculous fee to join their alliance society."

"M'lady, we might have paid exorbitantly, but it would have been to obtain coveted spots directly to the rear of the Kings' Caravan and under the direct protection of their knights. All others will not."

"Gwyness, we will all be under the protection of the Kings' Caravan by simply traveling with them. That is why we are all here. However, let us not fool ourselves. If the Caravan is attacked, Xenhelm will protect its kings alone, no one else—even those who have paid to be alliance members."

Lady Aylen noticed another rider approach—a man in a hooded cloak on a gray horse. He wore the colors of Xenhelm and trotted his horse along the different parties. She noticed him because of his eyes—the whites were yellow, and the pupils were unusually large. He stared at her, then his attention turned to Gwyness. His eyes frightened Aylen. He saw her staring back and galloped away to continue his inspection.

"I have never seen eyes such as his," Gwyness said.

"Neither have I, and I do not like that he seemed particularly interested in us."

They watched him as he seemed to stare at Traveler.

"Mr. Traveler has grabbed his attention, at the moment," Lady Aylen said.

The strange rider rode off again down the column.

"I do not like him at all."

"Do you think he is a seer of some kind?" Gwyness asked.

Aylen gave her maidservant a look of concern.

♦♦♦

The game of waiting drew on. No one knew how long the King of Ironwood would entertain the Four Kings. They had arrived in the morning of the previous day, and now dusk was falling on the second, so every group began to set up camp again for the night. Xenhelm nobles, in their colors of orange and white, rode to select camps to fetch their leaders and invite them into Ironwood.

An official-looking man carrying a large leather-bound book made the rounds from camp to camp by horse. He wore the attire of an Ironwood citizen—blackish-brown leather and chain mail. Two Ironwood warriors on horseback accompanied him from the main gates.

"Who is in charge of this camp?" he asked upon arrival at the Traveler camp.

"How may I help, sir?" Hobbs asked, with his pipe in hand.

"I am here on orders from the King of Ironwood to collect the Caravan taxes."

"Caravan taxes, sir?"

"Yes, any party taking up residence outside our walls, under our protection, shall pay for that privilege."

"Sir, such a provision was never communicated to us and there are no notices posted stating such."

"Nevertheless, sir, taxes are due. If you are not in authority to comply, then summon the one who has the authority."

Hobbs noticed Traveler and the dog were now standing beside him.

"We are not paying any extortion tax," Traveler said to the official.

"I will mark you down as non-compliant and inform our king."

"What you do is of no interest to me," Traveler said with contempt. "We have spent considerable money in your city on food, supplies, and weapons. Is this the dastardly way you reward such patronage? I have even hired an Ironwood man. I should dismiss him immediately and tell him that my reason is his city has no honor."

The official closed his leather book. "I apologize, sir, for my words. Your party would be exempt from any Caravan taxes due to legitimate purchases from within our walls. Please, do not take offense. The taxes were only instituted to deal with the influx of those who would squat on our land and take advantage of our protection, but not compensate us in return."

"Your apology is accepted."

The official nodded and rode away, with his two guards, back to Ironwood's main gate entrance.

Traveler turned to Hobbs and said, "Tell Bilfreth to double the guard shifts at once."

"Yes, sir."

◆◆◆

Night had fallen. Hobbs saw Traveler had turned in immediately, not even lighting a torch. His tent was completely dark, but Hobbs knew the dog would be on vigil, as he was every night. There would be no early night for Hobbs, however. Hobbs began his rounds through the camp, which the men welcomed and expected, especially with many of them being so young. A disciplined routine was what he demanded from the men, but he also made time to sit with them to chat and drink. He came to Estus's area, and the weaponsmaster seemed to be beginning his day, not ending it, tying and chaining up chests and boxes.

"Mr. Estus, do you need any assistance?"

"Mr. Hobbs," he greeted. "No, I simply want to ensure no thieves can slip into camp and be off with any of our weapons."

"Do you believe such a thing is likely?"

"I expect everything and anything, especially as we draw closer to the official start of Caravan. However, my work is almost done, so I will turn in shortly."

"Very good, Mr. Estus. I will leave you to it, then."

"Mr. Hobbs, I think it would be best for us to formally join with Lady Aylen's party tomorrow. No disrespect to Bilfreth and his men, but we have a clear deficiency in warriors. It is never good to have far more weapons than men to wield them."

"We need not concern ourselves with that matter. Mr. Traveler will not risk any of our lives venturing on without the proper contingent of men."

"Then I will not speak of it again. But know that it is gossiped about by the men."

"Yes, I know. Thanks and good night, Mr. Estus."

"Mr. Hobbs."

◆◆◆

Early in the morning, the horrifying flurry of bird shrieks and men's screams ripped the men from their sleep. Everyone jumped from their sleeping to their feet in panic. The Caravan camps were in two columns, about a hundred feet apart, one camp forty feet behind the other. A bright streak of blood ran down the middle.

The men instinctively looked to Hobbs, who ran to the front of the crowd in the Traveler camp, for answers. He expanded his new telescope from Mr. Estus to see if there was anything to be seen; there was nothing, but the screams did not stop. Then they heard loud flapping sounds, and high above, King Wuldricar appeared on his hippogriff with the remains of a horse in the beast's front clutches. The king flew over all camps and over the wall into Ironwood.

People were running toward something. Hobbs glanced back to see Traveler, who nodded. Hobbs followed the crowd, with Bilfreth and Estus at his side. It was a shocking sight of dozens of horses and men ripped to pieces and a river of blood.

"Why did they do this?" a boy yelled hysterically. Men tried to console him but he fell to his knees and burst into tears.

"They attacked you?" Hobbs asked a man in an adjacent camp.

"It was death from above," the man said angrily. "One of the fine Four Kings swooped down and took the prized steed of their camp's king. The men fought back, as is their sworn duty, so King Wuldricar killed all their horses and the men who raised their swords. What kind of evil men are we following?" The man's rage boiled within him.

Hobbs walked back to the carnage. He wanted to make sure he did not forget what he saw.

"Mr. Hobbs!" one of the camp lads yelled.

"Come quick, Mr. Hobbs."

The lad stopped and doubled back.

Hobbs ran as fast as his stocky legs could manage. Bilfreth sprinted past him with Estus.

♦♦♦

"You cannot do this!" Lady Aylen yelled from upon her white horse.

King Renfrey smiled from his hippogriff mount. "I see no reason to conduct my business with a commoner."

"I am not a commoner!" Lady Aylen yelled. "I am with the Royal House of Sirnegate."

The king looked at her master-at-arms, Samac. "My father is quite impressed by the presentation of your men."

"Thank you, m'lord," Samac replied.

"So again, the offer is quite simple. We wish to employ you and your men as official knights of our allied forces. You will oversee them, but be under our ultimate command structure. Your wages will be paid weekly and will not preclude any riches you acquire in Atlantea. All your food, shelter, and provisions will be provided directly by the Kings' Caravan. Is that acceptable to you, sir?"

"Samac, you cannot allow them to do this!" Lady Aylen yelled. "I hired you a year ago. I have financed you and your men all this time. You are honor-bound to live up to our agreement."

Renfrey added, "Mr. Samac, you are not honor bound to any but your king. But if you choose my father as your king, you will be rewarded far beyond anything this woman could offer."

Samac did not look at her from his mount. He turned to his senior knights, already upon their horses, too, and they all nodded. "We accept your offer, m'lord."

"Very good. Gather your men then, and join us immediately."

"There were other fighters I wished to add to my ranks, m'lord."

"Under your direction, they are also welcome."

Samac gestured to his men, then rode across to the Traveler camp. "Bilfreth!" The swordsman looked up. "Gather your men and follow me. We are officially joining the Kings' Caravan."

A smile came over the man's face.

"Bilfreth!" Hobbs yelled.

"Sorry, Mr. Hobbs. You would do the same if you were me." He and his men ran after Samac and his knights.

In the span of a few moments, Lady's Aylen's impressive one-thousand-strong party of knights and warriors rode into Ironwood, following the Kings' Caravan's newest horsemen. The Traveler camp was equally decimated losing all of its fifty warriors.

"I cannot believe this," Hobbs said to himself, feeling winded. He lowered himself to sit on the ground.

Two new Kings' Caravan horsemen appeared next to King Renfrey, carrying a metal chest between them. "Ah, yes. I do not want you to spread vicious lies about the Kings, Lady Aylen. Here is a chest of money to more than compensate you for all that you have expended to date on your former knights." The horsemen threw the heavy chest to the ground before her horse's feet.

"How am I going to replace one thousand knights now?"

"Lady Aylen, I do not care in the least."

King Renfrey kicked his hippogriff onto its hind legs. It shrieked and leapt into the air, almost knocking her off her horse. It disappeared over the Ironwood wall, and the two horsemen rode back through the main gate.

Lady Aylen had to fight mightily with her white horse to calm it. She looked at the empty space that once was her party; they even took all the wagons of supplies. What remained was her tent and a few hundred servants, all staring at her with open mouths. She cursed in anger, jumped down from her horse, and stormed into her tent, closing the flap. Her maidservant rushed in after her.

Hobbs looked up to see Estus standing above him. The steward cast his gaze back down to the empty ground. The bliss of the Caravan had been shattered.

♦♦♦

All the camps were in shock at what was wrought by Kings Wuldricar and Renfrey. For those not among the Kings' alliance society, the appetite to join the Kings' Caravan was gone. But what other alternatives were there?

"Hobbs!"

It was nearing dusk. Hobbs had been sitting on the ground all that time, in shock, not even making sure the noon meal was served. He snapped out of his daze to look around, and the remaining man—and boys—were equally downfallen and seated silently on the ground. Some had tears in their eyes. None of the men would have eaten, and none of them would eat anything for supper either.

The voice was Traveler's, appearing from his tent, with one of his swords in hand—the smaller one. It was strange to see it not strapped to his back.

"Yes, sir." Hobbs jumped from the ground and dusted off his backside.

"Go to Lady Aylen and have her join our camp—her maidservant and all her remaining men, straight away."

"Yes, sir. Is something the matter?"

"Perhaps."

At that moment, the screeching sound of the Ironwood portcullis coming down echoed through the air, and knights could be seen also closing the massive steel doors.

"Hobbs, get them over here immediately."

"Yes, sir." He ran to Lady Aylen's command tent even as he heard yells in the distance.

They came! Marauders, the nomadic killers that roamed the lands, swarmed in from the distance. There were so many of them, and as they neared the men saw their matted hair reached down to their waists. They wore a patchwork of animal skins and rusted armor. All the camps readied themselves as the human animals, armed with every manner of bloodied weapon, ran at them. As they drew closer, their savage yelling grew in intensity.

Traveler's men braced their weapons—swords and spears, mostly—for the attack. Now, Estus was who they looked upon to lead them in battle. He had hastily thrown on chainmail armor and stood with the largest mace he could find.

"Stay close together!" he yelled. "Shoulder to shoulder and back to back is how we will defeat them."

"Lady Aylen!" Hobbs reached the tent, and Gwyness appeared. "Please, come with me! We need to get all of you to our camp." Hobbs gestured to Lady Aylen's camp servants. "Move quickly to our camp! An attack!"

Lady Aylen appeared behind her. Her face was worn from crying.

"We must go!"

The women ran with Hobbs; all the Aylen servants followed. Hobbs realized he had no weapon on his person save his dagger. Traveler was waiting with a long polearm. "Mr. Hobbs, your running of the camp is impeccable. Your regard for your personal safety is not." He tossed the weapon at him, then ducked back into his tent.

"Hobbs!" Gwyness yelled.

He turned and saw that the marauders were almost upon them. Hobbs braced his polearm. Gwyness pulled a longer dagger from the sheath at her side. A blur flashed by them. The marauder about to reach Hobbs was slashed down by Traveler as he and the dog ran into battle.

Hobbs, Gwyness, and Lady Aylen stood mesmerized. Every marauder that reached Traveler was cut down. Marauders not directly in his path were killed by the dog. The dog leapt into the air from shoulder to shoulder of advancing marauder, clamping down on the top of each skull and snapping each neck with one sharp pull. Man and dog fought so ferociously that the marauders began turning back to escape.

Estus moved to Hobbs. "Is our employer a berserker, and have you ever seen a dog kill a man in such manner before?"

"In all my many years, I have not," Hobbs replied. "I wager none of us have ever seen a dog kill in that manner."

"Either of them alone could cut down an army, but together…Notice he did not take his true broadsword with him. So, there is much more to Mr. Traveler then we have yet to see."

"We need to secure the camp," Hobbs said to them. "Lady Aylen, will you put your servants under my direction?"

"Of course," she answered.

"Mr. Estus, how should we equip men who are not fighters?"

"Two-man teams. One shieldman, one poleman. The longest polearms we can put in their hands. We can only fight defensively with no knights or warriors."

"Except for Mr. Traveler," Hobbs said.

"And his dog," Estus added.

"When the time comes, you will see that my maidservant and I are capable fighters." Lady Aylen said defiantly.

"Lady Aylen, you are not required to fight," Hobbs said to her. "That should be the task for the men."

"They took my knights!" Lady Aylen was now enraged.

"There is nothing we can do, m'lady," Hobbs said to her. "We will figure out a plan when Mr. Traveler returns."

"He returns," Gwyness said.

They saw a silhouette approach but knew it was him from the canine at his side. Traveler held his blade in his right hand. As Traveler and his dog came closer, they could see the aftermath—both were covered in blood.

◆◆◆

Hobbs ran to a couple of the camp lads and directed them to fetch water immediately. Man and dog walked past into their tent. Hobbs appeared with two of the lads carrying buckets of water.

"Set them close," Hobbs said to them.

Estus appeared, and it was the first time he had ever stepped into the master's tent. "I'll take that blade, sir. Return its shine."

Traveler handed him the sword. "Thank you, Mr. Estus." Traveler grabbed a cloth and after dampening it with water quickly wiped the blood from his dog's coat. The animal visibly enjoyed the grooming. Traveler took another cloth and threw it into the second bucket. He wiped his head and face clean then his arms. He turned and grabbed a large, thick leather satchel. Before he left the tent, he knelt before the dog. "Guard the camp."

The dog dashed out of the tent.

Traveler stood and walked out. Hobbs, Estus and the women looked at each other. Traveler was walking towards the other camps.

"I'll follow him," Hobbs said to them. He pointed to the two camp lads and gestured for them to follow.

Traveler stopped at a shell-shocked boy sitting on the ground and crouched down. "Are you wounded? Cut anywhere?"

"No, sir."

"Where's this blood on your tunic from?" Traveler asked as he checked the boy for any wounds.

"From my friend. He was killed."

"Get up from the ground. Go back to your camp."

"They are all dead, sir."

Traveler stood and turned to Hobbs. "Take charge of this boy and get him settled in our camp."

"Yes, sir."

Traveler continued on.

Hobbs pulled the boy to his feet. "Take him into camp and get him something to drink," he said to one of the camp lads, "anything he wants, and return promptly."

"Yes, Mr. Hobbs."

Hobbs and the remaining lad followed after Traveler.

The first obvious casualty was a man prone on the ground with his sword near his hand. He held his side, and Traveler knelt beside him.

"How deep is the gash?" Traveler asked.

"Not too bad."

Traveler lifted the man's hand, and blood oozed from the wound. He pushed the man's hand back down. "Hold it very tight." Other men from his camp gathered around them. "What is the strongest drink you have? Fetch it." One of the men dashed away and returned with a bottle. "It is not for me." He pointed to the wounded man. "Make him drink all of it." The man took the bottle and began drinking as Traveler opened his bag. When he saw the hook and thread, he stopped drinking.

"Please no, not that."

"Do you want to live or to die? Your choice."

"Will I feel it though?"

"We shall see." Traveler stabbed him in the side, catching the man off guard and startling all of the men. He screamed out and almost immediately passed out.

"Hold him down!" Traveler set the line on his thread quickly. "And I need water!"

One of the men handed him a canteen. Traveler doused the wound then wiped it. He applied a mud-like paste to it from a small jar from his bag then began to sew the man's side closed. He cut the thread with a small knife from his bag then laid a couple of leaves from a folded cloth on top of the stitches.

"I will need help. You two lift up his front. You two lift him up from the back. I need to bind his chest tightly." As the men lifted, Traveler wrapped white cloth from his bag around the man's chest. He pulled tight, allowing no slack, then clipped it with large pins. "Put him in a breastplate, so he is unable to move his chest. He has to remain flat for at least a few days, if possible. Keep his activity light for at least a fortnight after that. Check the color of the cloth beginning tomorrow. There should be no new blood or other fluids. If there is, change the cloth, clean it again and rebind him."

"How can he go on Caravan like this?" a man asked.

"He cannot and will not. Take him away from all this to recover. Hopeshire would be best."

The next wounded man sat nearby. Traveler knelt and looked at the deep multiple slash wounds across his chest. The man's body below the waist was soaked red. He was sitting in a pool of his own blood. Traveler shook his head. "There is nothing I can do."

Tears welled up in the man's eyes. "Yes, I know. At least I can die as a warrior."

"That honor belongs to your men, not I," Traveler said in a respectful tone.

"We shall give you all the time you need," a man said. Several warriors stood nearby, one looked at his sword in hand. All the men were in tears.

Traveler touched the arm of the swordsman. "You need not do anything. He will drift off and never awake."

The warriors sat with their dying comrade as Traveler moved to the next battle victims.

The crowd of men watching Traveler grew larger as he moved through the camps, but one warrior among them that Hobbs noticed was unlike any he had seen before. He was a large man, clad in an earthy armor that seemed to be more like the scales of a snake than metal plates, but there was an invincibility to the material. Fastened on his back, somehow, was a mace made of the same scale-like material with an ax blade so massive, that the very look of the weapon incited fear. The olive-skinned warrior had watched Traveler closely with a few menacing fellow warriors at his sides.

"I have never met a swordsman who was also a healer," one of them said.

"I was a healer before I was a swordsman," Traveler answered. "One day, I grew tired of men in one long campaign being sent to me injured, half-dead, or dead for my care, so I learned how to kill them so they would not send any more."

Traveler washed the blood from his hands before he tended to more gravely wounded men. However, he was soon covered in blood again but continued on.

"Time is short for many of them. I do not want to see those who get to me first, but those who are closest to death," he instructed the camps. "I will not leave until every man is seen. Every man in battle deserves that."

The words had special meaning to the men. They were all warriors and lived by a universal code.

"No!" The man had to be held down by his colleagues.

Traveler knelt at the man's mangled right leg. The very bone of his thigh was visible. Men had wrapped the leg with many pieces of fabric, but they were red with blood.

"We will have to cut if off. I can save the leg from above the knee, but it has to be done immediately. You may have already lost too much blood."

The man shook his head. "I would rather die, then. There is no life for me unless I can be a whole man. Please, I am a warrior. I choose death."

Traveler looked up at his comrades. They looked back at him, nodding.

The man grabbed two of them. "Avenge me by staying on the Caravan. Get to Atlantea for me. Get there despite those dogs of Xenhelm! Promise me!" His skin grew more pale as he continued to lose more blood from his terrible wound.

"We swear it," one man said.

"We shall," another said to him. "We swear." A man next to him, tears in his eyes, drew a knife.

Traveler was true to his word. The sun had risen for noon, and now dusk approached as he saw the last man. All he had to do was close the man's eyes. He had died while waiting. Traveler reflected for a moment.

"You did what you could," one of the camp's men said. "You did more than anyone could have asked."

Traveler nodded. He closed his healer's bag.

"Let me carry it, sir," Hobbs said and took it from him as they walked back to camp. The two boys followed.

"Hobbs, you can dismiss the lads so they can get some sleep."

"The lads would prefer to stay, sir." Hobbs told him the boys, after watching Traveler work, now wanted to be healers too, one day.

"Very good. Hobbs, have some men set up a large tent, solid and able to be closed properly. I will need several others to move wounded men to it."

"Beyond what you have already done, sir."

"Yes, hippogriffs are not merely chimerical beasts made of eagle and lion parts. They are magical beasts, so any damage they inflict on a human is of a magical nature too."

"Yes, sir. A tent will be set up immediately, and I will have bearers for you."

♦♦♦

Hobbs oversaw the movement of dozens of men, who had been severely wounded by the hippogriff, to a new large tent. At first, the tent raised was not large enough to accommodate the wounded, so Hobbs had the men join two into one to comprise the size they needed.

Meanwhile, Traveler stood at a table in his tent mixing a variety of powders and herbs on a thick cloth. Outside the tent, several large black pots set on rocks boiled water over fire. Curiosity had taken over the camp, as Traveler did not work alone at his table. The women watched beside him, and others, especially the boys of the camp were eager to see what he was concocting. The two lads who helped him and Hobbs the whole night would not trade sleep for the opportunity.

"You are not only a healer, Mr. Traveler. You are some kind of herbist or apothecary," Lady Aylen said. "What will this do?"

"Medicines can be made into liquids to drink, made into ointments or pastes to apply to wounds, but medicines can also be made into vapors so that the wounded can breathe them into their lungs. For afflictions of a magical nature, this latter method is best. You and Maiden Gwyness should observe closely. There is no reason I should be the only one in the caravan who possesses this knowledge."

"What is this method called?" Gwyness asked. "This administering medicine by—"

"It has many names. It was taught to me under the names of *arbularyo* or *kulam* or *pagkukulam*. Magic of the earth, herbs, and candles. My interest was to see the true wounds and afflictions of a man to know how to heal him best as a non-sorcerer."

"Our guide and trailmaster, Gwyness, is no ordinary healer," Lady Aylen said.

"How does it work?" Gwyness asked.

"I will pour the medicine in the boiling water, then move the pots into the tents with the wounded men, and seal the tent. The men will breath in the vapors and be healed," he explained.

"Is this knowledge common?" Gwyness asked. "I have never seen it before."

"In most of the Seven Empires, no, but in remote regions of Laurasia, it is a known art."

"Mr. Traveler has not only traveled the magical lands, Gwyness," Lady Aylen said. "He has traveled all our lands too."

Traveler continued, "This yellow powder is the most important."

He did as he said. He poured the medicine into all the pots, had them moved into the large tent, and closed it. The men would sleep as normal, only they would breathe the medicinal air from the pots.

"Have someone check on them in a few hours," he said to Hobbs.

"Yes, sir."

"Now, Mr. Hobbs, I go to sleep too. Good night." Hobbs could still see the sadness in Traveler's eyes.

"Yes, sir. Good night," Hobbs answered.

"We begin again tomorrow."

Hobbs felt a twinge of anger. What would occur tomorrow, after today's treachery? It would have been so much worse if their guide and trailmaster was not also an accomplished swordsman and healer. The next day the Four Kings would act as if nothing had transpired, that no men had died at all. He would curse both Xenhelm and Ironwood tonight. But what of the Caravan? Was it all to end before even beginning?

There was the dog watching them—never far from its master. Lady Aylen, Gwyness, and Estus sat by a fire. Traveler had said nothing as he walked past them and into his tent, his dog following. He dropped his healing bag to the ground, and like any accustomed to outdoor life, he cared not about who may or may not be watching. He stripped off his blood-soaked tunic and trousers to reveal his undergarments, threw them in the corner of the tent, and in moments, he was fast asleep under his thick fur blanket. The dog curled up next to him and also set its head down to sleep.

"We have some major decisions to make," Estus said.

"We do," Lady Aylen replied sadly, "but a key one was already made for us. For us, the Caravan is over before it even began."

"Unless a miracle happens," Estus said.

"The Fates have done nothing for us to this point," Lady Aylen said bitterly. "Why would they start now?"

◆◆◆

With the new dawn, the strangely earthen-armored warrior approached their camp, but not alone. He led over a dozen men to the Traveler camp.

Hobbs was already about, seeing to the camp's functions. He saw them draw near.

"May I help you, sir?"

"We are here to speak to the master of your camp," the main warrior replied.

"Wait here, and I'll see if he can be disturbed."

Hobbs ran to Traveler's tent. He had learned to look to the dog for his clues. If the dog was sitting up, it meant that Traveler was not really sleeping, as it was doing now.

"Sir, are you awake?"

"Yes, Mr. Hobbs," he answered. "What is it?"

"There are men from the other camps who wish to speak with you."

"Warn them I am not dressed and have no intention of doing so. But I am sure they will not be too put off by that. Show them in."

"Yes, sir." Hobbs gestured for the men to gather. Estus and the women were sitting by a nearby fire, waiting, and got up to listen.

The warrior in earthen armor led in the men. Traveler looked up, but remained on the ground, most of his body under his fur blanket.

"Sorry for the intrusion, sir. My name is Pangolin, the Berserker." It was then that Hobbs noticed the tattoos on his face, a common practice among berserker warriors.

"The Gondwanan warrior in Laurasian armor. Yes, I remember you," Traveler said.

Pangolin paused for a moment, surprised. "How could you possibly know that?"

"It is not important."

"I am not a man easily impressed by anyone in life. But, you, sir, have impressed me twice in one day. Your skill with the blade against the marauders. Then your skill and compassion with the men as a healer. Many will remember what you did for the men here."

"I did what I had to and what they deserved."

"You did more than that, sir. You could have kept the secret and benefit of your healing skills to your camp alone. What are your plans now for your camp?"

"I did not come this far to be thwarted by the likes of the Four Kings."

"Since you possess knowledge of the origin of myself and my armor, did you know of the true dark nature of these Four Kings?"

"I had heard rumors, but in these matters, rumors are plenty; truth is scarce. I am a suspicious man by nature, so I was on guard, as I am always."

"Then what are your plans for your camp?"

"I must say, if we cannot survive this setback, no matter how unjustified and vile, we have no business joining the Caravan to begin with. In the magical lands, yesterday's violence will seem so mild an occurrence that it will not warrant even a fleeting consideration."

"You speak as if you have personal experience."

"Because I do, Mr. Pangolin. My intention is simple. We will wait here until we assemble again the men we need to continue, then we will continue."

"But how will you make the journey without the guide of the Kings' Caravan?" a warrior asked at Pangolin's side.

"I do not need the Four Kings to guide me, because I know the way through Titan's Trail. I should. I traveled through and back myself."

The revelation started a commotion amongst the warriors as they looked at each other; their spirits lifted.

"Your honor is not in question with me, sir," Pangolin said. "But you know well that men claiming to know the way through Titan's Trail are as common as those claiming to be a wizard of unimaginable power."

"Your caution is more than wise. I would do no less. However, Mr. Pangolin, the problem with your question is that neither you nor your men would have any way to know the difference between a lie or the truth. You have never been there. I could explain in detail the Lands Between; Faë-Land Minor, the domain of fairies, sprites, and giants; or Faë-Land Major, the domain of the elves; and all the markers of Titan's Trail. It would mean as much to you as if I were speaking a foreign language or gibberish. All I can say is have faith. A liar can fake their way at the start, but they cannot fake their way though a year-long journey. Every step of the way, every day, I will have to prove myself every bit as much as each man on our caravan. But that is how it should be when we will all be responsible for each others' lives and the success of the journey to Atlantea."

Pangolin nodded. "Your answer is sufficient enough for me. And based on my observations of your conduct and those of the high Four Kings, I place my faith in you. For all I know, the Four Kings would strand us in some hellish place along the Trail to be devoured by some evil beast. They care for themselves and the money from their alliance society but none other. I am satisfied with your answer, and I trust so are my men."

"Very good, then."

"We spoke amongst ourselves," Pangolin continued, "after we buried our dead. Passions remain very hot in regards to the lowly behavior of these Four Kings. I was told they took all your knights and other fighters. If you are agreeable, my men, the warriors who have joined us, and those from the other camps—all whom have joined forces, and have every intention of continuing on the Caravan—would join with you. We will add two thousand men to your party—all warriors. We do not have any servants or the niceties that you have, so it would be a perfect match. However, I have one condition."

"Which is?" Traveler asked.

"I command the warriors as master-at-arms."

"Mr. Estus?"

Estus appeared at the tent's opening. "Yes, Mr. Traveler."

"Did you hear? I would not want you to feel slighted in any way."

"Mr. Traveler, that is by no means a problem for me. I am a weaponsmith, not a warrior, and definitely not a commander of warriors."

"I would say you did quite an able job yesterday."

"Thanks for saying so, sir, but I am happy to relinquish those duties to another. My skill is equipping warriors, not leading them."

"Then it is settled. Mr. Hobbs, settle Mr. Pangolin and the new men into camp. It would appear there will be no need to wait after all. We will continue as our own caravan. Where is our royal? Is that agreeable to you, Lady Aylen?"

"Yes, yes, it is, Mr. Traveler," she replied, peeking in from the main entrance.

CHAPTER NINE
Quillen the Scribe

With the caravan to move forward again, Hobbs was in high spirits. It was early the next morning, and he had the men breaking camp. This time Traveler accompanied him as he surveyed the men's progress, the dog following a few paces behind them.

"Sir, others have asked to join us, especially now that word has spread that Mr. Pangolin and the warriors he has assembled will be joining us. Most of them are not fighters at all, but they refuse to abandon the journey."

"Take them on."

"Very good, sir. It will give us two thousand fighters and increase our servant complement from the nearly 50—"

"We lost some men?"

"Yes, about half our own left to return to their homes. The same with Lady Aylen's party. Combined we had nearly five hundred, but with the new servants from all the unaffiliated parties, we may have as many fifteen hundred."

"Mr. Hobbs, when we get to the magical lands you will see we do not have enough non-warriors."

"Not enough, sir? I feel we have too many now, and we still do not have archers."

"We will have to address that deficiency along the way."

"Yes, sir."

"How is the mood among the men?"

"Sir, the anger among the men about Ironwood's complicity with the Four Kings is barely containable," Hobbs informed Traveler. "They feel that, rather than warn the camps, they purposely locked us all out. Mr. Pangolin and his men, especially, feel the marauders were doing the bidding of the Four Kings. I do not believe that, though with so many dying in the marauder attack, I can fully understand why the men would believe such. How do you feel about it, sir?"

"It matters not either way to me."

Hobbs lowered his voice as they continued through the camp. "There is another matter, sir, that I did not share with anyone. Mr. Pangolin is aware. It appears that the Kings' Caravan has already left for Goodmound."

"Yes, they left in the middle of the night."

"You knew, sir."

"They have more than one hundred thousand men in their party. They could have left three days ago and we would still catch up with ease. Have Misters Pangolin and Estus meet with me immediately. It will not be long before all the men in the camp know of this."

The two men had circled the camp and returned where they began—at Traveler's tent. Hobbs rushed off as Traveler noticed Lady Aylen and Gwyness seated at a fire in front of their tent, watching. The women's tent was adjacent, and they had heard the men speaking.

"Shall we attend the meeting, too, Mr. Traveler?" Lady Aylen asked.

"If you wish, m'lady," Traveler answered, as he disappeared into his tent. The dog flashed a quick snarl at her and followed him.

Pangolin appeared, marching to Traveler's tent. Estus, pulling on his tunic, apparently having changed his clothes, ran up quickly behind him. Inside, on Traveler's collapsible table, was a map of the end-lands of Avalonia.

"Mr. Traveler," Pangolin said as he entered, "you requested my presence."

"Gentlemen, make the preparations to strike camp for Goodmound's Castle. We depart before sunset tomorrow."

Estus joined them at the map table, his eyes scanning the roads from Ironwood. The women strolled in, and Hobbs followed, quietly.

"The scoundrel kings left last night," Pangolin added.

"Yes, I know, but they cannot move faster than we can." Traveler pointed to the map. "I know exactly where they are even at this moment."

"Mr. Traveler, do we intend to follow in the Caravan's wake after what has transpired?"

"It is a fair question, Mr. Estus. However, we have little choice until we pass beyond the Lands Between. There is but one single path to proceed forward. We can cheat after Goodmound to Last Keep, but we have no chance to move ahead of them. If we wish to make the journey, our nearly three thousand men is significant, but the Kings' Caravan has the advantage. Not because of their size, but the fact that they have undoubtedly negotiated their path to Atlantea. Without such agreements, no amount of men or griffins and hippogriffs would allow them through the magical lands every three years. We despise them, but we can use the Kings' Caravan to our advantage."

"They tried to kill us," Estus said.

"I believe, as do most of my men, they sent those marauders at us," Pangolin added.

"So do I," Estus said with heightened agitation.

"We need them for the moment," Traveler said, calmly. "But only for the moment. Pretend we are a party joining them, in case they have allies ahead. Once we pass beyond the Lands Between we will be free of them."

"My view of the Four Kings has dramatically turned," Lady Aylen said. "And not only because they took my men. I agree with the men that the Four Kings allied themselves with the vile nomadic marauders that plague these lands. This shows them not only to be dishonorable and petty, but would mean they, these royals of Xenhelm, are no more than common murderers. I appreciate your plan, Mr. Traveler, to use them, but they may not let us."

"True, m'lady, but the very reason you do not want to follow them is my firm reason for following in their wake—these are dishonorable, petty, and murderous men. We cannot pass them so we would need to wait. I am not going to wait here for more marauders, or worse, to appear. We must press on."

"Worse?" Estus asked.

"You have seen a griffin and hippogriffs with your own eyes in the Lands of Man. I wonder if the Four Kings have other pets from their frequent travels through the magical lands. We can debate this all day and night. We do not need to join the Caravan, but we do need to follow them for now."

"Yes, Mr. Traveler, you have convinced me," Lady Aylen said. She looked at the nervous faces of the others. "You have convinced all of us."

Traveler smiled. "I thought as much. We follow them until we cross into Faë-Land Minor. Once there, we will take on the fae members of our caravan. Then, and only then, will we be ready to make the journey through Titan's Trail."

"Mr. Traveler, *fae members* of our caravan?" Estus asked. They were stuck on the same phrase.

Traveler looked at Hobbs. "This is why most have never succeeded in reaching the magical lands, and most of those who have, have never made it past the border regions of Faë-Land Minor.

"The journey through Titan's Trail is not a clear one and is more deadly than you can imagine. Believe me. In its lands, many different things live that do not welcome trespassers. We are not formidable enough, nor do we possess any other significant advantages to make the journey alone, even with Mr. Pangolin and his warriors. It is one thing to be prepared to fight the occasional battle along the way. However, I have no wish to engage in continuous war every step of the way for our year-long trek. None of us would survive. Our caravan is not complete. There will be a time, if we make it that far, that the human members of our caravan will not even constitute half our numbers."

"Less than half?" Estus asked with shock. "You mean elves, gnomes, dwarves and such, Mr. Traveler?"

"Dwarves live in the Nether-Lands far from the Trail, so it's doubtful we will ever encounter any of their kind, but yes, Mr. Estus. And many others."

"I—I don't know what to say, Mr. Traveler," Lady Aylen said, as overwhelmed as the others.

"Humans cannot get to Atlantea alone," Traveler said to her, almost with a smirk.

"Very interesting," Pangolin said. "We will have fae as part of our caravan. That will keep the men in gossip over the campfire for many moons."

"It shall, indeed. Without those fae, we will have no chance in vanquishing the deadly creatures we may encounter on the Trail, among the other dangers. But I should stop talking, before all of you decide to return to Hopeshire."

Hobbs laughed.

"Mr. Traveler, I do have one question for you," Pangolin said.

"Yes?"

"With magical armor and weapons, how do suppose I would fare against these dangers you speak of?"

"Mr. Pangolin, there are only three who could survive those dangers. You, me, and the dog. That is not good enough."

"No, it is not, when we have a party of three thousand. Yes, let's get to Faë-Land Minor and get the rest of the men we need.

"The Kings' Caravan will have more than a full day's start on us when we set out tomorrow. How long do you estimate it will take us to catch up, Mr. Traveler?" Pangolin asked.

"We will not follow them on their own path. We are still in Avalonia, so we can make our own way and arrive at Goodmound's Castle seven days ahead of them."

Everyone in the tent was stunned by the answer.

"Mr. Traveler, these are too many shocks for me all in one day. How can we possibly arrive at Goodmound seven days ahead of them?" Lady Aylen asked. "They may be one hundred thousand in number, but three thousand is not small. Do you have flying sandals for all of us, Mr. Traveler?"

Traveler pointed to the map. "The Kings' Caravan took this path out of Ironwood. Plenty of forest protection and available water for men and animals. However, it is a journey of twelve to fourteen days. We will take this path. Little forest, sparse watering, extremely mountainous, but if done, we can get to the castle in about seven days.

"Mr. Estus, you will lead the efforts to build the necessary rappelling equipment for the men. That is why we are not departing today. The construction is what will take the most time. The land of Ironwood is a mountain plateau, and we will scale down to the region below, rather than take the long, winding path of the Kings' Caravan."

"We have to go down the side of a mountain?" Gwyness asked with a worried look.

"Down the mountain to the bottom and then a clear path to the castle. Mr. Pangolin, you and your Cut-throats will be the first down the path. I doubt there is anything there, since no one is as foolhardy as we are about to be, but you will deal with anything that needs to be dealt with."

"Mr. Pangolin, we do not think of your men as...cut-throats," Hobbs added.

Pangolin burst out laughing and slapped the manservant on his back. "My men call themselves the Cut-throats, Mr. Hobbs. Traveler asked, and they told him that is what they wished to be called."

"I was drinking with the men, Mr. Hobbs," Traveler said, "as you instructed."

Hobbs grinned. "Yes, sir."

"Mr. Estus and Mr. Pangolin have their main tasks for the day. For the rest of us, our work is to prepare the camp for tomorrow's journey."

◆◆◆

With Ironwood at their backs, the Traveler party marched a well-worn path to Goodmound's Castle. The bordering lands were bleak forest—few trees or brush, as if decimated by fire in the past. The sun peeked across the horizon as they stopped to survey the course. To the left was the main path, which showed the signs of the one-hundred-thousand-man army of the Kings' Caravan that had passed two nights before. To the right, was not one main path, but a series of disconnected smaller footpaths. It was to the right where Traveler and his dog led the party.

"Does anyone ever take this way, Mr. Traveler?" Gwyness asked.

"No," he answered, "but my dog and I have traveled it before."

Traveler raised his hand high as they stopped at a precipice. Gwyness was especially keen to peer over. It was not as far of a drop as she expected, but anyone falling the distance would be seriously injured or killed.

"Mr. Estus!" Traveler called.

The weaponsmith appeared. "Yes, sir."

Traveler pointed, and Estus also peered over the edge. "We have this level to descend, then another to the bottom, which is about twice the distance."

"Is that all?"

"Yes, from there it is a straight path to Goodmound. The land is rocky and inhospitable, but after only two days' journey, the land becomes nothing but green woods. If there is no incident, we may arrive in less than seven days."

Estus nodded. He motioned to his team of men. Most of the party had thought it was a deficit not to have any horses—until now.

Traveler's estimate was correct. Estus and his men took the whole day to set up the rappelling gear for the party. The first leg was fairly quick work; the next took well into the night. An entire day and all they had traveled was from the front of Ironwood to the five miles beyond it. Hobbs had camp set up again for the night while Pangolin doubled the guards posted in case Ironwood had more treachery planned.

"Mr. Pangolin," Traveler said as he approached with the dog at his side.

"Mr. Traveler."

"For tomorrow, you will lead the men."

"Actually, since you are the only one who know how to get to Atlantea, you should not be point."

Traveler nodded. "Of course, Mr. Pangolin, you are correct. Once we get to the magical lands we will establish the proper marching structure. For now, take your Cut-throats down to the foot of the mountain and lead the party out of Ironwood's lands. When we reach the greens of Goodmound, we can change again."

"Are you expecting trouble?"

"No, but I want to know if Ironwood remains interested in us."

At dawn, Pangolin and his men had already rappelled down both mountain levels to the bottom. Estus directly oversaw the slow task of sending down carts, equipment, and supplies a few at a time. By noon, all of it was with Pangolin's men, then the party itself began down.

Estus, startled, noticed Traveler and his dog next to him as if they appeared from nowhere.

"Mr. Estus, once you go down, I shall break down your equipment and throw it down to you."

"How will you get down, Mr. Traveler?"

"That is my secret, Mr. Estus," Traveler answered, smiling. "Do not wait for us. Instruct Hobbs and Pangolin to carry on."

♦♦♦

Night had fallen. Hobbs stared up at the stars as he smoked his pipe. Across from him were the women, both with cups in their hands.

"Where do you think Mr. Traveler is now, Mr. Hobbs?" Lady Aylen asked.

"Not far, m'lady."

"I never did get a chance to thank him for his kindness. To have Xenhelm behave in such a dishonorable way—my journey could have been over before it had begun. His dog does not like me. Did you know that, Mr. Hobbs? All animals like me. I have a natural way with them, but not Mr. Traveler's dog."

"I imagine, m'lady, the animal merely needs time to get accustomed to those not its master."

"No, Mr. Hobbs. The dog does not like me at all. He likes you though."

"No, m'lady. He simply tolerates me. Not the same thing."

"Mr. Hobbs, which house did you belong to?"

"King Theogar."

"I believe I know of it. War was it?"

"War or the passing of a good king. They are the twin devils that end so many kingdoms, m'lady."

"It is why we go on Caravan, Mr. Hobbs. We wish to secure a place for Sirnegate at Atlantea."

"That is a long way to go for a kingdom's salvation, m'lady. Surely, there must be easier ways."

"I am more determined to get there than ever. Why should Xenhelm be the sole representative of Avalonia or the Seven Empires throughout the magical lands to Atlantea? Why not Sirnegate or any other?"

"An interesting topic, Princess."

The voice was that of Traveler, strolling into the camp with his dog following. He sat at their fire.

"Sir, should I have a meal prepared?" Hobbs asked.

"No, thank you. We have already eaten."

"So, Mr. Traveler, where did you have this meal?" Lady Aylen asked.

"It was a nice tavern in Ironwood."

"You were in Ironwood, Mr. Traveler?" Gwyness asked.

"I was. I wanted to ensure Ironwood was not plotting against us."

"Are they?" Lady Aylen asked.

"No."

"So the Four Kings paid for their treachery against us for the day?"

"It would seem so."

"Lady Aylen, have any of the kingdoms ever tried to form their own Caravan?"

"Why yes, Mr. Traveler. It has been coveted by my kingdom and many others ever since the Caravan began twenty years ago. There are many kings and queens who would like their own griffin steeds from fabled lands to prance around their castle courts and the untold riches they could add to their coffers."

"Indeed, though your reason sounds more noble."

"So, Mr. Traveler, is there something you learned from your visit to Ironwood?" she asked.

"Nothing. Only mere suspicion. However, we will have plenty of time to ponder it on the trail. I shall turn in for the night."

"Yes, sir. We will all do the same," Hobbs added.

◆◆◆

Five days. Traveler's party arrived in Goodmound's lands in a mere five days. The journey was uneventful from the time they left the mountainous lands surrounding Ironwood to when they arrived in the plush green woods of Goodmound's Castle. Pangolin and his men led the group every day, and Traveler and his dog stayed in the rear. Everyone wondered if it meant they were being followed, but Traveler always told Hobbs they were alone.

"Mr. Pangolin," Traveler said as he walked to the front of their caravan. The warrior turned to him. "Send three of your men to run ahead of us into the city and secure lodgings. Tell them to find a place as far away from the main gate as possible. I do not expect the Kings' Caravan to stop inside, but they will surely send scouts, and we do not want them to see us."

"When they arrive and pass, will they not be suspicious of followers?"

"You will see when we get inside the city. There will be many who will follow after the Caravan when they pass. We will simply be one of them. They might never even see us."

Pangolin quickly picked out three of his men. The trio were swordsmen and they bolted ahead of the group. The wall of Goodmound's Castle was visible in the distance.

"Mr. Hobbs," Traveler called out.

"Yes, sir."

"Accompany Lady Aylen," Traveler began, "with as many men as you need, and acquire the additional supplies we talked of."

"How far will we have to travel until the next town, Mr. Traveler?" Lady Aylen asked.

"At least a month to Last Keep, the last city we will see in the Lands of Man. Then we will cross the threshold into the Lands Between. After that, we enter the magical lands of Faë-Land."

Some of the men smiled, as did Gwyness.

"The magical lands of Faë-Land," Gwyness repeated. "How long will it take us to get there, Mr. Traveler?"

"Without incident, it may take us three weeks or three months."

"I do not understand, Mr. Traveler," Lady Aylen said. "Will it take three weeks or three months?"

"Or any duration in between. We shall know the answer when we cross the threshold into Faë-Land. You do not understand now, but you will. Distance and time do not necessarily work the same on humans in their realm. We are not beings of magic...or I should say, not all of us are."

◆◆◆

Goodmound's Castle was a massive structure, easily twice the size of Ironwood. The city stood on top of flattened earth. Looming in its center was the tower of Goodmound's Castle proper. The actual castle occupied the center of the city and was rumored to descend deep into the ground. The city grew around the castle over time and was now a city of fifty thousand—five times the population of Ironwood. Goodmound was a city of the forest, with much of the surrounding fields used for farming, and large hunting parties went out daily for meat for the royal court. Like Hopeshire and Ironwood, they used the coming Kings' Caravan every three years as a time to renew their city.

Pangolin's three men had long since disappeared through the city's gatehouse when the party arrived at the busy entrance, but there were no guards visible. People came and went as they pleased. Many cities had a criminal element that loitered near the roads into and around the main entrances; however, even without guards, there seemed to be none. A few unkempt men sat against the main wall as the Traveler party passed. The dog snarled at them; the men were not pleased by the attention, and moved on.

"Mr. Hobbs, we shall go this way." Lady Aylen pointed down one of the three different paths farther into the city.

"Yes, m'lady." Hobbs looked back at the men he had chosen.

Lady Aylen, with Gwyness at her side, led the way with Hobbs and a dozen men following. Already, they could see every patch of ground was occupied by a merchant of some kind—their goods prominently displayed for purchase or trade.

Traveler and Pangolin stopped. "Mr. Pangolin, lead the entire party to the lodgings your men secured."

"Where will you be?"

"The dog and I will wander through the city and see if we can gather any additional information about the Kings' Caravan arrival. Be wary of strangers. For all we know, the Four Kings could have spies in wait. We also do not know if the royalty of Goodmound are neutral or allied with them."

"Mr. Traveler, be not concerned. We will do our best to blend in with the common folk of Goodmound."

"That will be hard to do in your case with armor no one has seen before."

"But, Mr. Traveler, you have seen it before."

Traveler grinned and left with his dog, moving into the crowds.

◆◆◆

"Mr. Hobbs, Mr. Traveler will not allow us to have horses, and you say we cannot have donkeys either," Lady Aylen said. "Why? They are sturdy animals that will make our journey easier. I would like us to complete our journey in a year rather than three. It is my money. I want us to have as many donkeys as possible to help with our supplies and equipment."

"M'lady, I will not contest it, but Mr. Traveler did say such animals often become food in the magical lands."

"Food? We can become food for whatever beasts are in that realm, but we go. Purchase the animals and put them in the charge of our bearers. What other supplies do we need, Mr. Hobbs?"

♦♦♦

Hobbs had noticed the boy when they first entered the main gate. He had been watching Lady Aylen, but kept his distance. Hobbs had lost track of him as he went to the stables with some men to purchase donkeys and their equipment.

"Pardon me, sir." Hobbs turned to see the boy again. He had no visible weapon but he was aptly dressed for a long excursion, with a leather pack strapped to his back, and a smaller one in his hand.

"Yes, how may I help you, lad?"

"I noticed, sir, you are getting provisions. Will you be joining the Kings' Caravan when it passes?"

"We will. Why?"

"My name is Quillen, sir. I wish to join the Kings' Caravan, but I have not secured my place with a reputable party."

"How did you get to Goodmound's Castle? Did you travel here alone?"

"I did, sir. Though, it is not an experience I would ever wish to repeat in my life."

"What is your profession, lad?"

"I am a scribe by trade, sir."

"That is the profession of royal households and scholars."

"I was in the employ of the magistrate of my kingdom as an apprentice."

"Your kingdom where, lad?"

"Eastern Avalonia, sir."

"Why would you leave such a noble profession for this, lad?"

"I have my own mission, sir, that could not be fulfilled in that position. I endeavor to create the official bestiary of the magical lands beyond man. I need only to secure a place with a reputable party."

"Bestiary?"

"A compendium of the magical beasts of those lands, with illustrations and full histories. I intend to become the Avalonian expert of those beasts."

Hobbs began to laugh. "The only illustration that may end up in your bestiary is one of you being devoured by one of those magical beasts. As amusing as I find your quest, lad, we have no need for such a person."

"Oh please, sir, wait. My scribblings I will do in my spare time. For your party, I seek a position as a bearer or whatever position is required."

"Why did you not say that from the start, lad? Get your things. You are hired."

◆◆◆

The inn was in the farthest quarter of the Goodmound city, and the foot traffic was sparse. The shadow of the wall made it seem even more secluded, but there was also a nearby stable. Pangolin's men rented all of it—ten rooms, the stables, and a small cottage for the two women.

"A very good sign, Mr. Pangolin," Lady Aylen said as she arrived. "Stables for our donkeys and mules."

"You may want to hide them from Mr. Traveler, m'lady."

"Why? Has he told you the same tale? That our animals will be eaten by some beast or another on the Trail. Yes, we did see the hippogriffs make meals of those horses, but the magical lands cannot be overrun with hippogriffs and griffins. But, we need animals to transport our supplies. I have full confidence in your ability and your men to protect our party—two-legged and four-legged alike."

"Thank you, Lady Aylen. I will tell him that."

"Where is Mr. Traveler?"

"He is out looking for spies."

"Spies?" Lady Aylen's demeanor changed. She looked around.

"This area is completely safe, Lady Aylen," Pangolin said. "Guards will be posted at all the buildings we have rented. You and Maiden Gwyness have the cottage."

"Thank you, Mr. Pangolin. We shall get settled in then."

The two women walked to the cottage as Hobbs directed men to get their new animals into the stables.

"I see we have a new addition to the party, Mr. Hobbs."

"Mr. Pangolin, this is Mr. Quillen. He will serve as another bearer and general laborer."

"No new warriors for me?"

"Sorry, Mr. Pangolin. My judgment in that area does not seem to be very reliable."

"It was not your fault, Mr. Hobbs. I heard about the man Bilfreth and his men. Neither they nor the Four Kings are honorable men. Put it from your mind and do not think of it again. The Fates tend to bedevil such men and their accomplices."

"My only hope is that the Fates get us to Atlantea alive."

"We do not need the Fates for that, Mr. Hobbs. We have our own determination, skill and cunning—and Mr. Traveler and his dog."

"Yes, the two most important."

♦♦♦

Inside the inn, the ale flowed, and the men were loud, laughing, drinking, and dancing. Hobbs sat outside on the steps for his nightly pipe. Pangolin had men guarding all entrances to the inn, stables, and cottage. No one was on the streets, and besides the rowdiness of the men within the inn, the surrounding city was quiet.

No one had seen Traveler or the dog since they first settled in, but Hobbs knew they were close by.

"Mr. Hobbs," Traveler called out.

Hobbs stood. "Yes, sir." He dumped the contents of his pipe on the ground.

"A forest animal whispered to me that we have a stable of donkeys for our caravan."

Hobbs laughed. "Yes, we do, sir. Lady Aylen insisted, and she said it was her money."

"No sense arguing with her. We can exchange them for more suitable animals in Faë-Land. Do we have everything we need?"

"We do, sir. Will we not be able to get more supplies from Last Keep?"

"Last Keep is a closed city, Mr. Hobbs. A mistake many an excursion has made. They cater to those from Faë-Land entering into Avalonia, not the reverse. They will not let us in."

"That seems very odd."

"Not when you consider the residents of Last Keep are not human."

The revelation caught Hobbs off guard.

"Have you taken on any new men?" Traveler asked.

"Only one, sir. A Mr. Quillen. He is well-prepared for the journey, but was alone."

"Then all there remains for me to do is sleep."

"Sir, if you go into the inn, we have a room set aside for you."

"Hopefully, you did not pack three thousand men into a handful of rooms."

"No, sir, though that would be an interesting feat. There is open space not too far away where we have our camp set up. The inn has been designated for the entertainment."

"Then, by all means, give my room to the men. I would not be able to sleep anyway with all their noise. I'll join the men at the camp."

"Very good, sir. When do you think the Kings' Caravan will arrive, sir? With our arrival two days early, do you still estimate nine days?"

"They will be here in five days."

Traveler was already walking past the rowdy inn down the path to their camp. The dog followed.

◆◆◆

Quillen sat against Goodmound's curtain wall, waiting. He had risen before dawn to find a spot. It was barely past dawn, and already crowds were forming. Traveler was right—the Kings' Caravan would arrive on the fifth day, and it was that day. Town criers ran through the street the night before to inform the city. Most of the people were gathering on the mound itself, but Quillen wanted to be away from the commotion. He had his telescope in hand, his leather-bound notebook open in his lap, his quill pen in the book's spine, and was ready to see fantastical beasts. Today, he planned to write a full account of his direct observations of the griffin and hippogriffs of the Four Kings. He looked out across the main road to the castle city, eagerly waiting with a smile.

A roar cut through the air, and everyone, no matter where they were stationed, stopped. All eyes were focused on the main road into the city. Quillen and others sitting along the wall stood. There was another roar and the scribe touched his chest. He had heard the roar of a griffin had the power of a hundred lion roars. Then they all heard eagle shrieks—the hippogriffs!

People got more excited. More people flowed out of the city, including children. Quillen looked around. Nowhere did he see anyone who looked like royalty or a noble receiving delegation. He snapped his head back, his eyes darting up to the sky as people gasped. King Oughtred of Xenhelm flew through the air on his giant griffin over the city. Other than his flapping orange cape, man and beast were almost a blur. Another roar from the griffin echoed. Following fast were Prince Wuldricar the Savage, Prince Renfrey the Wily, and Prince Gervase the Fair, on their hippogriff steeds. Gasps from the crowd were replaced with sounds of disappointment and anger. Quillen slammed his book shut; he hadn't even had a chance to look through his telescope with his own eyes to see the magical flying beasts.

The rumble of approaching feet frightened the crowds, and some people began to move back towards the main gatehouse entrances. Xenhelm armored knights, garbed in muted silver, draped with sashes of the Xenhelm colors of orange and white, ran into view. They were not running to Goodmound's Castle but around it. Many wondered how they could run so fast carrying spiked polearms that rose at least ten feet in the air. The archers with their longbows and crossbows, quivers on their backs, followed.

Hobbs appeared and gestured to him. "Mr. Quillen."

Quillen followed as Hobbs ran back into the city. "Is something bad happening, Mr. Hobbs?"

"We leave now. Gather your things and join the men."

◆◆◆

The Kings' Caravan and their one-hundred-thousand-man army and thousands more in their alliance society were already gone. People were bewildered, asking why the Caravan had not stopped as it had always done in years past.

"I knew something was wrong," Quillen said to Hobbs.

"What do you mean?" Hobbs asked.

"There were no dignitaries from the castle to greet them."

Hobbs thought for a moment. "You are entirely right, lad. Curious."

Traveler led the party, but he was not pleased with the slowness caused by the donkeys. He gave Lady Aylen a look.

"Mr. Traveler, the animals are to make our journey easier."

There were other parties caught off guard by the Kings' Caravan's hasty passing. While the Traveler party made its way out of the city, all ready and prepared to go, it was clear that none of the other parties would be.

"Can we follow along?" a man asked.

"You should stay with your group, sir," Hobbs called out. "They will need your service more than us."

Other men, including warriors, watched as they passed.

"Why would they do what they did?" Gwyness asked. "I heard city folk say the Caravan usually stays at least two days and buys most of the goods of their market road."

Traveler and the dog were at point. Lady Aylen, Gwyness, and Hobbs followed next. Following them were the bearers, pulling carts and minding the donkeys. Estus managed the bearers with the long carts, which carried the most valuable items and the weapons. The rear was managed by Pangolin and his Cut-throats. All other warriors and swordsmen flanked the party on both sides with their weapons and shields.

"Mr. Traveler, can you see their path?" Lady Aylen asked.

"I can. Though, they are trying to confuse me with other trails in different directions."

"Why would they do that?"

"Obviously, they do not want any to follow."

"They cannot stop us," Lady Aylen declared. "At the very least, with their size, we would see their campfires at night from many miles away."

Hobbs ran closer. "Sir, I would like to mention something one of the men observed. There was no royal greeting party for the Four Kings. That is unusual. I heard people in the crowds say that had never happened before."

"If we did not know better, I would say the Kings' Caravan was purposely targeting us with their treachery," Traveler remarked.

Lady Aylen studied him for a moment. "Is that what you believe, Mr. Traveler?"

"I believe the same thing you do, Lady Aylen."

"That is no response, Mr. Traveler. You do not know what I believe."

♦♦♦

They made good time moving from Goodmound's Castle. No other party followed; they were the only ones on the trail of the Kings' Caravan.

Quillen looked directly above and saw it. Its giant eagle wings, golden fur, its tail swaying back and forth. He was so mesmerized by the flying beast that all he did was stare up as he walked. It was so majestic and beautiful in his eyes. He did not know griffins could glide through the air without a sound.

Kind Oughtred descended from the sky on his giant griffin in front of them. Traveler stopped their party in its tracks. They were all stunned and watched the Xenhelm King holding the reins of his griffin in one hand and a long staff in the other. It was the staff that frightened Traveler. The air around them began to darken and a vortex began to take form. Everyone looked about frantically, practically frozen in motion. A party of nearly three thousand men were helpless to act as their feet rose inches from the ground. The king lifted the staff in the air, and a blinding flash enveloped the Traveler party; they vanished in its light. King Oughtred lowered his staff and flew away on his griffin.

CHAPTER TEN
The Kings Elder

Lady Aylen felt cold damp earth against her body. The roaring sound of water was nearby, drowning out anything else that might be around her. She opened her eyes and slowly sat up, coming to her full senses.

"Oh no!" She jumped to her feet in shock.

Unconscious men—her men, Traveler's men, Pangolin's men—were scattered everywhere. Then she noticed Pangolin about twenty yards away, dragging a man from a river bank. They were near a raging river and she looked around, unfamiliar with the land. She was relieved to see Gwyness, also wide awake, doing her best to aid Pangolin by dragging one of the lads away from the river.

Lady Aylen's head turned to survey the area, and she froze as her eyes caught sight of it—the dog; its growl echoed. Its head was still dog, but dangled on top of a long, snake-like neck. Its mouth was filled with fangs as it growled again. Its body was elongated, sitting upon reptilian legs of more than eight feet in length. It stood next to its unconscious master then screamed in distress. Traveler, as with all the others, was lifeless on the ground.

"Lady Aylen!" Pangolin yelled.

She turned her attention slowly. The dog never cared for her in its normal state. In this condition, it could kill them all.

"Lady Aylen!"

"Yes," she responded, moving away to approach him, glancing back at the dog-creature.

"You must do something."

"Do something?"

"Your maidservant said you know of potions that could revive the men."

"I do not know if any will work. We do not know what was done to us. I am not a healer like Mr. Traveler or some apothecary. I intended to hire an expert to use them, not have to use them myself."

Gwyness walked to them. "We are no longer outside of Goodmound's Castle on the way to Last Keep."

"Where are we then?" Pangolin asked.

"We are south of Hopeshire."

Lady Aylen shook her head. "No! How do you know?"

"I recognize the land, and this river. Hopeshire is some miles north."

"Lady Aylen, you must revive Mr. Traveler immediately," Pangolin said. He was as fearful of the animal as they were.

"I do not know if I can. The animal will not let me near him!"

Pangolin angrily neared her. "Listen, Your Highness, I awoke before you all, but too late to save more of the men who were dropped into the river to be swept away."

"No! How many?"

"I ran as fast I could. I managed to grab a few, but I believe many more are lost."

Lady Aylen dropped down to the ground and pounded it with her fists. "King Oughtred!"

Pangolin knelt. "M'lady, you must use your potions to revive Mr. Traveler. We must calm his animal before it becomes more erratic.

Whatever knowledge you have, however small, is vastly superior to my own, which is nil. Reviving Mr. Traveler must be your only task. Gwyness and I will move the men away from the river. I fear this day's treachery is not over."

"What do you mean?" Lady Aylen asked.

"I do not believe King Oughtred sent us here to drown us but to await our final end. The three of us are supposed to be unconscious, too. We are not."

"Are you asking me why?"

"Lady Aylen, I do not care what magical properties you or Maiden Gwyness possess. I care that you revive Mr. Traveler as quickly as possible, even if temporarily, so that his animal does not take the form of an even more dangerous beast and kill us and everyone else in this land."

The princess looked at the animal. It screamed. Gwyness reached out her hand and helped Lady Aylen to her feet. "The animal is like any other," Gwyness said to her. "It is just as you have said to me many times. It responds to emotion and action. If you are fearful of it, it will sense that. Make bold motions, but slowly, so it sees clearly what you are doing. Ignore it and focus on Mr. Traveler. It will see that you are helping him."

"It hates me." Lady Aylen stared at it.

"He may hate you, but he is more concerned with his master. If it is you who can revive him, it will not trouble you."

"Gwyness, you should mix the potions and administer it to him."

Gwyness shook her head. "It has to be you. I know only my potions. The animal would sense any uncertainty and I would be killed."

"Lady Aylen, you must act now," Pangolin said again. "If you help his master, he will help us. We may need his assistance before the day is done. We are now a party of three that has to defend an unconscious group of over two thousand men!"

Lady Aylen looked around. "Here," Gwyness said and handed her a large yellow pouch. "I already found it for you."

The princess took it and gave a loud sigh. She turned towards the animal. It screamed at her, but she marched forward. Pangolin and Gwyness watched. When Lady Aylen came upon Traveler, she stopped and focused her gaze on him, not the screaming animal hovering over her, which seemed to become more reptilian and larger in size as she neared. She sat on the ground and dumped the contents of the pouch on the ground. There were small wooden flasks, thumb-sized boxes, smaller colored pouches, spoons, sticks, and other assorted items. She took a parchment and one of the pouches, then began to shake specks of yellow powder on the parchment.

Gwyness held her breath. The animal had craned its head back on its long snake-like neck, ready to strike her. Pangolin slowly touched Gwyness's shoulder to reassure her. Lady Aylen paid no attention to anything around her but her task at hand. She rested the parchment with its contents on the ground then took a stick and broke it in half. The parchment was on fire. She lifted it, and the powder produced yellow smoke that began to rise. Slowly, she moved the parchment near Traveler's nose so he would inhale the yellow smoke.

Traveler stirred. The animal was suddenly in its "normal" form—a dog. It whimpered as it tried to push Traveler to get up with his nose and then his two front paws.

"I shall help him," Lady Aylen said to the dog. "I need to get him into a covered tent and build a larger fire with the powder." She stood up. "Mr. Pangolin!"

Pangolin was already walking to her. "You need a tent."

"Yes. I will build a large fire with the powder."

Not only were the bodies of the men scattered everywhere, so were all the supplies. However, Pangolin found what he needed.

"I can help," Gwyness said.

"No!" Pangolin said. "Maiden Gwyness, you must keep watch until I finish this. You alone are keeping guard over two thousand men. Get yourself some kind of weapon."

"My weapon is lost somewhere—"

"Any weapon will do."

Gwyness grabbed a sword from the ground. Pangolin quickly put up the tent and tied the flap of one wall open. Lady Aylen set some cloth on one side of the tent as she set another fire. Pangolin lifted Traveler from the ground and set him inside the tent. The dog seemed to be panicking again and screamed at Lady Aylen.

"Stop that! I am moving as fast as I can," she yelled at the animal.

The dog screamed at her again then again. Lady Aylen slowly poured powder in the fire. Soon the yellow smoke was everywhere.

"You have this under control, m'lady." Pangolin left the tent and closed the flap to keep the smoke in. The dog burst out of the tent. He stopped and vigorously shook his head then used a paw to wipe his nose. The dog sniffled and slowly sat on the ground.

Pangolin was amused, but looked out across the unconscious men. The work was too much for two, but it had to be done.

♦♦♦

Gwyness stood watch in the center of the area. Pangolin approached her, and she turned.

"Did you see anyone, or anything?" he asked.

"Nothing."

"Good. It will take us well into the night, but we must move all the men together. We need to create the smallest possible perimeter."

"Mr. Pangolin, this is not the answer. We cannot wait here. We need help."

"Help from where?"

"I can run to Hopeshire."

"Run? How far away?"

"Twenty, maybe thirty miles."

"That is too far."

"Mr. Pangolin, I have run such distances before. That was for sport. This is for our very lives."

"That would leave only me. Lady Aylen has to stay in the tent to attend Mr. Traveler."

"I know it is taking a chance, but it is a chance we must take. If what you fear is true, then we are simply waiting to be slaughtered. If I leave now, I can get there before nightfall and be back by morning. We have no choice, Mr. Pangolin."

"Before you leave, find your personal weapons."

"Yes."

"You are certain you know where we are?"

"Yes. We are outside Hopeshire. There is no doubt of it."

"Go. Get your weapons and go. The sooner you leave and get there, the sooner you will return."

She touched his forearm. "Good luck, Mr. Pangolin. I shall return in the morning. I promise."

◆◆◆

Gwyness found her dual weapons—a pair of slender war hammers.

"Not weapons typical for a woman," he said to her.

"I am not a typical woman."

"Yes. Since both you and Lady Aylen survived King Oughtred's spell, I have come to that realization."

"What protected you? Your armor is magical, then?"

"Yes, it has saved my life many times, and I intend for it to continue doing so."

He helped her cross the river to the other side by simply tossing her across with all his might. She smiled when she landed and dashed away. She would need to keep a quick pace if she expected to reach Hopeshire by nightfall. However, he had no doubt she would succeed. Whether she could find help was another matter.

Pangolin looked at Traveler's tent. A cloud of yellow smoke escaped from between the flaps, and there was the dog staring back at him.

Why here? He thought.

It was the question that repeated in Pangolin's mind. He stood and carefully scanned the terrain. The key was the river. Was it to block escape? They were all expected to be unconscious. No, the river was to bring the instrument of their death.

Pangolin knelt on the ground and rested an ear on the top of his massive axe-mace. His eyes were closed and he concentrated his focus on what he could hear. He did not move; even his breathing had slowed to a deep meditative state.

He heard their approach from the vibrations through his weapon. His eyes slowly opened. Pangolin stood as he firmly grasped the handle of his weapon. He inhaled deeply then let out a yell—a berserker war cry. His eyes went bloodshot, then white as he ran.

Lady Aylen peeked out of the tent. She and the dog watched Pangolin jump across the river—miles across—in one leap and run into the forest with an intensity they had never before seen from him.

The barbarian in the lead of the war party on foot had pasty skin and wild, tangled hair. Like the other three men who followed, they looked like they had never shaved a day in their life and wore necklaces made of bone fragments—human bones.

Pangolin's axe-mace dropped from the air and crashed into the chest of the first barbarian, who never saw it coming. He dropped to the ground, dead; his sword fell from his hand.

The screaming Pangolin appeared from the forest. The other barbarians fired arrow after arrow at Pangolin, but they merely bounced off his earthen armor. He reached the dead barbarian and ripped his weapon from the man's chest. Pangolin threw it again as he rushed another wave of barbarians with swords and axes. His axe-mace killed another man, hitting him in the upper torso. Pangolin grabbed one barbarian and snapped his neck then stabbed another with an earthen dagger shard he pulled from his armor. More arrows rained down on him, but Pangolin's warpath never stopped. None of the barbarians would retreat; their code demanded to fight to the death. Death was what they received at Pangolin's hands.

Over twenty-five men lay dead on the ground as Pangolin walked past them with his blood-soaked armor and weapon. The battle was not over. The war party had come from a larger force. He could see the ship moving slowly down the river, and he waited in place until it came around the river's bend.

The pirate ship looked to be made completely of human bones and skulls. Pangolin had heard rumors of the ship for years, but always considered it a myth. On the deck of the ship were no less than a thousand men. It had one main mast with black sails and jibs.

Pangolin yelled and ran towards it. Again, a flurry of arrows rained down upon him and again none of them did any damage. His helmet's visor and faceplate were down and secure. Berserker war rage gave its warrior super-human strength and he jumped from the river bank through the air and landed on the deck of the ship, but he did not attack the marauder pirates. He slammed his axe-mace into the deck, shattering it to pieces, and he fell down to the next level. He repeated his attack and shattered the floor again. At the bottom of the ship, he swung again and when he shattered the floor, the water blasted through as Pangolin fell through into the ice-cold river.

Pandemonium overtook the barbarians' ship as it sank into the water and began to break apart. Men jumped from the ship only to be swept away by the power of the river. Pangolin emerged and climbed onto the river's bank to stand on solid land. He watched as the entire bone ship completely broke apart and screaming men disappeared down the river, helpless to swim to shore.

Pangolin turned and could see the dog in the distance watching him. The animal turned and disappeared in the direction of Traveler's tent. Pangolin breathed slowly to reverse his berserker rage. It would take a few moments of quiet to return to his normal state.

♦♦♦

Lady Aylen stood outside the tent.

"A thousand men?" she asked Pangolin.

"Possibly more."

"So, this really was to kill us all. Not simply to send us away."

"It would appear so."

Lady Aylen touched the top of her lip to think.

"Did you know of Xenhelm and its Four Kings before?" Pangolin asked.

"I knew what everyone else did. They created and led the Caravan every three years. It began almost twenty years ago—I was but an infant. My kingdom had no special contact with them. There are kingdoms that do but not Sirnegate. I cannot believe any of this. Their behavior has been of common street ruffians, not that of a royal family."

"Maybe you are being naive, as I have known many a king and queen to act like a common street ruffian."

"Yes. You are correct, of course, but I never heard that Xenhelm was such a kingdom. Well, Mr. Pangolin, it would appear that our journey is over—again."

"Why do you say that? Mr. Traveler knows the way. Do you doubt he knows the way through Titan's Trail to Atlantea?"

"No, I am certain he does, but look at our state of affairs. Mr. Traveler said we could not go alone unless we were a strong party. We are no force of any consequence now. Gwyness will get to Hopeshire. I also have no doubt of that, but who can she get to help us?"

The dog appeared and started screaming at Lady Aylen.

"Stop that!" she yelled at the animal, but it continued.

"Looks like your presence is required."

"You are a miserable animal!" she yelled at the dog. "I am doing everything I know to help your master."

The dog continued to scream at her. Lady Aylen relented and went back into the yellow-smoke-filled tent. The dog peeked in then backed out. It sat on the ground, looking in.

Pangolin looked up at the sky. Darkness would fall in only a few more hours. He would be the sole sentry for over two thousand men for the entire night. His eyes were filled with sadness. Not one of the men had awoken from their magic-cursed slumber.

◆◆◆

Pangolin had set up as many fires as possible to encircle the men. Now, he walked their perimeter the entire night without pause. There was no visible moon due to dark clouds, so the night was even blacker than usual. The only sound in the night was the raging river, and if anyone was stalking them, he would not know until they were upon him. He did glance at the dog from time to time; it sat quietly in front of Traveler's tent. Pangolin would have to rely on the animal's heightened senses as a beacon.

At dawn, the dog leapt to its feet and ran off into the distance, opposite the river. Pangolin stopped his march and watched. Suddenly, he saw dark shapes rise from the trees. Pangolin watched several bloodied, mangled bodies sail overhead and crash into the river. They were another barbarian hunting party but were no more. The river, as it had done so often before, swept them away into oblivion. Pangolin watched the dog trot back into camp and return to its spot in front of the tent.

◆◆◆

Pangolin sat on the ground with his ear on the top of his axe-mace, but this time he was more sleeping than listening. Lady Aylen, with sword in hand, replaced Pangolin in his march. The dog followed her, screaming.

"Go away from me!" she yelled. "Your master is sleeping." The dog screamed at her again. "I will not be bullied by you, animal!" She stopped, and the dog also turned to sounds in the distance.

"Mr. Pangolin!" she yelled.

The berserker was asleep. She ran to him and tapped him on his shoulder. He snapped awake and rose to his feet. The sounds were of approaching horses. They neared the river bank, and the dog joined them. Pangolin took a firm grip of his weapon. The riders appeared—over a dozen knights.

"Gwyness!" Lady Aylen yelled with delight.

Her maidservant was also on horseback, riding with the knights.

"Lady Aylen, we are sending someone over to you. Keep the dog at bay," she said.

Lady Aylen looked at the dog, who snarled. "Behave!" It growled. "This animal hates me. I help his master, and he still hates me."

More riders appeared and a few wore cloaked robes. They dismounted their horses and walked to the river.

"How are they going to get across?" Lady Aylen asked.

"Let us watch and see," Pangolin answered.

Many more riders appeared, and among them were men who looked to be royalty from the crowns on their heads. More men appeared on foot, axes in hand, and after speaking to the royals on horseback, they rushed to the forest and began chopping down trees.

"They are building a bridge," Pangolin said.

"The river is too wide," Lady Aylen countered. "To build a proper bridge would take many days."

"I believe…" Pangolin gripped his weapon. Lady Aylen and the dog noticed a bearded man in a hooded cloak on their side of the river, standing quietly. The dog growled at the stranger. Lady Aylen stepped in front of the dog.

"There is no need for alarm," the cloaked man said. "I am with the Kings Elder."

"The Kings Elder?" Lady Aylen said, smiling.

"You know of my lords?"

"I do, sir. I am Lady Aylen of Sirnegate."

"Ah, yes, m'lady. I know of your kingdom. I was told by your maidservant of your encounter with King Oughtred."

"You mean his treachery and plot to murder us," Lady Aylen said angrily.

"I do not doubt either. It has been rumored they have done so before. We know the rumors are true now. Please give me a clear account of the spell he cast upon you and your men."

"He was on his griffin and raised a staff in his hand."

"Describe the staff, m'lady."

"It was nearly five feet in length. I believe it was of a translucent material, but the tip had an….orb. He raised the staff, and the air about us began to change. We found ourselves in a whirlwind, and our feet rose from the ground. Then there was a blinding flash of light, and we were here."

"Where did he cast this spell upon you, m'lady?"

"Outside of Goodmound's Castle."

"He cast you and your men quite a distance."

"Are you a sorcerer?" Pangolin asked the man.

"I am, but I am not certain my magic can undo his. There are two choices. I can lift the spell and allow the men to recover naturally. In a month or so, they would be almost themselves again. Depending on the man, they would be completely themselves in six months or sooner."

"That is not acceptable," Lady Aylen said. "Why so long?"

"M'lady, think of it as if King Oughtred picked us up and violently threw us through the air, unimaginable distances, and we slammed, equally violently, to the ground. That is why your men are as they are. Their bodies are in shock from the magical attack. It is why your animals, the donkeys, will surely die. Most of your men, if left on their own, will also die." The sorcerer looked at the dog. "Your dog, m'lady."

"He is not my dog," Lady Aylen said. The dog snarled at her.

"So I see. The dog is not magical, but it is something else. Something shielded it from the spell, but I cannot say what." He looked at Pangolin. "You were protected by your magical armor. Your Maiden Gwyness possesses a magical amulet. M'lady, what is your special magical protection?"

"I shall keep my secret, sir."

"Very good, m'lady."

"The men, though, is there not another way to restore them?"

"The second choice, m'lady, is not to reverse the spell, but to nullify it."

"What would that do?"

"It could do many things. It could return them to their exact location outside Goodmound's Castle where the spell was cast on them. It could pull the malignant magical effects from their bodies and they would all jump to their feet. It could also kill them."

Lady Aylen and Pangolin looked at each other.

"Sir, can we not have them jump to their feet and nothing more?" Lady Aylen asked.

The sorcerer smiled. "Yes, that is the outcome I would choose also. I will do my best."

"Have you done this before?" Pangolin asked.

"Once, but this teleportation spell was purposely perverted to injure in this way. A normal teleportation spell is a rather benign spell. But again, I will do my best, and I will have help."

"Sir, I must warn you in the strongest possible terms," Pangolin began. "To address your earlier observation, the dog is more than a dog. It is a shape-shifter, and its master is one of the men. If his master were to die, he would assuredly kill you, and there is nothing anyone could do to stop him."

"Then none of the men shall die."

◆◆◆

The sorcerer instructed them to position each man on their back with their hands at their sides. They did not know how they got across, but the other two cloaked men joined their fellow sorcerer. Pangolin moved quickly to complete the task. Lady Aylen positioned Traveler, but then the dog screamed at her, not wanting her to leave his side.

"Go away!"

The dog not only screamed but blocked her path when she tried to walk away.

"Lady Aylen," Pangolin said. "Stay with Traveler. We need you to keep the dog calm."

"You are a miserable animal!" she yelled at the dog.

Pangolin could hear the cloaked men having a laugh.

While they positioned the men, knights across the river were indeed constructing a bridge. It would not be a permanent one but to be hoisted across, securely rested on either edge of the river bank, and allow people to cross single file.

"We are ready," the sorcerer said to Pangolin.

"That is the second time, sir, you have approached without me sensing your presence first."

"I am a sorcerer."

"We shall find out for certain. What do you need Lady Aylen and me to do?"

"Keep the dog calm."

The sorcerer stood in the center of the unconscious party, with the other two cloaked men on either side, as he raised a polished oak staff. He tapped it on the ground. Light flashed from the bodies of every man and beast on the ground.

The dog started to go hysterical, jumping and screaming. Lady Aylen knelt next to Traveler and placed an ear on Traveler's chest. The dog immediately calmed down and pushed his face in. She lifted her head and the dog listened to Traveler's chest too. Lady Aylen looked around at all the men. She saw Hobbs slowly open his eyes, then another man, and another. Traveler stirred and sat up.

The dog went wild with happiness and jumped on his master, its tongue hanging out. The dog bolted away and then ran back to jump into Traveler's lap. The dog bolted away again. It wanted to play. Traveler stood to his feet. The dog jumped and stood on its hind legs to place its front paws on Traveler's chest.

"What happened?" Traveler asked groggily.

Every unconscious man had awakened and began rising to their feet.

"Mr. Traveler, you look like you are about to fall over," Lady Aylen said.

"That, I believe, is because I am." Traveler fell to his knees, which startled the dog. "I am fine," he said to the dog, rubbing its head and neck. "I need a proper sleep." With that, he rested down on the ground.

Traveler was not the only one. Other men began to return to the ground to lie down.

"Mr. Hobbs." Quillen's voice rang out. Hobbs slowly walked to him. "The donkeys are all dead, sir."

Traveler raised his head to look.

"Mr. Traveler, sleep," Lady Aylen commanded.

"Yes, princess," he said as he lay back down and closed his eyes.

◆◆◆

Traveler remembered men lifting and moving him into a new tent. He awoke a few times to see many men around him setting up camp. He remembered the dog nudging him with his nose to wake him up and make sure he was fine; otherwise, the dog rested his head on Traveler's chest. It was nightfall when Traveler awoke again fully, but this time he would not sleep again for the rest of the night.

The camp was well-lit by campfires and torches. There was a basin of water on a table near Traveler's sleeping mat, and he washed his face. When he wiped it dry with a cloth, he turned to his dog. "I almost did not survive this time."

The dog whimpered but remained lying on the ground.

Hobbs appeared at the entrance to his tent. "Sir, you are awake."

"Had your nightly pipe yet, Mr. Hobbs?"

"Actually, a few times already, sir—waiting for you, sir."

"How are the men?"

"There are a few things I need direction on, but Lady Aylen wanted me to inform her as soon as you awoke. She wants you to meet our saviors."

"Yes, that would be welcome. Tell her I am ready to meet whomever."

Hobbs left him but returned soon afterward. Traveler noticed there were two new camps—one joined with theirs and a larger one across the river. The tent they walked to was a large crimson one at the edge of the camp. It was well-guarded by knights, and another escorted them in. Inside, at a series of tables were several men. Some were dressed as knights, others wore hooded cloaks. Lady Aylen and Maiden Gwyness stood with three men wearing crowns.

Traveler turned to Hobbs. "Where is Mr. Pangolin?"

"Here, sir." The berserker warrior walked in after him, led in by another knight.

"Mr. Pangolin, please stand with Lady Aylen and Maiden Gwyness." Pangolin moved to do so. "I do not have the whole story yet, but I heard the men talking amongst themselves all day while I rested. Maiden Gwyness, I wish to thank you personally for your courage in saving our lives. Your decision to race to Hopeshire, on foot and alone, for help is what rescued us from disaster. Mr. Pangolin, I hear you alone dispatched an entire pirate ship of barbarians to the bottom of the river as well as a war party sent to finish off the men. Finally, Lady Aylen, yes, my dog does not care for you, but both he and I recognize your efforts in trying to save me. We both thank you sincerely. You saved the men, and I thank you—we all do."

"Thank you, Mr. Traveler. I did what I had to do," Gwyness said.

"You did much more than that," Traveler said. "Mr. Hobbs, how many men did we lose?"

"Sixteen men, sir," Hobbs answered. "It could have been much worse if not for the quick action of Mr. Pangolin."

"That lad you brought on from Goodmound's Castle."

"Yes, sir. Mr. Quillen."

"He can scribble about whatever creatures he wishes at night, but I want his other official task to keep a ledger of all the men we have lost and will lose on this journey. I do not want any of them forgotten."

"Yes, sir. I will make it so."

"But maybe I am speaking prematurely, as I do not know if there will be a journey to have in our current state."

Lady Aylen stepped forward. "Mr. Traveler, thank you for the recognition, though my efforts were far less than stellar when compared to theirs, but I welcome your words, nonetheless. However, this is my meeting, and if you bear with us, you will learn that all is far from lost."

"Yes. Who are our saviors that you have assembled, Lady Aylen?"

Lady Aylen gestured to the crowned royals. The men walked to Traveler. "This is King Aereth of Helm Earldom."

The royal had silver gray hair, mustache, and beard, though he was not all elderly. "Mr. Traveler, it is a pleasure to meet you. Already, we have heard many stories about you, your exploits, and your dog, but I suspect it is but a fraction of the stories to come.

"Let me introduce my colleagues: King Eothelm of Strongbridge and King Sigbard of Eastmoor."

Eothelm was a man with graying-black hair. Sigbard was the largest of the three kings; he was mostly bald, except for the remaining white hair on the sides of his head.

"We are known throughout Avalonia as the Kings Elder. Aereth the Wise, Eothelm the Blessed, and Sigbard the Humble. So, Mr. Traveler, what kingdom are you from?"

"My kingdom no longer exists, sire. I was a healer as a boy who became a swordsman, and I have my dog as my companion. I would say that, if our journey was to continue, I would tell you more over a campfire meal."

"Why do you feel our journey will not continue, Mr. Traveler?" Lady Aylen asked. "I am as determined as any to complete it."

"We can catch up with the Kings' Caravan," Aereth said. "I am sure of it."

"We do not need to catch up with them. Mr. Traveler knows the path to Atlantea," Lady Aylen revealed.

The expression on the faces of the three kings was a combination of joy and surprise.

"Mr. Traveler knows the way through Titan's Trail?" Aereth asked.

"He does," Lady Aylen said. "We do not need King Oughtred the Wicked or his Kings' Caravan. We can create our own."

"King Oughtred the Wicked," Sigbard repeated. "No truer words have ever been spoken."

The kings looked at each other with smiles. "We have waited years for this moment," Aereth said. The king stepped closer to Traveler. "Do you truly know the way to Atlantea, or is it a boast?"

"It is not a boast. I was there before."

"You have been there before?" Eothelm asked. "Why would a mortal ever leave such a place of riches?"

"It was a different time. I arrived there after much tragedy and the loss of many I called friend. I arrived, and I did not feel the journey was worth it. My heart was not in it, despite its riches, so I left. And I met my dog."

"You must tell us more, sir," Aereth said. "The Kings' Caravan has journeyed there for twenty years. Does Atlantea live up to its legend?"

"It does, sire, and much more."

"Then what is it, Mr. Traveler?" Lady Aylen asked.

"The journey is not my concern. I know of the dangers and am ready for them. My concern, which should be the concern to us all, is why King Oughtred, of a kingdom with a long and revered history, tried to murder us at least twice? We have not even left the Lands of Man. I need to understand this fully before I go anywhere. If I am not satisfied, I will not go."

"If you do not go, we cannot go," Lady Aylen said.

"Then convince me. Do you have a sorcerer, sire?" Traveler asked.

"It was how we revived all your men, Mr. Traveler," Aereth answered. "We have three."

One of the cloaked men approached. "It was I."

"Then I neglected to thank you, as well, sir."

"No need, sir."

"What did King Oughtred do to us? It was a teleportation spell, but it was not."

"You are very astute, sir," the sorcerer said. "It was a corrupted spell meant, not only to teleport across long distances, but to render all within it unconscious."

"Unconscious for how long?"

"For some, forever."

"You speak as if you knew of this spell."

"We heard about it from another noble who returned from Last Keep. He and his party had joined the Kings' Caravan the previous outing. He claimed the Four Kings used it on his party, and only a few of them lived."

"Did he say why the Four Kings engaged in the treachery?" Traveler asked.

"No, and he did not have any theories as to why either."

"Was there any black mark on their reputation before this?"

"You said it yourself, Mr. Traveler. The Four Kings are of a kingdom of nobility and reverence," Aereth answered.

"You say that with an edge of sarcasm, sire."

Aereth smiled. "I despise King Oughtred. I always have. He killed my only son in battle many years ago. However, it was a fair battle, so there was no grievance to bring against Xenhelm."

"Do you believe the battle was fair?"

"It was, but I am a father, Mr. Traveler. I hate the man and always will, which is why I have never entertained even my own suspicions against the Four Kings. I am forever biased."

Traveler turned to the sorcerer. "Are you familiar with any magic revealing spells?"

"You seem to know quite a bit about magic for one not a sorcerer."

"I told you. I was in Faë-Land for a period of time. There, magic is a daily experience. As a human, you learn, leave their lands, or die. The magic eye. Do you know the spell?"

"I do, but I cannot conjure it. I used all my power to destroy the effects of King Oughtred's teleportation spell upon you and your men."

"No matter. How long will it take for your power to return?"

"To conjure such a spell? A week."

Traveler nodded. "Then we will wait."

"Why do you want to do this, Mr. Traveler?" Lady Aylen asked. "We know what and who is of magic in our party."

"No, we do not, Lady Aylen, not everyone. That is what I want the spell for. I want to ensure we do not have a spy of any kind among us."

The three kings looked at each other. "Mr. Traveler, why do you believe we might?" Aereth asked.

"We reached Goodmound's Castle before them, but they rushed by as if they knew we were in wait. It could have been for a dozen other reasons not known to us. However, King Oughtred also ambushed us. How did he know we had left the castle and where we were? No, I want to be sure."

"Mr. Traveler, I suspected a similar thing," Eothelm said.

"Why, sire? What tales do you have to add to ours?"

"We were supposed to have joined the Kings' Caravan at Ironwood. However, we were detained, if that is what it can be called. Our camp was attacked by an army of marauders. We never saw them coming. They simply appeared around us. We battled them for ten days until we defeated them. I had a deep feeling they were sent to delay us, as they were not powerful enough to defeat us, and they did."

◆◆◆

Only Traveler noticed that his dog had slipped out of the Kings Elder's tent.

Quillen sat by the fire, writing in his book. He was drawing as much as he could remember of the flying griffin, but he was distracted. "Do you hear that sound?" he asked the nearest man, who was trying to get to sleep.

"What sound?" he asked with annoyance, his eyes closed.

"It sounds like...I do not know how to describe it."

Quillen looked up to see one of the men of the camp walking into the night. No one was supposed to go anywhere alone by day or night, but he held his tongue. The dog raced by, startling him.

It was one of the servants of the Traveler party. He looked for a tree as if to relieve himself, but instead reached beneath his tunic to pull out a giant amulet. The man's pupils disappeared. Only the whites of his eyes stared into the night. An eye opened in the center of the amulet. He heard a noise, and his pupils reappeared; the amulet's eye closed.

"No!" The man tried to cover the amulet with his hands.

The dog transformed into a giant humanoid form, picked him up, and threw the man high in the air, plunging him into the raging river.

◆◆◆

The dog returned to the tent. Only Lady Aylen and Traveler noticed.

"Three kings, three sorcerers, and our entire party are what you would acquire," King Aereth pronounced. "Mr. Traveler, we want you to lead our new, second caravan to Atlantea. We have sought to form an alternative to the Kings' Caravan for years."

"You said King Oughtred killed your son, sire. Have he or his sons ever done anything against you since then?"

"No, though Eothelm still believes the marauder attack we faced was his doing."

"It is a wise assumption," Eothelm said.

"I agree, based on what they attempted against your party. Though let us not forget that many, far and wide, are plagued by marauder attacks. Sigbard, your thoughts?" Aereth asked.

"My mind has been swayed to Eothelm's side. We have seen treachery, heard of it from others, so we should assume even when we do not have the facts to support it. No harm can come from such a position."

"Did attempts to form an alternative to the Caravan begin before or after your son's death?" Traveler asked Aereth.

"Before, but again, the battle was not Oughtred's doing. It was my son's."

"Were you there?"

"I was."

"Then, I will not speak of it again, sire. However, we must be honest with ourselves."

"Mr. Traveler," Aereth began, "we know what you are about to say. We can sit, talk, and ponder for days and weeks. We know King Oughtred has tried to kill us, he may have killed others, and he may try to do so in the future. However, those facts are irrelevant. We have before us all that we require for our own successful caravan through Titan's Trail to Atlantea. We must act, now.

"You have over two thousand men, we understand, from merging with Lady Aylen and warriors under Mr. Pangolin. We have another eight thousand men—four thousand are our best knights, three thousand other fighters, including archers, and the remaining one thousand are servants. That is ten thousand men, Mr. Traveler. Not the hundred thousand of the Kings' Caravan, but that can be our advantage. We shall move quicker. Additionally, we have not one but three of the chief sorcerers of our kingdoms to protect us."

"Mr. Traveler, we are, all of us, back to the beginning. The only difference is the Fates have brought us all together to start our caravan as one, as it was destined to be," Eothelm added.

Traveler smiled. "Destiny?"

"Do you not believe in destiny, Mr. Traveler?" Eothelm asked. "A man of your experiences and knowledge. An animal companion such as yours. To travel through the magical lands to Atlantea and back, alive. What other word could there be for that?"

"I was there, and it did not seem to be anything other than frantic chance."

"Destiny, Mr. Traveler," Eothelm repeated.

"Mr. Traveler, have we not convinced you?" Lady Aylen asked. "Ten thousand men, the majority knights and warriors, three kings, three sorcerers, you and your miserable animal." The dog snarled at her. "It always knows when I am speaking ill of it. Mr. Traveler, we have more than we had before, and then you had no objections. We know it is dangerous and a long journey, but none of us shrink from the risk. I am convinced that we will reach our fabled destination. Do you say we cannot?"

"We can reach and even overtake them. I have no doubt of that. One hundred thousand men move through a land at a snail's pace."

"Then we should gather our forces and set out first thing in the morning," Lady Aylen said.

"What is the reputation of the Kings Elder in Avalonia?" Traveler asked.

"Our kingdoms are some of the oldest and honored in Avalonia, Mr. Traveler," Sigbard answered. "However, each of us is burdened with no heirs. The journey to Atlantea has much more meaning to us than simple riches. It is our way to create a lasting legacy for our people."

"I am heartened, sire, that you did not say you wished to have your own pet griffin like the Four Kings."

"Never, Mr. Traveler. We are quite satisfied with our natural steeds that remain on the ground," Aereth said, half-laughing.

"Will you, the Kings Elder, be joining us?"

"Most definitely, Mr. Traveler," Sigbard answered.

"What do you imagine will happen when King Oughtred learns of our own new caravan?"

"Mr. Traveler, he has already attempted to murder us," Aereth answered. "What more could he possibly do?"

"Succeed," Traveler replied.

PART TWO

THE LANDS BETWEEN

CHAPTER ELEVEN
The Grass Lands

The night camp buzzed with gossip—about the apparition and one of their own thrown into the river. The men did not know the full facts, but it did not stop the chatter.

Hobbs appeared at Traveler's tent, as he did each morning, to brief him on any news. "What should I tell the men, sir?" Hobbs asked. "Mr. Quillen saw the apparition."

"Mr. Hobbs, I leave it to you. I do not want the men to know about what Maiden Gwyness did, nor do I want them to know about the spy. Make up whatever story you see fit to calm them."

"Yes, sir."

Hobbs had no doubt that the gossip would continue for many days, but as long as each day's duties were done, it was of no concern. Men on long journeys needed something to talk about, whether real or imagined, or nearing a realm where the things of imaginations were real.

"I hope this does not become a common part of my duties," Quillen had said to him after recording the names of the men lost due to the treachery of the Four Kings.

Without bodies, there was little more they could do. For Pangolin and the other warriors, proper burial was a must, so they said words for the men in a somber gathering at the bank of the river. Hobbs reflected it was like any other battle he had seen throughout his life. The fallen were mourned, but life had to go on, and he seconded Quillen's comment.

Hobbs had the men break camp and ready themselves to cross the make-shift bridge to the other side of the river. The encampment of the Kings Elder was also ready to depart, and knights helped the Traveler party across, holding the bridge firm. The knights of the Kings Elder had done a fine job in such a short period; the bridge held, and when the last man from their camp came across, King Sigbard gave the sign for dozens of men to lift one side of the structure and push it into the river. They watched as it was quickly swept away.

"I wonder where it all goes," one of King Aereth's attendants said.

The Kings Elder were upon their horses, as were all their noble attendants and senior knights. They had lent a horse to any in the Traveler party who wished to have one of their own. Lady Aylen and Gwyness had been the first to accept.

Gwyness said to the men on the ground, "The river runs for many miles then becomes fiercer as it nears a series of giant waterfalls. If anything, or anyone, is caught in its grip, no one will set eyes upon it again."

"You do know these lands well, Maiden Gwyness," King Aereth remarked.

"Maiden Gwyness has always been gifted with direction," Lady Aylen said. "We both traveled through here, but I had almost forgotten. It was when Sirnegate was scouting the region to create its own caravan."

"How far did you get?"

"Sire, not far. Our scouting parties could never find Last Keep."

King Eothelm said, "The same with our scouts."

"However, we now have Mr. Traveler," King Aereth said as he patted the head of his horse. "We cannot fully express our anticipation at the prospect of crossing from the Lands of Man into the magical ones."

"Speaking of our esteemed guide, where is Mr. Traveler?" Lady Aylen asked. "I wonder if he will accept one of your steeds. Mr. Traveler does not seem to care for horses."

"I do not believe Mr. Traveler needs a steed from our stock," Aereth said as he and the other Kings Elder looked past her. Lady Aylen turned.

Traveler approached on a very large gray horse, its coat was unusually thick. It wore no reins or bridle; Traveler simply gripped the mane. He stopped his horse when he reached them.

"Mr. Traveler, you have a new companion," Aereth said with a smile.

"Or the same one," Lady Aylen muttered.

"My dog will rejoin us later tonight," Traveler said facetiously.

"Are there any limits to what he can change to, Mr. Traveler?" Gwyness asked.

"Yes, of course. No power of any shape-shifter is limitless." He turned his attention to Lady Aylen and the kings. "I defer to the four of you until we reach Hopeshire. You may lead on."

Traveler's "horse" snarled at Lady Aylen.

"He is definitely your dog," she said. "You are a miserable animal."

"Mr. Traveler, are not all shape-shifters either of magic or the undead?" Gwyness asked.

Traveler smirked. "You are correct. There are only two types of shape-shifters in this world. However, he is not from our world."

"Not of this world?" one of the sorcerers asked.

"We can speak of that later. There will be many a night at the campfire to pass with conversation and stories. What is our plan for the day, sires?"

Aereth answered, "Mr. Traveler, we shall gather our men from the Grass Lands and set out to Hopeshire."

"Arrive at Hopeshire again," Lady Aylen said angrily. "We have to repeat the first leg of our journey, and we did not even reach Last Keep."

"Lady Aylen, do not view the journey as a burden," Eothelm said. "View it as a chance to complete it as we should have from the start."

"Mr. Pangolin," Traveler called out. "No horse for you?"

"No, sir," the berserker replied. "I prefer to travel on foot and lead the men."

"Very good."

"Let us ride, then," Aereth said as he pulled the reins of his horse.

◆◆◆

The Grass Lands were a region of small towns and farms across lush green fields. The day was especially sunny, the tranquility in stark contrast to the previous day's ordeal. They rode among the plentiful grazing horses, cows, sheep, and goats. Many chickens and stray dogs ran about.

The senior knights of the Kings Elder rode first. The Kings Elder, Lady Aylen, Gwyness, Traveler, and Hobbs followed, then the three sorcerers. Pangolin led the rest of the men on foot, with his Cut-throats in the rear.

"We will have to travel to several towns. We thought it best after the attack it would be easier to hide our forces if we split them up," Aereth revealed.

"Sires, Mr. Estus told me you have heavy weapons to defend against attackers of any size," Traveler inquired.

Sigbard answered, "Yes, catapults, battering rams, giant crossbows, ten-foot polearms. For years, we have had our scouts make note of the weapons of the Kings' Caravan to assemble the same."

"All major weapons have their own team of dedicated fighters," Aereth added, "separate from the knights and archers."

"Mr. Traveler, since we now have the numbers, we ought to have as many warhorses as we can, despite your objections," Lady Aylen said. "How many do you have, King Aereth?"

"Two hundred fine steeds," he answered.

"We also have donkeys or mules, and we can buy any additional mounts we need," Eothelm added.

"Whether now, or as we cross into the Magical Lands we will need to leave the horses. Take the donkeys or mules if you must. Nothing else."

"Mr. Traveler, I need you to explain why," Lady Aylen insisted. "We have lost all our donkeys, and the bearer cannot possibly be expected to handle the burden alone. Are you so afraid that the Four Kings' griffin and hippogriffs will make food of them? We can protect them."

"What happens when our horsemen encounter the first centaur?"

"*Centaur?*" Lady Aylen asked.

"I do not make my objections arbitrarily, Lady Aylen. I do it to keep us alive. If you are so set on the horses, use them. But we cannot take them past Last Keep. Since we will be denied entrance to Last Keep, you would have to leave them in Ironwood, which based on their collusion with the Four Kings, I would not do."

"What happens when centaurs come across a horse, Mr. Traveler?" Gwyness asked.

"Horses without humans riding them, nothing. Ridden by fae, nothing. Ridden by humans is quite another matter. They would attack us and take the horses. Centaurs attack in groups, often as many as a hundred, and like elves, their arrows never miss their mark. We must avoid conflict, not invite it. We will have plenty of opportunities to do battle in Faë-Land, all of it unwelcome, and every battle we have, even if successful, means that men die on our side. We will acquire steeds in the magical lands but not horses.

"Horses also attract malicious fairies and sprites, which would be the best outcome, as the more likely outcome is that we would be visited by dark creatures that consider horses to be an exotic meal worthy of many leagues of travel to kill for. Griffins and hippogriffs are not the only ones. Many look to feast on our horses, including lycanthropes."

Gwyness and Lady Aylen were particularly shaken. "Lycanthropes?" Gwyness asked. "Wolves that—"

"Maiden Gwyness, there are many types of lycanthropes in the dark regions of the magical lands. Werewolves may be one of the most ferocious, both known and feared in our lands, but they are the most rare. The other varieties of lycanthrope are much more plentiful. Those are the ones I fear, but we can avoid them if we do not carry with us the food they covet."

"No horses," Lady Aylen said.

"Thank you, Princess."

"Incredible. To know all that you know of the lands we will travel," Aereth said to their guide.

"You said 'even if successful,' Mr. Traveler?" Eothelm asked. "Surely we are not doomed to lose men for every battle we undertake?"

"Let us get out of the Lands of Man first, sires, and through the Lands Between. At this moment, we have not even reached Hopeshire. For a party that is supposed to get clear across Titan's Trail to Atlantea before the Kings' Caravan, our beginning is not very impressive.

"Also, know we may be quite formidable as warriors here in the Lands of Man. There, in the magical lands, a handful of fairies could easily defeated us if we do not keep our wits."

The kings and women laughed.

"Surely not, Mr. Traveler," Sigbard said. "We expect to do fierce battle with some demonic beast not a tiny flying humanoid."

Traveler turned his attention to the road. "Let us exit the Lands of Man first, before we brag about how invincible we are in our own minds."

"Mr. Traveler, get to Atlantea *before* the Kings' Caravan?" Lady Aylen asked. "Why before?"

"Yes, Princess, I was about to inquire about that as well. Mr. Traveler, you have added another dimension to this journey," Aereth said.

"Sires and Princess, this is not a journey. This is a race. It could be that Xenhelm wishes to remain the sole kingdom from Avalonia with the knowledge to venture through Faë-Land to Atlantea. However, their actions have been of such a low and evil nature that I suspect that they may, in fact, be waiting for us, or at least have a party waiting for us."

"Waiting for us?" Lady Aylen asked with a look of astonishment, the same as was on each of the Kings Elder's faces. "How would they know we survived their plot?"

"We did kill *all* their men, did we not?" The realization gripped them. "I hope I am wrong," Traveler said, "but we must proceed as if I am not. Remember, they had a spy in our camp."

"I wish your dog had not killed the man," Sigbard said.

"He is an animal, sire. The world is a simple one of black and white. The man was a threat; he killed the man. There is nothing to be done about it now. But even without their spy, I am certain the Four Kings already knew we were alive and would resume our trek. Also, keep in mind that they sent that spy along to be murdered *with* us."

"The evil you are ascribing to the Four Kings is beyond what even my comrade Eothelm believes," Aereth said.

"Murder from royals is nothing new, even from the supposedly honorable, but you suggest his nature goes deeper to evil, not simply wanting to keep others from forming their own caravans to the fabled lands." The conversation had caused the Kings Elder to stop their horses, with all the men waiting. Eothelm waited for Traveler's response to his inquiry.

"Let us move forward and collect your men, sires. I do know what we may encounter in Faë-Land. However, I am not amused by the level of danger upon us here in Avalonia. King Oughtred, himself, seems to have taken a special interest in all of us as individual parties. Now we are joined together as one. And we have not even begun the caravan, not really."

◆◆◆

Despite the noon sun being hours away, the climate had become especially hot as they neared the small town. The Grass Lands had no central authority—each town managed its own affairs. People paid the caravan no mind as they worked their farms and tended to livestock. A dog ran to them and immediately took to Lady Aylen.

"Good morning, dog." She glanced at Traveler. "What a wonderful animal."

Traveler smiled. His horse snarled at her.

"This is what I am accustomed to," she said. "All animals are fond of me. Mr. Traveler, do you have any objections to adding a few guard dogs to our caravan?"

"That is fine, Lady Aylen, so long as they are kept on a rope, they have their own servants to manage them at all times, and they are never allowed to run off on their own. However, there may come a time in the future when any animal from our lands, save my dog, may need to be put down."

"Why would that be, Mr. Traveler?" the princess asked. The kings listened intently.

"Ask the sorcerers. They know why."

"M'lady, I imagine Mr. Traveler is referring to the magical ability to easily mesmerize an animal of our lands to do violence against its own master," the lead sorcerer uttered.

Aereth interjected. "Mr. Traveler, I can see you are entirely correct. We have no inkling of the true danger of this journey, do we? May I ask, is there any value we mere humans bring to this caravan?"

"Yes, sire. We are humans. Atlantea is fond of humans; fae, not so much."

The Kings Elder and Lady Aylen held their tongues though they wanted to ask many more questions. They turned their attention to a man running to them from one of the small towns. He was dressed as a commoner, wearing a cloak.

"Sires," the man said when he reached them.

"Gather the men immediately. We depart," King Sigbard said to him.

"Yes, m'lord." The man turned and ran back the way had come.

In moments, men started to appear from the town, which was but a collection of hamlets surrounded by farms. A few horsemen bolted from the town in different directions.

King Sigbard turned to one of the senior knights. "Find us a secluded area to gather." He pointed to a wooded area with plenty of trees in the distance. "There may be suitable."

"Yes, m'lord," the knight said. He pointed to two other knights and they all rode toward the trees.

"If it is suitable, it will be our base until we ride out," Sigbard added.

◆◆◆

As night fell, all the men of the Kings Elder party had come in from nine different towns in the Grass Lands. The Kings Elder had all horses sold, save for six—one for Lady Aylen, three for the Kings Elder, and two additional. All in the region knew that the official Caravan was gone, but this did not deter numerous men from begging for acceptance into the new caravan. Hobbs relented and took in another two dozen, mostly for sentry duty.

"I have never been outside the Grass Lands, Mr. Hobbs," said one man.

"The journey will take over a year."

"That will be no problem for me, Mr. Hobbs. Atlantea, you say? You did tell me about the magical lands of fairies, sprites, and elves. It would be a treat to see such beasties, Mr. Hobbs."

Hobbs felt that a routine for the party was vitally important for morale. They may have been traveling long distances across dangerous lands most men would never see, but it did not mean discipline should be lacking. The men needed a set routine, and so did the leadership. He arranged for the leadership to have their night meals together and added the newest members of the Traveler camp. The Kings Elder sat on stools in front of the campfire. Traveler sat opposite them across the view.

"Mr. Traveler, I hope you did not relent on the horses on account of us," Aereth said. "I can assure you that despite our age, and royalty, we can walk any distance the men can."

Traveler smiled. "Sire, I have always assumed that even royalty have the ability to walk. No, the adjustment to my ban is for another reason. They are fine steeds, and when we arrive in Faë-Land, we will trade them for more suitable ones. There are kingdoms where they would be welcomed and well cared for. The magical lands have kingdoms too, so I hope I did not imply otherwise."

Lady Aylen arrived with Gwyness, and they both sat. Hobbs nodded a greeting to them.

"Mr. Traveler, it seems there is much we will see for the first time when we get to these magical lands called Faë-Land," Eothelm said.

"We call them the magical lands, but they have vast and different regions. The first of these regions is Faë-Land—Faë-Land Minor and Faë-Land Major. We will pass through the former first."

"How long ago were you in Faë-Land, Mr. Traveler?" Aereth asked.

Pangolin and Estus arrived to join the campfire. Hobbs had servants pass out plates of food and cups of drink.

"I was but a lad when I went," Traveler answered as he sipped from his cup. "Nearly twenty years ago."

"Before the Caravan," Aereth remarked.

"Yes."

"How long were you there, Mr. Traveler?" Lady Aylen asked.

"I believe it was ten years, maybe longer."

"Ten years!" Lady Aylen repeated. "Maybe longer?"

"Mr. Traveler, we assumed you merely passed through," Aereth said.

"No, I lived there."

"What do mean, you believe you were there for ten years, but it could have been more, Mr. Traveler?" Eothelm asked.

"Time and distance does not work the same in Faë-Land for mortal humans. I was there anywhere from ten to twenty years, maybe more."

They all looked at each other.

"How much time had passed when you returned to the Lands of Man then, Mr. Traveler?" Gwyness asked.

"I am not sure."

"You do realize what you are saying, Mr. Traveler?" Eothelm began. "One could conceivably go into Faë-Land and its lands and return to the Lands of Man, and many years could have passed."

"Yes, or worse, return aged beyond their years."

Everyone stopped eating.

"Mr. Traveler, what are you saying?" Lady Aylen asked.

"Do not worry yourself. Aging beyond our years will be the least of our worries. The important thing to remember is we will be passing through and not remaining. So, in that sense, we will be fine. The rule to remember is that if you stay in one place for more than seven days, the magic of the lands will begin to affect you."

◆◆◆

Quillen sat at his campfire alone. As he did every night, he focused on writing in his notebook. He looked up to see Traveler's dog. Quillen smiled and stood.

"You have returned." He touched the dog's side to pat it.

The dog jumped back and bared his teeth.

"I'm sorry. I meant no harm."

The dog growled as it lowered itself to the ground, ready to pounce. Quillen backed away. The dog seemed to grow more humanoid as it lifted itself on its hind legs. Quillen turned in fear and ran.

"Mr. Hobbs!"

When Quillen appeared, Hobbs rose from his stool.

"What is it, lad?"

"The dog."

"What dog?"

"Mr. Traveler's."

Traveler stood. The dog came out of the night and crouched behind his stool. "Mr. Quillen, did you try to touch my dog?"

"Yes, sir. I did, but—"

"Mr. Quillen, do not touch the dog—ever."

"I am sorry, sir."

"You did not know. However, I must warn you."

"Warn me, sir?"

"He may retaliate."

"Retaliate, sir?"

"There is nothing to fear. I am merely warning you."

Quillen could not help but be frightened.

"Can you not tell him I'm sorry, sir?"

"I will do what I can, but I am warning you."

"Mr. Quillen, get some sleep. You will be all right," Hobbs said.

Quillen walked away slowly.

Hobbs turned to Traveler. Both men sat down. "He is a good worker, sir."

"What will your dog do to him, Mr. Traveler?" Lady Aylen asked.

"Nothing will happen to Mr. Quillen."

"Mr. Traveler, we have seen what your dog can do. That lad has not. He is well justified in his fear."

Pangolin leaned over to Estus. "I would not want to be that boy." The men laughed.

♦♦♦

Traveler vigorously rubbed the dog's neck. The animal responded playfully, his tongue hanging from his mouth.

"Mr. Estus," Traveler asked, "how do you find the new weapons, courtesy of the Kings Elder?"

Estus finished his ale. "Mr. Traveler, all I can say is they are impressive. We will be able to give a good hurt to any who cross us."

"Very good."

"I do have a question though, Mr. Traveler, since you have elfin, dwarven, and goblin steel."

"Wait," Sigbard interjected. "You have weapons forged by their hands?"

"No, sire. He has the blade fragments of those weapons," Estus said.

"Is your weapon that powerful?" Aereth asked.

"It is," Traveler answered. "That is why I remained in Faë-Land so long. I had to learn how to use it, lest I sever my own body in half and burst into flames, or the reverse."

"Very wise indeed," Aereth said, chuckling.

"What is your question, Mr. Estus?" Traveler asked.

"Can our weapons withstand their steel?"

"We must never have a battle with elves. If we did, only a handful of us would survive. It is not simply their superior weapons, but their superior abilities. Goblins and other wicked races are another matter. They are worrisome, but we will be able to deal with them when the time comes. Again, we will not see any dwarves. They live far from where we will pass. However, their weapons are popular among the races."

"What other wicked races might we encounter, Mr. Traveler?" Lady Aylen asked.

"Trolls, hobgoblins, troglodytes. Maybe gremlins and imps, both of which are incorrectly characterized as merely mischievous when they can be far more deadly. I doubt we will ever come across any ghouls."

"Ghouls? Mr. Traveler, as I sit here listening," Lady Aylen began, "I used to wish I knew all that you did of Faë-Land and beyond. I no longer desire that. You talk as a man who knows more about things than he should. Their mention almost overwhelms me, but you have fought one or more of these creatures up close, and there is so much more."

Traveler placed his metal plate on the ground. "No need to be overwhelmed. I will educate everyone as we move along the Trail. However, we are talking much about Faë-Land when we have such a long journey to get there."

"How long will it take to get there, Mr. Traveler?" Aereth asked.

"It could take as long as four months."

"So long?" Lady Aylen asked.

"The Lands Between are not empty of life, Lady Aylen. Far from it. Also, I still believe we will have to deal with agents of the Kings' Caravan again."

"Mr. Traveler, we have complete faith in you to see us through to Atlantea," Eothelm reassured. "Whether man or beast, we shall triumph."

"King Eothelm the Blessed of the Kings Elder speaks it, so it must be true." Traveler said it lightheartedly, and his statement drew chuckles. However, Eothelm's smile wavered. He was not as certain of his declaration as he let on.

CHAPTER TWELVE
Return to Hopeshire

The party departed the Grass Lands at dawn. Lady Aylen looked back from her place alongside the King's Elder. Gwyness rode with a few senior knights and the long column of men. She smiled.

"You are pleased, Lady Aylen."

"King Aereth, I came to Hopeshire with two thousand. Today, we ride with ten thousand. I cannot be anything but pleased."

"As I said to Mr. Traveler, the Fates are with us on this journey," Eothelm said.

"Speaking of Mr. Traveler, he seems to be very negative about our chances. Not once have I heard him say an uplifting word of the journey to come. Even his words that Atlantea is fond of humans seem to have a double meaning."

"His caution is understandable, Lady Aylen," Aereth said. "Do we not prefer a guide and trailmaster who speaks the truth about the dangers to come over one who engages in a fiction of no danger at all? We all listened intently to his accounts at the night fire. Goblins, trolls, and centaurs. He is simply setting our minds where they must be—in a realistic state. He will supply the pessimism and fear; we will supply the optimism and luck. If the reverse were true, we would be in trouble."

"Though, in his favor, I have no doubt he and his dog will defend this caravan to the death."

"Nor do I."

"I spoke unwisely. We should take his advice and focus on Avalonia and reserve our speculation of the lands beyond until we actually arrive there."

Traveler was in conversation with Pangolin at the rear of the caravan. As the sight of Hopeshire came into view, he rode back to the front of the columns.

"Sires, what are your intentions in regard to Hopeshire?" he asked.

"We see no reason to stop, Mr. Traveler," Aereth said.

"Then I will ride ahead and see if anything remains in their markets that we might need. Particularly since we are a far larger party, I should acquire more herbs and such for my medicine bag. In fact, I will dedicate a wagon for my medicinal supplies."

"Excellent idea, Mr. Traveler," Eothelm said. "We should acquire additional healers if any are to be found, to ease your burden. Guide and trailmaster is job enough for you."

"Doubtful here though, sire."

"May I accompany you, Mr. Traveler?" Gwyness asked. "I can also search the markets."

"Of course."

"Sir, do you need me to go as well?" Hobbs asked from the ground.

"No, Mr. Hobbs. You can attend to the men. We should be done before our caravan reaches the town center."

♦♦♦

Traveler, Gwyness, and two warriors, assigned by Pangolin, rode out. Most of the settlements that had surrounded Hopeshire for the Caravan were still in place, but they rode past. Upon their arrival in Hopeshire proper, Traveler had both warriors accompany Gwyness through the markets still on Caravan Row.

"I will find you before our caravan arrives," Traveler said to her and rode off.

Gwyness dismounted and walked her horse through.

"What do you need, lass?" one of the market sellers asked.

"Do you have an apothecary, sir?"

He pointed down the road. "Go to the very end of the market row and turn left. At the very end will be such a place."

"Thank you."

◆◆◆

Caravan Row still had plenty of men in the streets who had hoped to join the Caravan but had arrived too late. After her walk through the markets, Gwyness found Traveler on Hopeshire's Caravan Row. She had a few sacks tied to her saddle as she rode to him with her two guardsmen. Traveler stood with two pull carts stacked high with supplies.

"Did you hire others, Mr. Traveler?" she asked.

"Let me introduce myself, mistress," One of five men appeared and bowed. "We are the Brothers Brimm. Traveling music at your service, my fair lady."

"Mr. Traveler, if someone said to me that you had hired a band of musicians for our caravan, I would have said to that person, 'Stop telling me lies. That is not our Mr. Traveler.'"

Traveler smiled. "I am a man of surprises, Maiden Gwyness."

"May we play a tune for you, lass?" one of the musicians asked with a flute in his hand.

"No, you may not," Traveler answered for her. "You may come here and do some work."

The five musicians picked up their satchels and bags and walked to him. They threw their things into the pull carts.

"Maiden Gwyness, did you find what you needed?"

"I did, Mr. Traveler."

"Our caravan is not far."

◆◆◆

As the caravan drew near, people in the settlements stopped their chores to watch them pass.

"We shall simply ride around the town," Aereth directed.

"I hope no one is foolhardy enough to follow us," Lady Aylen said. "Oh, what is this?"

Traveler slowly rode to them on his "horse," with men in colorful clothes pulling the carts behind him. Gwyness and her two warriors followed on horseback.

"What do we have here, Mr. Traveler?" Lady Aylen asked. Gwyness tried not to laugh. "Mr. Traveler, have you hired jesters to join our caravan?"

"Yes, Lady Aylen, I am sure you will have much to tease me about at the campfire. They are musicians, not jesters."

Lady Aylen smiled broadly as she looked at the Kings Elder.

"I do not even know what to say at the moment, Mr. Traveler," she said.

"That is the best thing you have said to me all day." He could not keep the smile off his own face. "Mr. Hobbs."

"Yes, sir."

"Get these men settled in and add these to our medicine carts."

"Very good, sir."

Hobbs led the new men into the column.

Traveler was serious as he watched the crowds of people within the settlements staring at them. "Soon everyone in Hopeshire will know we are passing."

"Do you suppose any will attempt to follow us, Mr. Traveler?" Aereth asked.

"Some may try, sire, but we will take on no more. And based on our last encounter, it is wise to steer clear of Ironwood."

"We have ten thousand men now, Mr. Traveler. How can we avoid Ironwood's people seeing us? We must scale their region."

"Lady Aylen, we did that last time to get to Goodmound's Castle ahead of the Caravan. This time we will travel their same path."

"Meaning it will take us longer than five days," she noted.

"Correct. Also, I will lead us through a different path to avoid Ironwood altogether, so we will take a full fortnight to reach the Goodmound's Castle."

Lady Aylen sighed loudly. "I know it cannot be helped, Mr. Traveler."

"At least we have fine weather for the journey, and it seems it will last," King Aereth said.

"When we arrive at Goodmound's Castle, we can secure any final supplies or men we may need then move past Last Keep. It is a dreary place, but I will feel more at ease when we cross into the Lands Between—far fewer places to attack without being detected long in advance."

"Where do you believe the Kings' Caravan is now, Mr. Traveler?" Eothelm asked. "Do you truly believe they wait for us, simply to destroy us? That is not evil but madness."

"Sire, it is both, and yes, I believe it."

CHAPTER THIRTEEN
Return to Ironwood

There was no hint of its coming. They awoke the next morning to dark, ominous skies and, soon after, intermittent downpour. The rain slowed their progress toward Ironwood, as there was little vegetation to mitigate the slippery or muddy earth.

They had only just set out when several riders came upon them. Hooded knights Pangolin and his warriors readied for an attack, but the Kings Elder signaled that the horsemen were allies. The knights were visibly exhausted and distressed as they neared the kings.

"We rode as quickly as our steeds would carry us, sires," the lead rider said. "You must return with us immediately."

The riders bore the colors of the Kings Elder's kingdoms. The kings looked at each other then rode to the side to speak privately with the riders. All could hear Sigbard loudly say: "Impossible."

The kings led the riders back to the caravan leadership.

"Repeat your news," Aereth directed.

"They came without warning, sires," the lead rider said. "Riders from the east said that Cirencester under King Rol is on the war march across the region. They defeated every army in their path and destroyed five nearby kingdoms. Cirencester's forces are two hundred thousand strong and will be upon our kingdoms within several days."

"Where did they get such an army?" Sigbard asked.

"Why are they making war on Western Avalonia?" Aereth asked.

"We do not know from where they amassed such an army, but our kingdoms will take the brunt of their attack," the rider added. "People are fleeing the region."

"Also, sires, there are rumors that they are in possession of magical weapons," another rider said.

"Sires, you must return to Helm Earldom, Strongbridge, and Eastmoor immediately to take charge. The lands are in complete panic and chaos," the lead rider said.

"Will eight thousand men really make a difference?" Sigbard asked.

"The three sorcerers of the Kings Elder will, sire," he answered.

"No." Lady Aylen could not contain her silence any longer. "If we lose your men, the journey to Atlantea is over."

"What do you suggest, Lady Aylen?" Aereth asked.

"I apologize, sire. I cannot help my frustration at once again being denied the chance to continue our journey. Instead of moving forward, we are continually pushed farther back. I am sorry. Obviously, you must attend to your kingdoms."

"Mr. Traveler, anything to add?" Aereth asked.

Traveler was very quiet, though his facial expressions from the time the riders began speaking indicated he had much to say. "Nothing, sire. You must decide what is best for you and your kingdoms."

"That is a very diplomatic response, Mr. Traveler," Eothelm said. "A response that is not a response at all."

"The decision is this: Our eight thousand men stay," Aereth said.

"Thank you, King Aereth," Lady Aylen said, relieved.

"And we should stay, too," Aereth continued.

"Sire?" the rider asked.

"Take the sorcerers with you and get to the kingdoms as quickly as possible. Defend our region," Aereth said.

"Not you, sires?" the riders asked.

"Eight thousand extra men will not turn the tide of such battle. If they came at us with magic, we would be of little use. No, our chief sorcerers are required," Aereth said to the men.

"M'lord, then the new caravan will be without a single practitioner of magic," the main sorcerer said.

"Aereth," Eothelm interjected. "This is much more than a matter of magic. It is one of leadership. The kingdoms of the Kings Elder cannot be led in battle without the Kings Elder. As much as it pains me to say it, we must abandon the new caravan. Let them keep the men, but we must accompany our sorcerers back to our kingdoms."

"Sires, you cannot leave Kings Elder knights under the command of others," said one of the king's knights.

"Mr. Traveler, do you have a less diplomatic response now?" Aereth asked.

"Sire, you know what I have to say. This is deliberate. We killed their spy within our ranks. I would wager the very next morning was when this kingdom of Cirencester began its war march to your region to destroy it with their new army and new weapons of magic. The intent is so transparent: Force you, the Kings Elder, and your sorcerers to abandon our caravan and return. Already, we have attributed madness and evil to the Four Kings, but another emotion is at work here."

"Which is?" Aereth asked.

"Desperation."

"What should be done, then?" Eothelm asked. "We must repel the invaders of our kingdoms and protect the region."

"Here is my counter suggestion. King Aereth remains with us to properly command your men of our caravan. Kings Eothelm and Sigbard return with all three sorcerers."

"Not even one sorcerer to remain?" Aereth asked.

Traveler looked at the chief sorcerer. "Is not your power amplified by your fellow sorcerers?"

"It is. How did you know?"

"I have seen such before. Trinity sorcerers exist in the magical lands, too. Yes, sires, all three sorcerers must go. The reason for this war upon Western Avalonia may be contrived, but I have no doubt that the war will be devastating and will spread if it is not stopped. You must destroy them all and save your kingdoms and all the regions around them."

"And I should stay?" Aereth asked.

"King Aereth, you will do your battle with us. Your comrades will do battle with King Oughtred's agents in Avalonia. We will do battle with the villain himself when we reach him. None of us will be escaping anything. It is a war in two places."

"But without the protection of our own sorcerers?" Aereth asked.

"We will hire our own when the time comes. Do not fret, sire. I had planned to do so anyway when we crossed into the magical lands. However, sires, you must be sure about this. Once we separate, we will have no way of knowing what has happened with each group. If we continue onto Atlantea, it could be years before you hear news, let alone see each other again. Remember, time does not work the same for humans in the magical lands. That could be a very heavy burden to carry."

The Kings Elder remained in deep thought for a moment, then looked at each other as if conversing without words to agree on a final decision.

"We appreciate your counsel, Mr. Traveler," Aereth said. He looked at the sorcerers, then his colleagues. "This is where we shall say our goodbyes until we meet again."

Kings Eothelm and Sigbard managed smiles. They moved their horses alongside each other and took turns embracing. Sorrow was etched in the sorcerers' faces; each bowed his head to King Aereth.

"I will be able to sleep these long nights only by knowing that you will all do whatever is necessary to defend our region."

"We will destroy Cirencester's forces," Sigbard promised. "They will not be allowed to ravage and make blind war on innocents."

"King Aereth, we swear by it," the chief sorcerer added. He looked at King Eothelm and Sigbard. "Sires, we ride for the kingdoms."

"May the Fates protect you," Aereth said sadly.

"And may they protect all of you along your journey. Aereth, the Kings Elder will be reunited one day," Eothelm said.

Kings Eothelm and Sigbard, the sorcerers, and the riders rode hard into the rain.

"Mr. Traveler," Lady Aylen began, "if the Four Kings do not want us to create an alternative caravan, then such desperation almost suggests—"

"Fear," Aereth interjected.

"But why?" Lady Aylen asked. "They are the ones who have ten times more men than we do. They have objects and flying beasts of magic, and undoubtedly their own sorcerers. If they wanted, they could leave us so far behind, we would never catch up, and yet they do all of this."

"Maybe we have advantages we are not aware of, but are known to them."

"Yes, King Aereth, I believe you are right," Traveler said. "However, we should move on. This setback and the rain will weigh heavily on the men, but we have much ground to cover."

◆◆◆

The previous day had seen a renewed vigor within the caravan with the addition of the Kings Elder and their full complement of men. Now, as the caravan moved on under darkened skies, the loss of two of the three kings—and, more importantly, all three sorcerers—was all that the men talked about in hushed tones.

"Mr. Hobbs, I want you to take special note of the morale of the men," Traveler said quietly, leaning toward him.

"Yes, sir." Hobbs walked next to Traveler's "steed." The rain had not left the region, so the march remained slow going.

"There is little to be done to change the dark mood of the men."

"Sir, as we journey past Ironwood, the men should forget what troubles them."

They stopped for the midday meal but could not find a patch large and dry enough for their size. No one had much appetite, but the cooks did their best to prepare and offer hearty meals.

"I hope we made the right decision." Aereth had no appetite either but ate for the sake of the men. They were quiet but watching for signs—either of reassurance or despair—from him or any of the leadership.

"Sire, I am poor counsel in this matter," Lady Aylen answered, "but I do believe we have taken the best course available to us."

"To make war upon us as a ploy to get us to abandon the caravan," Aereth said. "Could the Four Kings have been bewitched in their journeys through this Faë-Land? Men seldom change so radically, especially from such goodness to such evil."

"It would explain much," Traveler said. "There is no way to tell. However, men have turned from good to evil throughout time without any prompting of magic."

Traveler scouted ahead, as he often did. He returned and led the caravan to a secluded, defensible wooded area, where they set up camp at day's end. It took hours to properly set up the tents and defenses, and to prepare the night meal before settling in. The men who would be the night watch were always the first to bed and had learned to sleep despite the commotion around them. They would be awoken at midnight for their duties.

Before the final meal of the night, Traveler relaxed alone in his tent. Hobbs was a stickler for routine and insisted that the leadership eat their night meals together, especially these days. Hobbs entered Traveler's tent with a pitcher of water. He had learned that the dog would not even drink water unless Traveler did so first.

"I will leave the water here, sir." Hobbs set the large pitcher in the corner.

"That is fine, Mr. Hobbs. How are the men?"

"Nervous, sir, but I think, as we continue on, they will become at ease. We are now three different groups together as one. They will become accustomed to each other and the strength of our caravan."

"Yes, they will."

The dog walked into the tent and curled up near Traveler's feet.

"I feel special, sir. He does not even acknowledge my presence anymore."

"You are part of the family, Hobbs."

The rain clouds had moved on. With dawn, the men struck camp to set out.

"Sir." Hobbs entered Traveler's tent just before their trailmaster was about to exit.

"Yes, Hobbs."

Hobbs moved closer. "Sir, one of the men is gone."

"Gone? Who?"

"One of the servants, a bearer. He was near the perimeter, but—"

"What did the men around him say?"

"They were all sleeping and the night guards heard and saw nothing."

"So, a man has disappeared?"

"Yes, sir. I did privately inform Mr. Pangolin. He was out searching with a few warriors but returned a moment ago with no news. He will speak with you later, but he told me to say you should not delay our departure. Nothing would be gained."

Traveler lifted his hood to cover his head. "Not a word of this to anyone else."

"Sir, I have already instructed the men who know of him not to speak of it."

"No one else, either."

"Yes, sir."

♦♦♦

It was the first time any had seen Pangolin on a horse. He and Traveler rode ahead of the caravan to scout.

"What do you know, Mr. Pangolin?"

"I saw nothing to indicate the man ever left the camp."

"That is even more disturbing."

"I have taken great care to ensure the guards on night watch do not fall asleep or even nap. They saw nothing. There were no footprints from any others in the camp, and there were no signs of any disturbance in the surrounding woods. I am certain of it."

"I will join the watch tonight."

"No, you must not change your routine. Your dog also did not sense anything. Though neither of us believes it to be chance that this happened the very day we lost our three sorcerer protectors."

"There is nothing more for us to do, but I suspect our nights will not be very restful going forward until we bring all this to a resolution."

"Mr. Traveler, we must be very careful here. The men are fearful enough. If they come to believe our caravan is cursed, then we are truly lost. The men grow fearful of their own shadows. We cannot lose another man. I will take on the burden. If I join the night watch, the men will not regard it as unusual."

Traveler nodded, and the two men rode back to the main caravan.

Night fell, and the leadership gathered for dinner at the fire. Hobbs bustled about ensuring everything was in order, from the cooks to the servers to the sentries.

"Mr. Pangolin will not be joining you tonight," a lad informed them. "He apologizes, sire."

"That is too bad," Aereth said. "I hope Mr. Pangolin is not working himself too hard."

Traveler appeared with the dog and joined them.

"Mr. Traveler," Lady Aylen began, "now that these storm clouds have left us, it should be a smooth journey to Ironwood."

"I hope so, Princess. However, I have never been one to try predicting the future. We will face what we must as we travel."

"Should we speak more about the Four Kings, Mr. Traveler?" Gwyness asked. "I mean—you believe they wait for us. What if they attack us with another teleportation spell? We have no sorcerers this time."

"Maiden Gwyness, the men are nervous enough. Let us not add to their apprehension. We will postpone this conversation at least until we reach Goodmound's Castle. I have already devised a plan for that."

"Goodmound's Castle again," Lady Aylen said angrily.

"What happens at Goodmound's Castle, Mr. Traveler?" Aereth asked.

"There we may be able to find someone who can perform a true magic-revealing spell."

"But your dog threw Xenhelm's spy into the river and killed him," Aereth said.

"Why one, sire?" Traveler took a bite of his meal. "Why not more than one, or several?"

Lady Aylen shook her head. "Mr. Traveler, maybe we need to ban you from these nightly meals. You have an uncanny ability to say things that make it very difficult to sleep at night."

The dawn of the new day arrived. The men had struck camp to set out. Hobbs appeared at the trailmaster tent; Traveler knew something was wrong.

"Sir, another man disappeared last night."

♦♦♦

The caravan was ready to go, but it remained in wait. The leadership took to a hill as all the men watched from afar.

"Who was the man?" Aereth asked.

"Sire, one of the servants," Hobbs replied.

"Is there any pattern?"

Hobbs looked at Pangolin.

"No pattern, sire," Pangolin answered. "The first man was closer to the perimeter of the camp. This man was farther in and with another group. Both servants, bearers. The first man was with Mr. Traveler's original party. This second man was with Lady Aylen's party."

"What is the plan, then?" Lady Aylen asked. "Look at the men. They are frightened, and understandably so. The prospect of being snatched away in the night."

"There is nothing to be done now," Traveler said. "The dog and I will be on night watch and move through the men. That should calm nerves."

"What if it happens again tonight, Mr. Traveler?" Aereth asked.

"Then we will have another meeting on the hill, sire." He started back down the hill. "Let us move out."

Whenever the caravan had marched, the men conversed, told jokes, and laughed. Now, as they marched through the woods, no one said even a word. At the noon meal, they ate quietly. The leadership could see it in their faces—the fear of the coming night.

"Sir." Hobbs was at Traveler's tent with Pangolin. "Mr. Pangolin and I feel that we should set up camp differently tonight."

"Mr. Hobbs, set up the camp in whatever manner you and Mr. Pangolin see fit. It is under your authority. The dog and I will join the night watch at midnight."

"Do you need me to wake you at that time, sir?"

"No, my dog will wake me."

Extra fires were set. Rather than a large camp circle, the camp was set up in smaller connected circles. Men were in groups of ten with two men on watch at all times. Most were too frightened to sleep at all. Pangolin also increased the patrols through camp.

When Traveler and the dog began their night patrol, relief spread among many of the men. In his hand, Traveler held his sheathed broadsword. Men began setting their minds at ease to sleep. With so many on watch, including Traveler and his dog, nothing evil could befall any man during the night.

♦♦♦

An hour before dawn, a man yelled out. Traveler and the dog reached the circle of men moments before Pangolin and a few of his warriors.

"Who is it?" Traveler asked.

"One of the warriors," Pangolin answered.

Traveler touched the ground where the man had slept. "Did any of you see anything?" he asked.

"We were asleep," the men answered.

Traveler stood from the ground. The dog sniffed the ground but sensed nothing. Traveler saw the panic racing through the camp. Hobbs joined them.

"Hobbs, break camp right now."

"Yes, sir."

It was not at all what they had hoped. The leadership gathered on another hill as the frantic men waited and watched.

"We cannot go farther," Traveler said, "until this matter is resolved."

"What can it be? How is this happening? Magic?" Lady Aylen asked.

"Whatever the means, we must discover and stop it. We must return."

"Return, Mr. Traveler?" Lady Aylen asked.

Traveler answered, "Back to Hopeshire."

"No!" she yelled.

"We have no choice. Do you wish to be here again tomorrow morning or the morning after? The men will abandon the caravan."

"Lady Aylen, Mr. Traveler is doing the correct thing," Aereth said.

"Mr. Traveler, I may have an idea," Estus said.

"Yes, Mr. Estus. Please speak up, then, and share."

"Chains, sir. At night, let us chain all the men together."

"Chain us?" Lady Aylen asked. "We do not have enough chains to do such a thing with ten thousand men."

"If we return to Hopeshire, we can acquire what we need. Mr. Estus, I concur with your idea. These disappearances have been happening as the men sleep. There is no noise or commotion. I imagine, Mr. Estus, that you would need to metalwork the chains."

"Yes, indeed, Mr. Traveler."

"That is our one and only task for the day. Return to Hopeshire, purchase the chains we need, help Mr. Estus with his tasks, and be ready for tonight. Mr. Hobbs, inform the men that we have a possible solution to our dilemma. Lighten their spirits a bit."

"Yes, sir. It will help."

"Mr. Estus," Traveler said. "Today, you are the man in charge. Tell us what to do and what you need, and it will be done."

The weaponsmaster smiled. "I have never commanded a king before."

"Mr. Estus, not to ruin your moment of commoner ascendance over royalty but remember that your plan must be done by nightfall or tomorrow you, not us, will be on this hill with the men."

Pangolin and his Cut-throats set out, leading Estus on horseback with a thousand men, most with pull carts.

"I do hope they return by tonight," Aereth said.

Traveler turned to their steward. "Hobbs, have the men set the camp back up, and give them the details of our plan. Keep the men busy and their minds off the coming night."

Hobbs nodded and left them.

"Sire, they will be back in time," Traveler said.

Gone were the days when the Traveler party could set camp in no time at all. It was done so, in over an hour. Hobbs did not chastise any of the men for moving slower than normal. He could feel their fear. They did not have to speak at all for him to know that, if Estus's plan failed, they felt the camp would become the dark grave for another unfortunate soul when the sun set.

Traveler and King Aereth sat at the campfire. They could do nothing but wait. The two men glanced at Lady Aylen and Gwyness sitting in their tent, speaking quietly.

Hobbs joined the men. "Do either of you care for any drink or food?"

"No, Mr. Hobbs, thank you," Aereth answered.

Hobbs glanced at the women.

"Lady Aylen is quite distressed," Traveler remarked.

"You cannot blame her," Aereth said. "In her mind, it is a caravan that keeps going ever backwards. Remember, Sirnegate has scouted these lands before. Her kingdom has failed to find Last Keep or move beyond it."

"We shall," Traveler assured them. "We must trust in Mr. Estus's plan."

◆◆◆

At the sound of hooves approaching, echoing through the woods, the men expected an attack. However, it was Pangolin on horseback, followed by Estus steering a horse-drawn wagon, with more following. Men cheered as they entered the camp.

Traveler greeted him. "Mr. Estus, we were getting worried."

"Mr. Traveler, acquiring the amount of chains required for ten thousand men was no small feat, but I know what you are about to say. Yes, I can do what I must to accomplish in the hours we have left before nightfall. I had forgotten an item, so we had to go back."

"Go back?"

Estus smiled as he jumped down from the wagon. Pangolin appeared at the wagon with a stern face. "Mr. Traveler, know that should you plan to put Mr. Estus in charge of a mission again, neither I nor my men will bodyguard him."

"Why did you go back?"

"He did not tell you?"

Estus raised one of the items in his hand. "I forgot these."

Traveler leaned forward a bit. "Is that a tiny metal...bell?"

To complete all his work, Estus had used the sole furnace of the blacksmith in Hopeshire. He fastened the tiny bells on the chains. Endless banging with his hammer, but by the time night fell, he was done.

"Wrap yourselves securely, men," Pangolin directed as he marched through the camp. Hobbs accompanied him.

"I am a woman of noble birth, and here we are, wrapping ourselves in dirty chains to sleep," Lady Aylen said to Gwyness in their tent. "Have you seen Mr. Traveler at all?"

"I assume he is out on watch," Gwyness replied.

"Ah, sire. You have your sleep chains for the night, too."

King Aereth smiled. His tent was close. "Lady Aylen, I am feeling quite reassured about tonight. Mr. Estus's plan seems a good one."

"Yes, and the bells," Lady Aylen added. "As if we are stray cows on the plains somewhere."

"A flash of genius," Aereth declared.

Lady Aylen glanced at Traveler's open tent but saw nothing. "Sire, let us wish for a quiet, normal night."

♦♦♦

Pangolin walked through camp and reached another guard on patrol. "Have you seen Mr. Traveler tonight?"

"No, none of the men have, nor his dog. All seems quiet, though."

"It was quiet the last two nights too, but we lost a man each. Continue with your duties."

The man's yell shattered the sleep of every person in the camp. Men jumped up and ran to him. Even Lady Aylen ran from her tent, with Gwyness following. Yells, chains clanging, and bells ringing—the camp was in pandemonium. Everyone was out of their tents—except King Aereth.

Traveler and the dog had been watching from another nearby tent all along. They bolted from the darkness and into the tent of the Kings Elder. Traveler dived and grabbed the pale hand before it disappeared into the earth. With all his might, Traveler pulled as he got back onto his feet. He yelled as pulled an unconscious King Aereth out of the ground, but a green arm shot out and grabbed at Traveler to pull him down, too. The dog grew in size and became humanoid as he grabbed the green arm. When the dog yanked it up, its form was revealed—a monstrous mass of green serpentine arms. The dog grew larger, knocking down part of the tent, and threw the creature into the sky.

"What is that?" a man yelled.

Everyone looked up to see the creature rise in the moonlit sky, then fall back down.

"Archers!" Pangolin yelled.

The creature landed back in the camp, directly in one of the larger fires, but it did not burn. Archers appeared and fired arrow after arrow into it. Warriors attacked with their swords and axes. The creature violently defended itself.

Traveler looked back at King Aereth on the ground, still unconscious and pale white. He realized there was a portal just underneath the soil, but it was closing. Traveler grabbed at the edges and strained to keep it open. A human hand came out of the portal and grabbed his face. The giant humanoid dog reached down into the soil. When the dog's giant hand appeared, in his grip was a cloaked man with yellowish eyes. The dog struck at him, but the wizard had already encased himself in a translucent, yellowish magical bubble; the dog's hand bounced off it.

Outside, the creature of many hands grabbed several men and repeatedly struck at them. Pangolin leapt into the air with a yell. His axe-mace crashed into the center of the creature's body. It exploded in a bright flash, blasting Pangolin and every man within fifteen feet onto their backs, and blowing out all the nearby fires.

The dog grew larger again, and his body changed into something simian. All the men in camp knew of the dog's shape-shifting abilities and were seeing its evidence for themselves for the first time. However, without the fires, no one could see clearly. It stood on four legs but still towered fifteen feet or more above them. In one hand was the cloaked man within his magical bubble. The beast slammed the bubble violently against the ground, but it did not give way. The man within the bubble laughed, then started to chant in an ancient tongue. The beast continued to beat the bubble into the ground in a frenzy.

Traveler appeared with his true broadsword; the weapon had a special glow from the moonlight. Both hands on the hilt, he lunged into the bubble with the tip of the blade. He pierced it and the cloaked man. The wizard screamed. The beast raised the bubble in the air and, with increased force, slammed it into the ground. Instantly, the bubble vanished, showering everyone within twenty feet and beyond with a sickening spray of blood.

"Bring torches!" Hobbs yelled.

Most men in the camp had stood frozen; others had backed away, not knowing whether to run or stand their ground. The dual battles seemed to be over.

Even as the men approached, they saw the giant dog beast shrinking in size. When the torches arrived in the hands of servants, there stood the dog on all fours. Traveler stepped forward. All that remained of the wizard was a portion of his upper torso from his head to his shoulders, his two hands to the wrists, and his feet to his ankles. The cloaked man's yellowish eyes were fixed open.

"That was the man with the yellow eyes from when the Kings' Caravan first arrived at Ironwood," Lady Aylen said, joining the gathering.

Traveler looked up at her. She could see his simmering rage.

"Hobbs!" Traveler yelled. "King Aereth."

Lady Aylen looked up from the remains of the wizard and followed Traveler to the king sprawled on the ground. "Oh no," she said.

Gwyness appeared, with Hobbs following.

"Bring the torches here," Hobbs yelled. "I need blankets too."

"He is ice cold!" Lady Aylen remarked, touching the king's face.

Pangolin had stepped from the crowd of men to look down at the face of the dead wizard. "You killed our men," he said to the corpse. "But you will kill no more." He raised his axe-mace and crushed the man's skull into the dirt.

◆◆◆

No one could sleep. All waited until the sun rose, with barely a word spoken. Pangolin had all the knights and warriors on duty. Hobbs had all the servants waiting, sitting around campfires.

"Did we lose anyone, Mr. Hobbs?" Traveler sat at the main fire near his tent. His shimmering sword was still in his hands.

Hobbs sat next to him. "We did lose a man, sir. The armed creature snapped the neck of one of the warriors who fought it."

"So we still lost a man last night."

"But, sir, you saved the king and saved the men. Mr. Pangolin destroyed the creature. You and the dog destroyed the wizard behind the evil deeds."

Traveler's anger was clear, but he calmly said, "Ensure that the man's name is recorded."

"It already has been, sir. Mr. Quillen has been very diligent in his duty."

Traveler walked into the king's tent. Aereth was still asleep in a cot close to the ground. Thick blankets covered with him. Lady Aylen and Gwyness sat watch at his side.

Traveler checked his pulse.

"He has the same ill symptoms as when you and the men were teleported, Mr. Traveler," Lady Aylen said. "Unconscious and extremely weak."

"His heart beats strong. He needs rest."

"What are our plans now, Mr. Traveler?"

"We shall stay here for a day or two to collect ourselves and rest. Also, we need to confirm that the nightly disappearances of the men are over."

"What is next for us after our day or two of rest?" Lady Aylen asked.

"I am very reluctant to continue."

"Why, Mr. Traveler?"

"I am not comfortable moving forward until a magic-revealing spell is cast upon the entire camp."

"Is our own sorcerer a requirement on caravan?"

"Not in the Lands of Man, Lady Aylen, or it is not normally. We cannot simply react to their attacks. We are losing men. We are losing men and we have not even left the Lands of Man."

"I can conjure the spell," Gwyness said softly.

Traveler turned to her. "What do you mean? You?"

"Yes."

"You are a sorceress?"

"No, but I can conjure a version of the spell."

"A version of the spell?" Traveler asked.

"Yes, but it will have the same power to reveal."

"Why did you not reveal this before?"

"I had my reasons. It is not something I wish to speak of."

"What do you need for the spell?"

"A few items. I can fetch them."

"Do so, then."

Gwyness rose and left for the women's tent. Traveler also exited, leaving Lady Aylen alone to watch over the king.

♦♦♦

Traveler returned to the Kings Elder's tent with Pangolin. Lady Aylen noticed that Traveler had sheathed his sword. It was strapped to his back, but he had only one sword.

Gwyness returned moments later. Her right hand was tightly clenched.

Traveler's face bore a look of displeasure. "If you are not a sorceress, will casting a spell cause you harm?"

"No, not this spell."

"Then conjure your spell, Maiden Gwyness."

Gwyness walked to the center of the tent and threw the contents of her fist to the ground. It appeared to be simple dirt, but when it touched the ground, a white cloud erupted from it. A translucent fire rippled up to the tent's ceiling. A ghostly form rose from the fire.

"Maiden Gwyness, what is about to happen?" Traveler asked.

"The apparition will pass through anyone or anything of magic," she answered.

"You might have told us that. I do not like surprises."

"Yes, I am sorry, Mr. Traveler. I have never done this before."

"Is it dangerous?" Traveler asked.

"No, not at all. Where is your dog, Mr. Traveler?"

"He is sleeping. We can proceed."

The apparition rose higher, then passed through Traveler.

The sheathed sword strapped to his back began glowing with a bright, ghostly fire. The intensity grew until Traveler's entire whole back and legs were ablaze with a giant ghost fire and the sword was visible through its black sheath. The brightness and size of the ghostly fire enveloped his body and then most of the tent. It was a weapon of incredible magical power.

The apparition passed through Lady Aylen. Her skin, nails, and eyes glowed a bright blue. The apparition passed through Gwyness, and the amulet around her neck glowed a ghostly white. Then it was Pangolin, whose armor and massive axe-mace glowed a smoky, earthen brown. The apparition passed through a locked chest in the tent—belonging to the Kings Elder. They could see through the chest, which was filled with colored stones.

The apparition rose into the air and flew out of the tent.

"Follow it!" Gwyness yelled.

Traveler was already out of the tent, with Pangolin following.

◆◆◆

Quillen was on sentry duty over the horses. Not very exciting work, but important. He had to fight the impulse to take out his notebook and start writing. Instead, he thought about what he would write when he was able. Dawn was not far away, he thought, looking up at the sky.

He jumped as he saw the apparition pass through one of the men. From underneath the man's tunic, a giant amulet glowed yellow and red. The apparition flew above and passed through other men, and giant amulets glowed from beneath their clothes. Quillen stared at the man closest to him with a glowing amulet beneath his clothes. The man saw him staring and gave a wicked smirk.

The man bolted. All the men whom the apparition had revealed were possessing secret amulets around their necks ran in different directions from the camp. Everyone, including Quillen, had no idea what was happening. The apparition dissipated.

Traveler and Pangolin almost knocked down Quillen and others as they took chase.

"Archers!" Pangolin yelled, pointing to the closest escaping man.

One archer fired, missing. Three others did the same and missed. Pangolin was enraged; he ran and grabbed a polearm from a man, then threw it. The escaping man was impaled through the back and fell to the ground.

"Follow!" Pangolin yelled, running out of the camp after the other spies. His Cut-throats ran with him. Pangolin waved them on, indicating they were to pass him. Pangolin was fearsome, and he could run forever, but he was rarely the fastest. The Cut-throats passed him with their weapons in hand. Five spies were ahead of them, running as if on fire.

Traveler ran in another direction after four men. Three other spies split off in another direction.

"Mr. Traveler!"

Traveler turned to see Quillen running with a few spears in his hands. He slowed to grab them from the boy, then increased his speed. He stopped and threw one and then another. The spear grazed the shoulder of one spy, but the second planted itself in his back. He collapsed to the ground.

Traveler turned to the boy. "When you reach that man, make sure he is dead!"

A look of fear came over the boy's face. Traveler was leaving him behind. Quillen reached the downed man on the ground. He was trying to get up.

"Sorry, sir," Quillen said. He jumped on the man's back, held the spear, and thrust it as far as it would go. Quillen stood on him until the man stopped moving—stopped breathing.

Knights on horseback took chase after the three spies. In no time they reached the spies and killed them with swings of their swords. Two of them then rode hard to help Traveler.

Pangolin ran hard and could see his Cut-throats gaining on a few spies, but they didn't have enough men in their chase. As he turned back to see who was following, Lady Aylen dashed past as if the wind were carrying her. She was holding something in each hand. Pangolin watched as she quickly caught up to the Cut-throats and passed them.

Traveler finally reached another spy and slashed him apart with one stroke of his blade. However, the other two were too far away, and they split again. He could only follow one. Two horsemen raced by. One of the riders acknowledged him. They caught and killed the spies. Traveler stood to catch his breath. He looked back; at least a dozen men behind him were also on the chase. He first gestured for them to go back, but then had them draw closer.

"Collect their bodies," he said to them. "I want to know exactly who they were and which of the original three camps they came from."

Lady Aylen threw her weapons. The first trident landed and killed one man. The second killed the other spy. She stopped her chase and walked to the bodies to collect her weapons.

◆◆◆

Quillen struggled to drag the spy back to camp. Two other lads joined him in the task. However, the man was so large that, even together, they still struggled.

"Let me assist, lads," said one of the knights on horseback. Already, one body was draped across his horse's withers. He got down from his horse. "Lift the body." The four of them lifted the body onto the horse.

The knight walked his horse back to camp. Quillen watched as Traveler and other men, some dragging bodies, neared them.

"Too bad we didn't have the aid of your dog, sir," Quillen said.

"My dog did his part last night," Traveler said.

"Yes, sir. He did, indeed."

Not far away, Pangolin waited for his Cut-throats, dragging three bodies behind them. Lady Aylen neared, dragging her two spies alone.

"She said she could do it herself," one of the Cut-throats said to Pangolin.

"And so she can."

The princess dragged the dead men along the ground with no effort at all.

"Lady Aylen, I did not know you could fight."

"Mr. Pangolin, I can."

"Those dual tridents you wield. Do you ever miss your mark?"

She smiled. "Never."

"Maybe you should train my archers, since they apparently cannot hit a man standing still in front of them."

"Ha. Mr. Pangolin, do not be too hard on them. Your archers are warriors accustomed to slashing and gutting men with swords and battle-axes. Leave the archery duties to those of the Kings Elder."

The men of the camp watched as the bodies of the twelve spies were dragged together. Everyone had to see their identities and the gossip had already begun. Hobbs looked at each body, as did Pangolin and his men, Lady Aylen, and the knights of the Kings Elder.

Traveler had them convene in the Kings Elder's tent. Aereth lay silently in his cot, his eyes weary but open.

"Mr. Hobbs?" Traveler asked.

"None of the men were from our original camp, sir."

"Mr. Pangolin?"

"None of them."

"Mr. Bard?"

"Eleven of them," the knight of the Kings Elder answered.

"Lady Aylen?"

"One, Mr. Traveler."

"So, the Four Kings had their spies in place to monitor the activities of the Kings Elder. Then they added a couple when they became aware of Lady Aylen of Sirnegate."

"Thirteen spies, including the one whom your dog dealt with in the river." Lady Aylen shook her head. "Mr. Traveler, we must acknowledge your wisdom in demanding we cast the magic-revealing spell. Who knows what other evil deeds they would have done against us?"

"What now, Mr. Traveler?" Pangolin asked.

"We stay here for at least three days. If we have no other incidents or disappearances among the men, we will set out."

"We have lost three days in moving out. But will we not get to Goodmound's Castle faster by avoiding Ironwood, Mr. Traveler?" Lady Aylen asked.

"When we set out, we will be changing course and heading straight to Ironwood."

Traveler's change of mind surprised them all.

"Why would we do that, Mr. Traveler? Ironwood was in collusion with the Four Kings."

"Lady Aylen, we have been running and avoiding danger here in Avalonia. That is to change. It is a very simple thing. When someone tries to repeatedly kill you, it is a good wager that they will continue doing so until you kill them. We will wait here three days, then we will set out for Ironwood. If they attack us in any way, we will reduce the city in its entirety to rubble."

Traveler gestured to Hobbs and led him out of the tent. "Assemble all the archers."

Hobbs had two thousand men quickly assemble. Traveler looked at Hobbs, and nodded approvingly at his efficiency in gathering them.

"Do you know the colors of the Kingdom of Xenhelm?" Traveler asked the archers. The leadership stood nearby, looking on.

"Yes, Mr. Traveler, we do," they answered.

"From this day forward, if you see any man with those colors, you are to shoot on sight."

The archers looked at each other.

"Shoot on sight. The Kings' Caravan is our mortal enemy and they will not be allowed to kill any more of our comrades. They have killed with hippogriffs, evil creatures of magic crawling beneath our feet in the night, drowning our men in raging waters, marauders, spies within our ranks, and a wizard. It ends."

"Yes, sir!" the men yelled.

"Begin your drills," Pangolin said to them. "No man will remain an archer if he cannot hit even a stationary target."

The men laughed as they returned to their duties.

"This is a huge gamble you make, Mr. Traveler. To turn the caravan into a war party."

"Do you disagree, Mr. Pangolin?"

"I am a berserker, Mr. Traveler. I live for war, but be sure there is logic to your decision. You have said so yourself: Every violent encounter we have, men will die."

"Yes, but I hope to change that. It is obvious that the Kings' Caravan is determined to kill us before we even cross the Lands of Man. So, we will be the war party we must be until we are beyond them. However, before all of that, this will be a crucial night for us."

"No man must die or disappear."

"Yes, I am as concerned about the men's morale as Mr. Hobbs. The battle last night and finding the spies were a good start in uplifting their spirits, but we must maintain that morale."

◆◆◆

Night fell upon the camp. Some men still wrapped themselves in Estus's chains, but most did not. However, brave or not, they all slept with one eye open. Pangolin marched through the camp all night. Traveler confined his night watch to guarding the Kings Elder's tent.

"All men are present and accounted for, sir," a smiling Hobbs said to Traveler at dawn.

"Very good, Mr. Hobbs. I am going to sleep until noon. Keep the men busy. I want the servants drilled on defending themselves as a unit with shields and polearms."

"Are we preparing for battle, sir?"

"We would have had to do so anyway. It was my intention to start preparations after we reached Last Keep, but circumstances forced us to start early."

"Very good, sir."

Pangolin did not sleep but had his archers practicing their aim and speed at various targets nailed to trees. All other fighters drilled with sticks in two-person teams. Then Pangolin had them run around the camp until they dropped.

"Mr. Pangolin, might you tire the men so much that they will be unable to fight?" Hobbs asked.

"Mr. Hobbs, when a man's life is at stake, he will always find the spark of energy to defend it."

◆◆◆

The second night was far more relaxed for the men. However, it was only the second night after the wizard and its creature had been killed.

"Sir." Hobbs was at Traveler's tent at dawn again with a smile. "All men present and accounted for."

Traveler nodded.

"We will continue our duties for the day, sir."

"Good, Hobbs."

"May I ask, sir, how your dog is doing?"

"He's still sleeping." Traveler looked at Hobbs, smiling. "You really want to know where he is sleeping, don't you?"

Hobbs began to chuckle.

"I am not going to tell you."

◆◆◆

Lady Aylen and Gwyness sat on stools at their fire for their noon meal. They watched as Pangolin ran the men around the camp for their final laps.

"Mr. Pangolin is quite the taskmaster," Lady Aylen said.

"We are fortunate to have him, m'lady."

Lady Aylen gave her a look. Gwyness looked away to eat her food.

From Traveler's tent came the dog. It walked slowly, and its mouth opened wide in a yawn. Then it yawned again.

"Well, look what we have here," Lady Aylen said.

The dog snarled at her, but it was more instinctive. The dog sniffled.

"He is still sleepy." Gwyness laughed.

The dog proceeded to shake each of its legs vigorously, then walked away from the women. Some of the men who were not training saw the dog and smiled, but they knew not to touch him.

"Off to find his master," Lady Aylen said.

"Was he in the tent all this time?"

"It's a shape-shifter. For all we know, it changed into an insect and hid in the dirt."

"No, m'lady. The dog would not do that."

"It does mean, though, that we will be setting out soon."

"But what of King Aereth?"

The princess looked back at their tent. The king was still in bed but guarded by a knight.

"He is not getting stronger," Gwyness added.

"No, he is not."

"What about what you did last time? Those potions."

"Gwyness, those potions were useless. I was doing that more to keep the dog from killing us all. It made Traveler conscious for a moment. That is all. King Aereth is already conscious."

Traveler appeared, walking to his tent with the dog following.

"Mr. Traveler, do we set out tomorrow?" Lady Aylen asked.

"Princess, the day after tomorrow."

The trailmaster entered his open tent, grabbed his healer's bag from his things, and walked to the king's tent.

"How is he today?" he asked the knight.

"King Aereth has been awake from time to time."

"He is not recovering fast enough."

Lady Aylen and Gwyness entered the tent.

"What are you going to do, Mr. Traveler?"

"I am going to make a tonic for him. I fear the magic of the ground creature is not leaving his body. I need a fire and a steel pot."

Hobbs brought three cooked fowl on a plate as Traveler stirred the pot's boiling water. It sat on rocks over a large fire in the ground.

"Where do you want your meal, sir?"

"Not mine."

Traveler walked to Hobbs and grabbed one of the pieces of meat. He bit off a piece and threw the entire fowl to the dog. The dog snatched it with his mouth and trotted over to a secluded corner of the tent.

"How much will he need to eat, Mr. Traveler?" Gwyness asked.

"Much more," Traveler replied.

He ate pieces from the other two fowl and tossed them to the dog. The dog snatched all of them in his jaw and dropped them in front of himself.

Traveler returned to the boiling pot. He stirred it more and then used a hook from his bag to pick up the handle and remove the pot from the fire.

"Let it cool while we have our dinner."

Night returned, and Hobbs assembled the leadership for dinner. Traveler poured his tonic into a cup. Knights lifted the king into a sitting position; he looked worse than he had earlier in the day. Traveler handed the cup to one of the king's knight attendants.

He watched Aereth drink it and returned to his seat outside the tent with the others. Lady Aylen and Gwyness sat closest to the tent, watching. Pangolin, Estus, and Hobbs were opposite them.

"Will your concoction work, Mr. Traveler?" Lady Aylen asked.

"Tomorrow we will know. Oh, Mr. Pangolin, tomorrow will be our last day here. The following day we head out at noon. I want you to do a proper scouting before then."

Pangolin nodded.

"We are still heading directly to Ironwood, Mr. Traveler?" Lady Aylen asked.

"Yes we are, Princess."

The dog, lying on the ground behind Traveler, eating a big piece of meat, looked as if he were smirking.

"Mr. Traveler, maybe Ironwood will not be expecting us. I would not."

"Perhaps you are right, but I do not think so."

♦♦♦

The night and morning before moving out went without incident. The camp was struck at dawn and the men waited. Pangolin had set out with six warriors to scout ahead on the new path to Ironwood.

King Aereth sat on a stool, fully alert. Lady Aylen, anxious to get underway, walked to his side. "Sire, Mr. Traveler's tonic has indeed worked."

"He has promised to make more," King Aereth said, smiling. "We are fortunate to have a healer-guide-swordsman in Mr. Traveler."

"Yes, we are. However, today I feel he will be much more of the latter and none of the others. He wants to confront the Four Kings and their accomplices—fight and kill them. Though I cannot say I disagree in the least, I also do not want us to get bogged down in a drawn-out battle when we could be on our way."

Pangolin appeared from the woods, his men following, anger fixed on their faces.

"What is wrong?" Lady Aylen ran to them.

Traveler joined them with the dog. Pangolin and his Cut-throats stopped in front of them.

"What is the news, Mr. Pangolin?"

"If I had not seen it, I would never have believed it. A war party is in wait along the path we would have traveled. Many marauders, more than our number, I would estimate, and they are commanded by Ironwood knights. They are armed for war."

"Thousands of them?" Traveler asked.

"Yes, that is my estimate."

"Mr. Pangolin, you will lead the attack on the Ironwood army, which sounds ridiculous coming from my mouth because Ironwood has never had an army before. They are a mining town known for their superior weaponsmithing and the best weapons in Avalonia. Now it appears they are in the war business at the behest of Xenhelm. Mr. Pangolin, engage them and ensure that not one of their number walks away alive."

"And you?"

"I will personally visit Ironwood itself and have a conversation with their king. He will not enjoy that conversation and will likely not ever have another."

◆◆◆

Pangolin ran as a juggernaut through the woods, his fearsome axe-mace in his hands. The visor of his earthen helmet was down as he yelled, breaking through the foliage of the last of the wooded area before crossing onto the bleak rocky lands to Ironwood. The army of Ironwood saw him, and arrows rained down. All bounced off his armor. He ran straight toward the army; the Ironwood knights ran to engage him.

Boulders broke through the trees and sailed into the Ironwood army of knights and marauders. The Cut-throats appeared, yelling, weapons ready. Bard, the senior knight of the Kings Elder, followed in the next wave with hundreds of fighters. Archers of the Traveler party hid in the trees as they shot their own volley of arrows at the Ironwood army.

Pangolin the Berserker slashed and smashed his way through the Ironwood fighters with ease to attack his first target—the first of seven Ironwood catapults. He destroyed it and its men before they could engage, then threw his axe-mace at another. The weapon's blade cut the catapult's rope just before it launched. The massive boulder slid out and crushed one of the Ironwood fighters. Pangolin pulled a dagger from the base of the back of his helmet and killed his way through to retrieve his axe-mace.

The battle had only begun but already dead bodies littered the ground.

◆◆◆

Traveler watched from behind a tree. The entire city of Ironwood was locked down, with hundreds of knights standing guard in front of its closed main gate. At the top of the wall, archers waited.

"What is that?" an Ironwood guard yelled, pointing to the woods in the distance.

The ground shook as the giant beast rushed at them. Its head was similar to that of a ram and its body was of a scaled lion.

Archers fired at it; the knights braced for attack.

"It's growing!"

The beast rammed the iron gates of Ironwood, trampling the knights in front, blowing the giant doors off their hinges, and sending all the archers on the high wall falling to their deaths. The door fell back to the ground, crushing more knights.

Traveler ran into Ironwood, wielding his sword. He knew exactly where their king was. The barracks were near the main gate. As he neared, the door opened and armored knights poured out to meet him. They did not know his blade was of magic until, with one stroke, he cut them apart and a translucent fire engulfed them.

As he ran up the steps to the second level, Traveler killed more attacking knights. He dove when he reached the top, an archer's arrow barely missing him. Something broke through the roof and impaled the archer through the chest, then pulled him up through the hole. Traveler ran forward into the room to be immediately met by armed knights. He yelled as he cut both swords and men in half.

There, in the corner, stood the Great King of Ironwood—an elderly man with white hair. More knights ran in front of him with swords raised. They attacked, but the sword fight lasted mere moments. Traveler killed the last as the knight went for a morning star hanging on the stone wall. Their king wielded a similar weapon and attempted to whip the spiked ball at Traveler. Traveler cut off the king's arm, and the weapon fell with a thud.

The king screamed in agony and collapsed. He stared at Traveler from the ground, his eyes filled with hate.

"You will never make it out of the Lands of Man alive," he hissed.

"Doubtful, but *you* will not make it from this moment alive." Traveler thrust his sword into the man.

♦♦♦

Several knights burst into the room.

"M'lord!" one of them yelled.

When they saw the slain king on the stone floor, they yelled and attacked. Something impaled each knight through his chest and armor. The men collapsed to the floor. The dog entered. His tail, made of several long, pointed spikes, reverted to normal.

Traveler looked around the room. He went through all the drawers, bookshelves, and cabinets. Nothing. He set the furniture on fire with his sword. He led his dog from the room.

At the very bottom of the steps was a boy. The dog jumped down the steps in front of Traveler and growled.

The boy was not frightened. "I am king now. I know my father is no more. I could sense his death." Traveler watched the boy carefully. "I am no threat to you, sir. My mother, the queen, and I were adamantly opposed to aligning Ironwood with Xenhelm. We knew nothing but evil would come of it. Please forgive us." He lifted his hand with a book. "You should take this."

"Why?"

"It was my mother's, I mean, the queen's. Her diary. She recorded every meeting that my father, the king, had with the Four Kings. King Oughtred caught her and killed her. That was six years ago. He thought he had destroyed the book, but one of her wise attendants switched it with another book to save it. You should have it."

"What do you know?"

"You should follow me and see with your own eyes."

♦♦♦

As the caravan emerged from the woods, Traveler stood with the dog in front of the main entrance to Ironwood. Lady Aylen led the servants,

Pangolin the warriors, and Bard the men of the Kings Elders. From the caravan, they could see the bodies littering the ground and the entire front wall of the city reduced to rubble, as if a giant hand pulled it down.

"How was the *conversation* with the King of Ironwood?" Pangolin asked.

"With the old one, as expected, but with the new one, very enlightening."

A boy wearing a crown appeared at the entrance, startling the Traveler party. Pangolin gestured to calm the archers, who had trained their aim on him.

Traveler turned to him. "We will give you time to evacuate your city of its people."

"Thank you, sir. Xenhelm infected Ironwood with its dark magic. No one must ever live within its walls again. We will go past the Grass Lands. There are mountains there that may be very rich in minerals. We can rebuild there. Ironwood people need mountains."

The boy disappeared back into the city.

"Mr. Estus!"

The weaponsmaster appeared from the caravan.

"Yes, Mr. Traveler."

"I will lead you in first. Apparently, Xenhelm has been using Ironwood as its own vault of weapons."

"Weapons?"

"Weapons not of Avalonia. You will inspect the weapons, but we will take all of them. On the Trail, we will replace the ones in our possession with the least dangerous, as not all men can wield fae weapons without killing themselves or everyone around them."

"How will I know?"

"The ones that seem to weigh the same as our own human metals."

"Yes."

"Where is Mr. Hobbs?"

The steward ran to him. "Here, sir."

Traveler threw him the book. "That is the diary of the late Queen of Ironwood."

"Late, sir?"

"I did nothing. She was killed by King Oughtred years ago—for writing that diary. You are to read it from beginning to end. I want to know anything that can help us on our journey, anything we can use against the Four Kings."

Hobbs stared at the leather-bound book. "Yes, sir. I will do more than my best."

Traveler looked at Pangolin. "How many men did we lose?"

"Not as many as they did. They lost all. We lost some."

"Mr. Quillen recorded their names, sir," Hobbs said to Traveler.

"Good."

"This vault, Mr. Traveler," Lady Aylen began, "was for what purpose?"

"Lady Aylen, you should follow us. I believe that the Four Kings are using their triennial journey to Atlantea for a purpose other than attaining riches. Maybe that is how it began. However, I believe they are using it to acquire weapons and animals to equip themselves for war against all of Avalonia, maybe even all the Seven Empires. If that is so, then their mad behavior begins to make sense."

The weapons vault was more massive than any of them could have imagined. The secret entrance was behind the king's residence. It went down one level into the ground before opening up into a giant cavern filled with armor, hand weapons, and wagon weapons. Lady Aylen walked down the aisles.

"Mr. Traveler, do you know all the metals from which these weapons are forged?"

"Elfin and dwarven mostly, but many, many others as well, some I am not familiar with."

"But you have a notion of where those weapons could be from?"

"I do, but I would rather not say at present."

To empty the secret war vault, Estus had to use every last man to help him load up their pull carts and all the other wagons they found in the city. It would take many days for him to properly sort everything. As they worked, the Boy King of Ironwood led all the people of Ironwood from the city. None of them spoke or made eye contact. The caravan watched them disappear into the distance.

It was nearly dusk when Estus, now a mass of sweat, finished emptying the vault of everything they could use, including armor for horses he had found in an auxiliary vault. Traveler told them all to move far away from the city and set up camp. He did not accompany them as they left. It was a task easier said than done, but they made their way back to the wooded areas between the border of Hopeshire and Ironwood lands.

Hours later, they watched as the entire city of Ironwood was engulfed by flames so large, they turned night into day. The next morning, when the caravan passed by on the way to Goodmound's Castle, the men saw what was left of the once-great city of metal and stone—a giant crater with a black mass that seemed to be the city burning a hole down to the center of the world.

CHAPTER FOURTEEN

Return to Goodmound's Castle

Again, the men were quiet. It was so much to take in. Ironwood was gone. Traveler's dog could change into a beast that could burn an entire city of metal and stone. They were not in the magical lands yet, but there was much of an unnatural nature that they had already encountered. Hobbs could sense their unease, but though Traveler and his dog had joined them in the early morning, Hobbs had no chance to speak with him.

"Mr. Estus, sir?" one of the men asked.

"Please, lad, either sir or Mr. Estus suffices. I dislike titles to begin with. I do not need two of them at a time."

"Sorry, sir. Men are asking what happened to all the weapons we took from Ironwood. They were stacked high at night, a stash larger than the size of our entire caravan but disappeared by the time we awoke this morning. Did Mr. Traveler's dog turn into a beast and take them all somewhere?"

Estus thought for a moment then smiled. "Yes, that is it. He took it all away and buried them for safekeeping. We will have them once we cross into the magical lands. Magical weapons for the lot of us."

The man smiled, as did others who were in earshot.

◆◆◆

"How is King Aereth?" Traveler asked from his horse.

"He is alert but still weak, Mr. Traveler. The ill effects will not leave him," Lady Aylen answered.

"We will need something much stronger than my tonic to restore him then. I know what we must do."

"Mr. Traveler, how did you and your dog destroy Ironwood in that fashion?" Gwyness asked.

"He did not turn into an ancient dragon, if that is what you're asking. The beasts no longer exist, and he can mimic only living things he has encountered."

"Mr. Traveler!" one of the warriors called to them.

Pangolin and his Cut-throats were on point, ahead of the main caravan but always in view.

Traveler and the women rode ahead to where Pangolin and his men waited. They stopped when they saw what the warriors were looking at in the distance—a knight, his helmet in hand, wearing the colors of Xenhelm.

Traveler dismounted and lifted his sword, sheathed on his back, over his neck. Pangolin and his men followed closely as they neared the knight.

The Xenhelm agent smiled. "Traveler."

Traveler stopped.

"Do not be alarmed, sir. King Oughtred is also King Oughtred the All-Knowing. My lord has a proposition for you and your party."

"What would that be?"

"Return home."

"Say again?"

"All of you, take your men and return home. Proceed no farther and all will be forgotten."

"That is a strange request from your king, since he has attempted to kill us multiple times. But now he expects us to trust his word—or his word uttered from the mouth of a messenger."

"Do you think you are the first to try to usurp the Kings' Caravan through the Magical Lands to the fabled kingdom of Atlantea? The Four Kings own Titan's Trail!"

"Own? Do the empires of fae know that Xenhelm owns that part of their lands?"

"The empires of fae are the ones who gave the land to King Oughtred alone. If you are denied acceptance to the Kings' Caravan, there is no journey to be had by you—forever."

"Why are you really here?" Traveler asked. "The fae empires do not submit to humans, Xenhelm or otherwise. I wonder what they would think if they heard of the lies you spread. Xenhelm owns Titan's Trail. What is your true purpose?"

"Do you not know what occurs at this very moment? Cirencester and its allies ravage all of Avalonia. Soon they will move beyond. So as you fight a futile quest here, your home lands lay in ruins. Whether here or there, you have no concept of the power of the Four Kings. We will destroy you and then lay waste to the kingdoms unfortunate enough to have given you to the world. This is your one and only chance to live. Turn back and go no farther."

"Mr. Pangolin," Traveler said.

"Yes, Mr. Traveler."

"Kill that man."

"Archers!"

The agent was cut down in a hail of arrows.

"Since King Oughtred is all-knowing, he already knows our response."

◆◆◆

Traveler looked to Pangolin and his men. "Mr. Pangolin, keep our forces on high alert.

"What is it?" Lady Aylen asked when she reached them with the king.

"Mr. Traveler," King Aereth began. "If I can make a point." The king was still weak, but he stood confidently. "I have studied Xenhelm's strategies for years. A favorite gambit of theirs is to delay their opponent—"

"Until their stronger forces can move in for the kill."

"Yes. A preliminary force fully assesses strengths and weakness and location. They delay until the true attack force appears. They did so with us in the Grass Lands, before we combined our parties. They did so with you using their teleportation spell and the attacks afterward."

"Turn the caravan around now, Mr. Pangolin!" Traveler pointed to one of the senior knights. "Mr. Bard! Now! Turn the men around and back into the woods!"

◆◆◆

The first one appeared a day later. The battle elf was clad from head to toe in rust-colored armor, including a helmet that covered his face, with large insect-like eyes over his real eyes. His pointed ears stuck out from his head. He knelt to the ground, then a wolf the size of a horse appeared. The animal wore armor over most of its head and forelegs. His war-wolf steed sniffed the path and raised its head. More battle elves appeared on their giant war wolves to join the hunt. Others got down from their wolves and walked around. All the elves were at least seven feet tall. They looked around and circled for hours, bewildered.

"They cannot figure out how we or our trail simply disappeared," Traveler said.

From behind an invisible barrier, the leadership watched the elves. No one had dared speak before even though Traveler had told them that no sounds could pass through the barrier.

"Have elves ever ventured this far into the Lands of Man?" Pangolin asked.

"Many times. This area was once part of northern Faë-Land—many eons ago, long before men were anywhere close. However, never has a war party been this far into our lands in modern times. They go to Last Keep maybe, but even there they have never brought a war party."

"If we encountered them on the trail, Mr. Traveler," Lady Aylen began, "what would have happened?"

"I am certain they were waiting for us on the way to Goodmound's Castle. They tracked our steps when they realized we would not show. If we had encountered them, they would have killed every last one of us."

"Except your dog."

"My dog is neither immortal nor invincible. I have no doubt they would have killed us first with one of their arrows. See them in their quivers? Those are special arrows. They know who we all are."

"What kind of elves are they, Mr. Traveler?" Lady Aylen asked.

"Woodland elves. The best trackers of wooded lands. They would have come upon us, and we would never have known. Elves can turn invisible in their natural environment."

"Invisible," Lady Aylen and Gwyness repeated.

"Yes."

"It would seem you have saved all our lives again, Mr. Traveler," King Aereth said.

"The Xenhelm man called King Oughtred the All-Knowing," Pangolin said.

"He did." Traveler glanced at them. "We have our answer. The Four Kings know things about us all that are impossible. Obviously, by magical means."

"How long can we stay in this place, Mr. Traveler?" Gwyness asked, looking around.

Beyond the doorway, which looked like a hazy mesh from within but was invisible from outside, was a large wooded area surrounded by denser woods.

"As long as needed."

"What do they see from their vantage point?" Pangolin asked.

"Nothing. We are completely invisible to them. The entrance is flush with a tree, so even if they were to accidentally touch the doorway threshold, they would touch only the tree."

"Is this from the magical lands, Mr. Traveler?" Aereth asked.

"Yes, sire. We will use it as often as needed when we get there. I never imagined we would need it here."

Hobbs was not with them. He oversaw the men setting up the camp and the cooks preparing the meals within their magical "domain." It was unlike anything they had ever experienced. It was as if they had passed through a doorway to another world of a wooded forest. The trees, brush, and earth seemed real enough, though there were no birds, insects, or any other animals. Yet, there was no eeriness to the place, only a light breeze. There was no sun, but there was light above a thick cloud covering. They could see far into the distance, but that distance could never be reached. Men had tried, but no matter how far they walked, or even ran, the distance remained the same.

"What is this place exactly, Mr. Traveler?" Lady Aylen asked. "Mr. Hobbs said it looked like no more than a folded cloth."

"There is no word for it in our tongue. It is common in Faë-Land. It is a 'pocket' of an environment. It is used to hide your camp or town or city from outsiders. One could say that all of Faë-Land is a series of 'pockets.'"

"Like crossing a threshold into a private realm," Gwyness said.

"Yes. It is hard for me to explain. Think of it as a tent that is larger inside than it would seem from the outside. It's invisible outside, and on the inside is your own personal realm."

"But, Mr. Traveler, how long will we have to stay in here?"

"Until we are sure the battle elves are gone. We cannot fight them. They would kill us all. Therefore, we will not be going to Goodmound's Castle after all. When we are able to set out, it will be straight to Last Keep."

"If they can turn invisible and come upon us without a sound, how do we watch for them?" Pangolin asked.

"We need to get to the Lands Between. They cannot sneak up on us there. Once in Faë-Land, things will be more equalized. I will explain more when we arrive."

"As long as we are continuing forward," Lady Aylen said.

"Mr. Traveler," Aereth began, "is it normal for elves, any elves, to do the bidding of humans, even the supposedly great Kings of Xenhelm?"

"Very astute, sire. No, never. And this is more than unusual. Elves hunting to kill one group of humans for another is unheard of. For such acts, the kingdom of such elves could be cast out and exiled by all the elfin kingdoms. That is why this elfin war party is panicking. They expected to have quickly killed and disposed of us yesterday, but we have vanished. We still do not know the complete story here."

CHAPTER FIFTEEN
Last Keep

The men were greatly amused to see Traveler's dog sprint through the camp, circle it, and run through the woods of their 'pocket' realm. For the first time that any could recall, its behavior was very much that of a real dog wanting to stretch its legs and play.

It was day four of the party hiding inside, and all were taking advantage of the respite. Hobbs reduced the duties of the servants, and Pangolin did the same with the fighters. Quillen spent most of his time writing and adding to his bestiary. Though the musicians were not yet able to play their instruments, here they took the time to entertain the men with impromptu performances. Pangolin spent most of his time sleeping in his small, well-worn, one-person tent. Estus was in Nirvana, having the time to catalog every new Faë-Land weapon they had seized from Ironwood. Only a few knew that the weaponsmith had his own "pocket" inside his tent—a realm that looked very much like the inside of a castle, with endless tables and walls.

Traveler alternated between resting and playing with his dog, often doing his best to run along with him. The dog would sprint ahead then run back to him. This day, however, Traveler was in his tent writing. The women spent their time talking and overseeing the king's care.

"Mr. Hobbs?" Lady Aylen asked when the steward passed by.

"Yes, m'lady?"

"What is your impression of Mr. Bard, the king's lead knight?"

"Why, m'lady?"

"He seems troubled."

Hobbs looked into the crowd of men watching another performance of the musicians. "I will look into it, m'lady."

♦♦♦

"Mr. Traveler seems to be finished with his writing," Gwyness said. The women sat in front of their fire. Within the "pocket," it was now night, but there was not a hint of cold.

Traveler walked to them from his tent.

"Lady Aylen, may I speak with you privately?"

Lady Aylen glanced at her maidservant.

"Of course."

Traveler walked away from the tents, and Lady Aylen followed.

"Why all the intrigue and mystery, Mr. Traveler?" she asked when they stopped.

"Before we discuss that, Princess, I need to know if your secrecy will threaten us along the way."

"Nothing about me will threaten our caravan, Mr. Traveler."

"I hope so. How is King Aereth?"

"He is still weak."

"We need the proper potions to restore him completely, since we have no sorcerers of our own. When everyone is asleep, I will fetch you, and we will go to Last Keep."

"Last Keep? You said they do not let people enter who are traveling out of Avalonia."

"Their prohibition will not apply to you, Princess. Be ready."

"How can we get to Last Keep when it is so far away?"

"It is not far away. The city a month's travel from here is not the real Last Keep. The real Last Keep is on the mountain in view of Goodmound's Castle."

"What? We saw no structures the last time."

"Because it is in its own 'pocket' that is visible only to mortals returning from Faë-Land, as well as sorcerers and other magical beings."

◆◆◆

Under the light of a full moon, Lady Aylen rode slowly on her horse to the walled city. Last Keep sat on the mountain plateau just as Traveler had said, but she did not know why she had not seen it last time. There was both a massive door that was nearly as tall as the thirty-foot wall and, next to it, a nine-foot door.

She got down from her horse, held the reins, and walked to the door. She knocked three times. The wait was long, but she did not knock again, just as Traveler had instructed.

The door opened and she saw a hooded figure, his face obscured by the night.

"I am in need of supplies," she said, then pulled a note from her outfit to hand to the man.

Instead of taking the note, he grabbed her hand. "What tribe? What house?" he asked in a deep voice.

"I do not know what you mean."

"I will send you away if you do not answer."

"House of Faylen."

The man watched her from the darkness. He took the note from her hand and read it. "Did you write this?" he asked.

"Yes, of course."

"Do you know what it says?"

"We need supplies to restore our comrades."

He turned the note so she could see it. "You do not know what it says. Strange, since it is written in elvish. Are you not elf?" He spoke in a different tongue, but she did not understand. "An elf who does not speak elvish. That is a very dangerous thing. Why should I give you entry? An elf who does not speak elvish, who wishes medicine for non-elves. I see no reason to speak to you further."

"Did you truly read the note, or are you simply making up a reason not to help? I do not speak elvish because my people rescued me from my kingdom as an infant, before it was destroyed. Should they have left me there to be murdered? Elves do murder other elves, or do you believe in fairy tales?"

The hooded man laughed. "I will let you pass. Get your magic medicine. I trust you have someone who actually knows how to use it, because that someone surely is not you."

♦♦♦

The camp had devolved into horseplay, with the men so relaxed that many were not even wearing their boots anymore.

Hobbs sat at the campfire with his pipe. He tried to appear relaxed, but he was not.

"It is fine, Mr. Hobbs." Pangolin had risen from his slumber. "Think of it as a vacation for the men. Remember, our journey will last a year."

"Yes, Mr. Pangolin. You are correct. I am a creature of discipline."

"Yes, Mr. Hobbs."

"Oh, Mr. Traveler is ready."

Hobbs jumped up and ran to the Kings Elder's tent.

Traveler carried in a steaming pot. Lady Aylen and Gwyness waited at the king's side where he lay on his cot. A servant held a cup in hand, and Traveler poured the new elixir into it.

"Have him drink it all."

Aereth struggled to sit up to drink, almost trembling. He was visibly thinner than days prior.

"How long will it take to react—" Lady Aylen did not get a chance to finish her question to Traveler.

Steam seemed to emanate from the king. Aereth stood to his feet, his eyes open wide, his posture straightened. As the man rose, he seemed to grow a bit younger. Aereth smiled, then began to laugh. He marched forward and snatched Traveler into a bear hug. The trailmaster did not know how to react.

"You might want to let me go, sire, as my dog may think you are attacking me."

As soon as Traveler uttered the words, the dog rushed into the tent with a suspicious gaze.

"Well, Mr. Traveler, I do not know what you gave me," Aereth said, "but it would appear that you have made me more than whole."

King Aereth had been truly reborn. When he ate, it was as if he had not eaten for weeks. He also could not stop laughing.

Traveler was back in his tent, cleaning up from brewing the new elixir. Lady Aylen appeared at the entrance.

"Mr. Traveler, it would seem your potion is more successful than any of us could have hoped. What were all those other herbs and powders the merchant gave me? I also saw what looked to be animal parts in there."

"All for medicine. We need to be ready for the normal maladies, as well as the magical on our journey."

"How do you know all about this, Mr. Traveler? Healer and apothecary?"

"Remember, Princess, I was a healer before I was a traveler or swordsman."

"Yes, and guide. Mr. Traveler, when do we leave?"

"Two days. Give the men one more day of rest, then back into a full day of routine. We set out after that."

"Do you fear that the battle elves will be ahead?"

"No, I do not believe they are in our realm anymore."

"Then they went back to King Oughtred empty-handed. I do not think he will like that. Nor do I believe he will let it go at that."

"I agree, Princess. More surprises for us ahead."

"I simply want this to be a caravan, not a running battle every step we take. Will we stop at the false Last Keep?"

"Do you want to stop there, or continue past to Titan's Bridge?"

"Mr. Traveler, you must know by now that I am an impatient person. To Titan's Bridge!"

◆◆◆

King Aereth's new vigor astonished the men, especially his own. All remarked that, in body, he was truly as he had been twenty years ago. He even joined the common work of the camp. Hobbs was glad to have the order of the work routine return.

"Sir, I am gathering everyone for the meeting of leadership." Hobbs had entered Traveler's tent on his rounds.

"Very good, Hobbs," Traveler replied as he looked through a variety of maps from a chest in the corner of his tent.

They assembled in the Kings Elder's tent. Traveler stood at the table as those invited began to arrive. Pangolin and one of his Cut-throats were first, and they joined Traveler looking upon the map.

"Mr. Traveler, did you draw these maps?" Pangolin asked.

"I did. Though how accurate they are today, I cannot say, but they will suffice for now."

King Aereth entered with Lady Aylen, Maiden Gwyness, and Sir Bard.

"Ah, Mr. Traveler," Aereth said, nearing the table. "A map of the lands beyond Avalonia where we will travel. No one is more pleased than Lady Aylen, I imagine."

Estus and Hobbs arrived next. They quickly gathered at the table.

"Mr. Traveler, Lady Aylen informed me that the city all of us have known as Last Keep is not the true Last Keep at all," Aereth announced. "Will we be stopping there anyway?"

"I do not believe so, sire. However, we will pass nearby. My dog and I will make a night visit."

"Is that wise, Mr. Traveler?" Aereth asked.

"Wiser than not doing so at all. It is simply a precaution. I doubt there will be any presence of King Oughtred's agents. They are not that kind of people. They care for no one outside their own."

Traveler pointed to the map and continued. "I want to familiarize you all with what we will encounter once we cross Titan's Bridge. We may not have time to do so again until we reach Faë-Land. I know we have gotten used to the security of the 'pocket.' However, once we leave it, we will not be able to use it again until we set foot in the magical lands."

"So, we will be exposed again," Lady Aylen said.

"Yes, for many miles. I know we were all growing quite accustomed to its sanctuary, but it cannot be helped. It is how its magic works.

"It will take us a full day to move across Titan's Bridge. We must start at dawn, and reach the other end before dusk."

"Is there danger associated with its crossing?" Aereth asked.

"It is a land bridge of such mass that it is larger than anything you could imagine, above a chasm said to be bottomless. It is not, but it cuts so far into the depths of the world that it might as well be. With that beneath us, having ten thousand men above is not the way to spend a night. The night winds are fierce, and the chasm echoes with strange noises that would frighten any man or woman and create panic. We must cross during daylight hours.

"Once we do, we will officially be in the Lands Between. The first region we will come upon is the Mist Mires. The mist is ever-lasting, but the mires are not as plentiful as the name suggests. However, we will also not want to cross it during the night, so we will make camp immediately after crossing the land bridge, then start again at the next sunrise. I expect the Mist Mires to be uneventful, though visibility will be impossible. We will rely on the ingenuity of Mr. Estus to rope the men together as we cross.

"Afterward, we will come to the Howling Mountains. The name says it all. We will either have trouble there or not. I will say no more until we arrive, as I do not want to alarm anyone needlessly. Then we pass the Stone Forest—"

"What makes the Howling Mountains howl, Mr. Traveler?" Gwyness asked.

"The way the mountains are—or were made to be. When the winds pass through them, the sound is exactly like that of howling animals."

"And the Stone Forest?" she asked.

"Only the women are asking questions. If the rest of you do not ask me questions here, do not bother me any time after this," Traveler said. He returned his gaze to Gwyness. "Are you certain you wish me to answer? I do not believe the answer to be anything other than a myth to frighten humans."

"Now you must tell us, Mr. Traveler," Lady Aylen said.

"It was said to be infested by gorgons in times past."

"Gorgons?" Gwyness asked with a look of fear. "Are those not the creatures that—"

"Yes, turn any who look upon them to stone. However, again, I do not believe the story. Trees do not have eyes—at least in our lands, so how could they turn to stone? I believe the truth to be different. Regardless, the Stone Forest is not a vast region. We can pass through it quickly.

"Finally, we come to the Mirage Plains, which is of pure magic. If you do not know how to cross it, you will never do so. You can walk through it for days or a lifetime and never cross its threshold."

"A mirage?" Lady Aylen asked.

"Yes, it makes you think you are seeing the way through when you are not."

"Fascinating, Mr. Traveler," Aereth said. "How long do you estimate it will take us?"

"A fortnight, sire, if we encounter no obstacles along the way."

"Is Necropolis not also in the Lands Between?" Gwyness asked.

"No, it is another myth. Those lands are beyond Faë-Land, to the west. We will not be anywhere near there. I believe the Lands Between to be a realm magically created by the empires of Faë-Land for the sole purpose of keeping men from their lands. Titan's Bridge is natural enough, if you believe in the pre-history of the Titans, but the Lands Between is not a naturally formed region."

"Do you not believe the legend of the Titans, Mr. Traveler?" Lady Aylen asked.

"I neither believe nor disbelieve. Remember, I have traveled across all of Titan's Trail. Some points fit the legend. Others do not. You shall see for yourselves."

"Ah, good, Mr. Traveler. Finally, a positive word from our caravan's guide and trailmaster about our chances on our fantastic journey."

"Yes," he said wryly. "As I was saying about the Lands Between, its purpose is more to frighten away than to kill. However, that may have changed."

"Why do you say that, Mr. Traveler?" Aereth asked.

"The Kings' Caravan."

"Yes, of course."

"Also, we should discuss the structure of the camp and the duties of the men going forward. We may not again have this extended time of peace to discuss these issues so casually."

"Mr. Traveler, before you begin," Lady Aylen said, "what of the elfin hunting party? Might they be waiting for us ahead?"

"They are not."

"How do you know that, Mr. Traveler?"

"The dog and I scouted ahead last night."

Traveler's revelation elicited chuckles and expressions of surprise from the group.

"What if you had encountered them, Mr. Traveler?"

"Lady Aylen, elfin war wolves cannot fly."

She smiled. "But Traveler's dog does. Where is your companion, anyway?"

"He is sleeping."

She laughed.

"Let us return to the matters at hand. Mr. Pangolin, you brought one of your men, as requested."

"Mr. Traveler, this is Nirgund the Slasher." The berserker slapped the Cut-throat on his back.

"The Slasher? Such creative names. He will be your second in command. In battle, I do not want the two of you standing together."

Pangolin nodded.

Traveler continued. "You and your men will take charge of point for our caravan and the rear. I want the best archers divided between the two areas. 'Best' meaning they can actually hit something."

"I have been drilling them thoroughly, Mr. Traveler. They will be able to hit at least a standing tree if needed."

"Or a moving one, hopefully. Also, I want a circle of fighters around the caravan with polearms and full armor. Mr. Pangolin, you had other suggestions?"

"Yes, to have teams of shieldmen who can move where needed in the caravan during battle."

"Very good. Sir Bard, you will be under Mr. Pangolin's informal command, as there should be only one master-at-arms for our caravan. However, the knights will remain under your command. You will do the same. Go where needed, and leave a contingent to protect the leadership at all times."

"Mr. Estus, you will always remain with the weapons. If we lose those, we might as well return home. They give us an advantage on this journey that we could only have dreamed of—and without spending a coin. You will command the team of men to protect our food and weapon wagons at all times."

"And, Mr. Traveler," Estus said, "I have been building a few gadgets and traps to aid in their protection."

Traveler smiled. "You are Estus the Forge, so I am sure they are especially wicked and deadly. King Aereth?"

"Yes, Mr. Traveler."

"We must have a team of fighters to man the heavy weapons—catapults, giant crossbows, and battering rams—to use at a moment's notice. You will command those teams. A fitting role for one who has commanded men on the battlefield countless times, as our princess has told me, and who still retains a strategic military mind. We are a caravan and not an army, but no caravan that cannot also ably conduct itself as an army when needed has ever made it through the magical lands."

Aereth nodded. "Very good plan, Mr. Traveler."

"Mr. Hobbs."

"Yes, sir?"

"Take on Mr. Quillen as your apprentice. He was essentially in that role already, but let's make it formal."

"My own second, sir."

"Mr. Traveler, you organize our caravan like a seasoned general in battle rather than a simple trailmaster," King Aereth observed.

"Sire, I have been on many journeys and with many groups. The ones most likely to reach their destinations whole were those that adopted a war mindset. On those journeys, I was a healer, not a warrior, so that is my perspective. However, attending to the broken bodies of men and burying them made me become a warrior.

"Lady Aylen and Maiden Gwyness will remain at the front of the camp."

"No, tasks for us, Mr. Traveler?" Lady Aylen asked.

"You will have many, Princess, and Maiden Gwyness, as soon as the Lands of Man are behind us and we cross into the magical lands. Your real tasks begin there.

"This is only the initial plan. I have no doubt circumstances will cause us to change our priorities many times on this journey. But, we must be able to work as a team and adapt no matter what we face. There remains one final thing I will ask you, sire, to answer, but there is no hurry. What will we name our caravan? I do not want the men referring to us as Traveler's Caravan, especially once we reach the magical lands. This is so much more than any one of us. There is the Kings' Caravan, and there will be ours."

"No need for us to ponder, Mr. Traveler," Aereth answered. "We came up with a name years ago, my fellow Kings Elder and I. It is through Titan's Trail we journey, so it is Titan's Caravan we shall be named."

◆◆◆

Hobbs awoke before dawn to the sound of yelling. At first he thought he was dreaming, but when he rose from his sleep, he saw the men's pained looks in the glow of the campfires where they gathered.

"What is happening?" Hobbs asked.

"Something with the Kings Elder's knights," a man answered.

Hobbs ran toward King Aereth's tent only to collide with Bard. King Aereth marched after his knight, anger and sadness on his face.

"Sire?" Hobbs asked.

He did not answer but held up his hand to indicate: not now! He brushed past Hobbs.

Hobbs turned back and saw the women standing quietly. He slowly approached them.

"What happened?"

"Sir Bard is returning to Helm Earldom," Lady Aylen answered.

Shock crossed his face. "It is all arranged. We set out for Titan's Bridge today."

"Soon the men will say that Titan's Caravan is cursed," Lady Aylen said in a huff and disappeared into the women's tent.

Again, elation was followed by setback. The men were looking to him, but Hobbs did not know what to say. All they could do was watch. The entire contingent of the Kings Elder, all its knights, fighters, and servants, were gathered apart as both King Aereth and Mr. Bard addressed them. They were far enough away that the men could not hear exactly what was being said, but they did not need to hear. They knew. Titan's Caravan was about to lose more men; the only question was how many.

"Has anyone seen Mr. Traveler?" Hobbs asked.

"No, sir. Some of the men said he set out sometime at night. He has yet to return."

"Did he have the dog with him?"

"Yes, sir. They saw the dog with him."

The often fiery exchange between King Aereth, Bard, and other senior knights went on for more than an hour. During that time, Traveler reappeared at his tent. As Hobbs neared him, there was no sign of concern in their guide's face. He pointed at Hobbs and then pointed in the distance. Hobbs stopped and turned to see a lone King Aereth marching back to his tent.

When the king passed by, Hobbs followed.

"Mr. Hobbs, assemble the leadership in my tent."

"Yes, sire." Hobbs turned to run, but he already saw Pangolin, Estus, and Nirgund approaching. He saw Quillen and gestured for him to come too.

The meeting did not start immediately. King Aereth paced feverishly in the tent, waiting. They all stood quietly. Finally, Mr. Bard entered with several of the senior knights.

He avoided eye contact with all except the king. "Sire, the knights will return with me. You will have most of the fighters and all the servants."

"Thank you, Bard."

"Sire, again, this is not against you."

"You do know what that Xenhelm messenger said was lies to get a reaction out of us. It seems, though he was killed, he has still succeeded."

"Sire, if you can show me proof that his words are lies, we will all remain. How can we travel idly, far from our home and lands, when they may be under siege? Our home, our kingdom, our families, our people. No, sire, this is too much to ask. We cannot ignore this duty. We must know in our hearts and minds that all is safe with Helm Earldom and our brother kingdoms of Strongbridge and Eastmoor. Yes, our sorcerers are there, but what if more is needed?"

"You made this decision of your own free will?" Traveler asked.

"Yes! I did, Mr. Traveler," Bard sneered at him with deep hate in his eyes.

"Bard!" Aereth yelled. "That is no way to conduct yourself. It is a legitimate question to ask."

"Yes, I did, Mr. Traveler," Bard answered again, calmer. "As we passed the remains of Ironwood, the great city of iron and stone, I thought to myself, this was all done with one creature pretending to be a wolf dog. What if the Four Kings sent an army of such creatures to ravage our lands? We, Mr. Traveler, were hiding like scared animals from battle elves that you admitted should never have been in the Lands of Man, but there they were with their giant wolf steeds, and we were hiding from them. What if the Four Kings sent an army of them into our lands? No, I can proceed no farther."

"Yes, Mr. Bard, you should not," Traveler said.

"I, sir, am a royal chief knight of Helm Earldom. I was born to fight and die to protect my kingdom and its people, not to take orders from commoner barbarians and berserkers on some quest for treasure we do not even know exists."

"Mr. Bard, you can take your leave."

Bard held his tongue. He calmed his agitation as he stared at the top of the tent. "I apologize, sire, for my perceived disobedience. I cannot proceed farther because, as powerful as the three sorcerers are, they are powerless to bring back the dead. I swear, sire, I will kill every Xenhelm and Cirencester man sent against our kingdoms and keep our people safe."

"Yes, Bard. I know you will. Tell Kings Eothelm and Sigbard that I am well, and we move to Titan's Bridge."

"Yes, m'lord." Bard saluted his king with his sword, bowed, and left. All of the knights did the same, then followed him.

Hobbs spoke up among the silence of the tent. "I will have a full accounting of how many men remain once they set out."

"Thank you, Mr. Hobbs," King Aereth said.

"Yes, Hobbs," Traveler answered.

♦♦♦

Titan's Caravan set out at dawn the next day. It was the first time the men had breathed the natural air in many days. They missed the security of the 'pocket' but were overjoyed by the fact that they were moving forward on their journey.

Pangolin scouted ahead over a ridge with a half-dozen men. The lands were a combination of those of Ironwood and Goodmound—rolling, hilly terrain and plush woods. Traveler led the caravan on foot; his dog was absent. King Aereth and the women followed a few yards behind on horseback, pulling the other unmanned horses with them.

"With Mr. Traveler's stride, he carries himself as fast as even a large horse's gallop," Aereth remarked.

"I wish, sire, that he walked with his companion," Lady Aylen said. "Our powerful shape-shifter does not benefit us if it sleeps often."

"M'lady, I believe Mr. Traveler is having his animal rest as much as possible because he expects danger ahead," Gwyness added.

"Or because both are fond of dangerous excursions in the dark hours of the night," Lady Aylen said.

"All for a good cause, I'm sure," the king said.

They noticed Pangolin and his men appear from the woods, running back to the caravan. Traveler met them.

"What did you see?" he asked.

"A large camp is ahead on our path—knights, other warriors, with horses, wagons, many heavy weapons. They fly the colors of a kingdom with which I am unfamiliar."

Traveler turned and motioned to King Aereth.

"King Aereth or Lady Aylen can ride ahead with you and identify their flag."

The camp was as Pangolin had described. Thousands of men sprawled out on either side of the road to the city known as Last Keep.

"Do you recognize the flag, sire?" Traveler asked from their hidden vantage point in the woods.

"Yes. It is the colors of the Kingdom of Fontaare. They are a long-time ally of our kingdoms."

"Before we expose you to danger, sire, let Mr. Pangolin and me show ourselves to the camp and see what our reception will be." Traveler slowly emerged from the trees to the road. Pangolin kept close to him.

They were seen immediately; several men of the camp stood from their seated posts to confront him.

"Good day, sirs."

"Who might you be?" one of the men asked, a sword in his hand.

"I wish to speak to the leader of your party. Are you from the Kingdom of Fontaare?"

"Yes, most."

"Wait, I know you," another man said. "You are the healer from that day of the marauder attack outside Ironwood. The same day one of the Four Kings attacked us with their hippogriff beast."

"Yes, it is I."

"How did you get here? We imagined you would be in the magical lands already."

"The Four Kings have the means to transport people back long distances with magic. That is what they did, but we were not deterred."

The men looked at each other. They were disgusted.

"Traveler, was it?" the same man asked.

"Yes. I am the guide and trailmaster of a larger caravan now. We joined with others on the way back."

"I remember you, too," the man said, looking to Pangolin. "The berserker. You saved a lot of men, protecting them from the hippogriff beasts."

"Yes, I did."

"What others have you joined with?"

"The Kings Elder. Do you know of them?"

"Yes, of course. Are they here?"

"Yes."

"Then we will take you to Prince Reinborne."

"We have two royals in our camp. I will have them join us."

Traveler had both King Aereth and Lady Aylen accompany him. They were led into the camp of men—a mix of seasoned warriors and simple commoners. In the center was a large tent—purple and white, the colors of Fontaare. A man with shoulder-length hair emerged with several knights behind him.

"Prince Reinborne!" the king yelled out.

"King Aereth!" the man greeted. "The Fates have smiled on us, indeed." He moved closer to them. "And fair Lady Aylen."

"Prince. I see you have not lost your charm."

"Where are your colleagues, Kings Eothelm and Sigbard, m'lord?"

"They are back in our kingdoms."

The prince took Lady Aylen's hand. "Please, please, join me in my tent. We have much to discuss. I will have the servants bring food and drink, because this is truly a celebration."

♦♦♦

"Mr. Traveler, many of the men in my camp speak of you with high praise," Prince Reinborne said. "You saved many lives."

"They deserved no less than my best."

"They told me of your master skills with the blade in the battle, and against the marauders—and your dog. I hope you did not lose him."

"He lives. He is simply resting."

"Good. An animal that can fight such as yours is worth ten fighters."

"Tell us what happened," Aereth said. "We did not know Fontaare was joining this year's Caravan. We could have set out together."

"We did not want anyone to know, sire. As with your kingdoms, and yours, Lady Aylen, Fontaare has been seeking its own caravan to Atlantea for years. My scouts came across several men who claimed to have been part of the last Kings' Caravan three years ago. Their stories were quite disturbing. As a fellow royal, I could not repeat the charges against them publicly, but my own counsel suggested both caution and secrecy. My intent was to ride up and join you at Ironwood, since we knew you would be there.

"However, we were plagued with one disaster after another that delayed us. We did not reach Ironwood until a week after everyone had set out. My trackers could not find their path, so I decided to simply wait here until we formulated a new plan. Since then, a steady flow of new men has wanted to join us. They were part of the Caravan but were attacked by the Four Kings or marauders and had to abandon their travels."

"How were you delayed when you set out from Fontaare?" Aereth asked.

"The night before we were to leave, my trailmaster, my master-at-arms, and our sorcerer were poisoned—all three men. Also, all our horses in the kingdom died. It caused such chaos in the palace, and we did not know how the evil was done. I was determined not to abandon our efforts, though we no longer had our advantage."

"An army of marauders attacked us on the way to Hopeshire," Aereth said. "We all had setbacks, but we have gathered together now."

"Do you have trackers who can find the Kings' Caravan's trail for us to follow?"

"We have something better, Prince," Lady Aylen said. "We have a guide."

"A guide?" the prince asked. "You have someone who knows Titan's Trail?"

"All the way to Atlantea," Aereth said. "In fact, that is the name of our new caravan—Titan's Caravan."

The prince could not contain his joy. He took Lady Aylen's hands and started dancing with her. "We are going to Atlantea!" he sang.

◆◆◆

Prince Reinborne introduced his knights to them.

"I have five thousand men to add to your Titan's Caravan—my best soldiers in Fontaare. They are at your disposal, and I defer to your command."

"Thank you, Prince. We are honored to have you and your men," Aereth said. "Mr. Traveler is our guide, Mr. Hobbs our steward, and Mr. Pangolin our master-at-arms. We can easily incorporate all of you. Mr. Traveler?"

"It will be no problem, sire. He can ride at the front with you and Lady Aylen. His men will be our new rear guard. Mr. Pangolin and I can go over the details with them later."

"Very good."

"That is agreeable to me," Prince Reinborne said. "I will send men into Last Keep and purchase our final provisions then."

"We will make camp here for the day to prepare and set out at dawn," Traveler said.

Hobbs had the camp set up quickly as the Reinborne camp sent dozens of horsemen into Last Keep for supplies. It would be an early meal courtesy of the Prince, but only the royals would attend—all others would be hard at work.

"Are you positive that your guide knows the way?" the Prince asked from the round meal table. Lady Aylen sat adjacent to him.

"We are positive," Aereth answered.

"Prince, did you encounter any other dangers while you waited?" Lady Aylen asked.

"No, fortunately. Though I had all but abandoned the Caravan. If you had passed by a few days later, we would not have been here. I was making the final plans with my men for the return to Fontaare."

"Prince, has Fontaare had any encounters with Xenhelm?" Aereth asked.

"We have not seen an agent of their kingdom in almost seven years, and they are not too far from our borders. It is rumored that since they began the Caravan, they have spent most of their time in the magical lands, returning every few years only to deposit riches in their castle vaults and, recently, to show off their fantastic beasts—a griffin and three hippogriffs, with more amazing things to come."

"More?" Aereth asked. "Such as?"

"Who could say, m'lord? To those of us in the region, it seemed that the Four Kings had since tired of the Lands of Man. One rumor said they had created a new kingdom."

"A new one? In Faë-Land?"

"You know the names of these magical lands better than I, m'lord. That was the rumor, but I believe it. One cannot keep one hundred thousand men on the road forever. They would need a base, and after all this time, such a base would become a city or kingdom."

"We should share this news with Mr. Traveler," Aereth said.

♦♦♦

Dusk fell with the expanded camp busy at work. Sentries were at their posts, the night watch was already asleep, and chores were underway. All was quiet at the Kings Elder's tent; the tent was completely closed up. An incredibly fiery glow came from within, then a lesser one.

The apparition rose from the top of the tent. Traveler immediately emerged, followed by Pangolin and Lady Aylen. Gwyness stepped past them to watch her spell rise above the camp. They all watched it as it flew toward the men of Prince Reinborne's camp, but it simply dissipated.

Gwyness looked back and smiled.

"What is happening?" King Aereth asked from within the tent.

"It would appear that we are free of any magical spies of Xenhelm, sire," Lady Aylen replied.

"We set out tomorrow morning, then," Traveler said.

"Will your companion be joining us, Mr. Traveler?" Lady Aylen asked.

"He may. He misses growling at you."

♦♦♦

"Well, good morning, Lady Aylen." Prince Reinborne rode up on his brown stallion, a wide smile on his face. "What a good morning it is, indeed." He took a position to ride next to her.

"Prince, good morning to you, too."

Gwyness hid her giggles well, seated on her horse just behind her lady. King Aereth, with his new vigor, quickly rode up to join them.

"Why, look at this, Lady Aylen," said Prince Reinborne. "What an impressive caravan we have. Do you realize that this time tomorrow our eyes will behold the very Titan's Bridge of Avalonia? One of the many legendary wonders we have heard of as children."

"Prince, I will save my dancing until we cross the threshold into Faë-Land."

He laughed. "That will be a sight to behold. I will need to remain at your side until that moment."

♦♦♦

"You boy," Prince Reinborne called to Hobbs. The prince impatiently waited with four expressionless knights.

"Yes, Prince." Hobbs had been talking to a few of the men.

"Assign me a man to give me a proper tour of your camp."

"Yes, Prince, immediately."

In his service to the Theogar Royal House for some thirty years, Hobbs had met many nobles and royals. In his role, splendor and high ceremony were commonplace. He wished he could say most of the monarchs and nobles he had met were respectful, mature, and dignified, but they were not. However, as a professional steward in a royal palace, his own feelings were irrelevant. Service to the crown was all that mattered. Rudeness and slights from royals and their staff were always to be ignored. Even abuse was to be overlooked.

However, this was not a royal palace in a revered kingdom. This was a caravan upon an amazing but dangerous journey to the magical lands. They had already lost men. They had already faced monsters and more and would do so again. Hobbs knew the prince's type because he had seen it so many times before. He could dismiss it, but would the men?

Though his new master was one he could bring any issue to whatsoever, Hobbs felt he had to hold his tongue. Prince Reinborne was a friend and ally to the Kings Elder.

The prince had his official tour of the camp. He cared not for any of the men he had met and Hobbs had introduced him to. The men were not royals.

◆◆◆

Pangolin and a dozen warriors stood in a clearing about twenty feet ahead of the caravan. They watched the way ahead, then the berserker glanced back.

"What is it?" one of his men asked.

"Do you not feel it? The ground is shaking," Pangolin replied.

"Could it be another group running to meet us?" another asked.

"Riders?" the first warrior suggested.

"No, it is much more powerful than that," Pangolin said.

Pangolin pulled his axe-mace from his back. His men drew their weapons, too, and they all walked back to the caravan.

The caravan's royals waited at the front on horseback. Three columns, ten thousand strong, lined up behind them, stretched back along the path. A warrior ran to the front. "Mister Hobbs," he said, pointing. "Pangolin and his front guardsmen have their weapons at the ready."

"Why?" Hobbs turned to look.

Quillen was also at the front. He looked at the ground, then knelt to place his palm on it. "Why is the ground shaking?" Quillen looked up and around as the shaking became more violent. Everyone began to feel it. "Something is coming!" Quillen stood as a noise burst from the forest and the trees moved.

The ogre pushed through the forest, uprooting an entire tree. The giant humanoid bent down, grabbed the tree before it fell, and threw it at the caravan. Pangolin and his Cut-throats had already reached the flank under attack. They managed to dodge the projectile, but one man was not so lucky. The ogre stood erect at thirty feet tall. Its skin was a sickly greenish color and its body looked malnourished, but it had a potbelly under the animal-hide clothing that draped over half its chest, its privates, and to its knees. When it yelled, they saw its gnarled teeth. The ogre smiled at the man crushed by the tree and reached for his body as its mouth watered.

The entire caravan readied for battle. "Fire!" Pangolin yelled. Archers fired volleys of arrows at the creature, but none did any damage. The ogre ripped another piece of a tree apart and hurled it at the archers. Several men were hit and fell to the ground. With one swing of its hand, the creature hit Pangolin center of mass, sending the berserker hurling back through the air and crashing into the trees.

"Protect the princess and King Aereth!" Prince Reinborne commanded his knights as he drew his sword but remained at Lady Aylen's side. The knights encircled them.

Rock projectiles and giant arrows showered the ogre from heavy weapons teams. The creature screamed as it swatted away as many of the incoming boulders as possible; most of the giant arrows bounced off its body. Pangolin's axe-mace sailed from the trees and toward the creature, striking its head with perceptible force; the ogre screamed and grabbed the side of its head as it started falling sideways. Pangolin appeared, running at it, yelling with full berserker rage.

The ground shook violently again; trees began to move, but everyone had already seen what was coming—another ogre, much larger, with a misshapen upper body. It looked to have two heads, one grossly deformed. It grabbed the first ogre, picked it up, and raised it above its head.

Pangolin had retrieved his weapon from the ground but stood in place. The new ogre locked its gaze on him. It looked at the rest of the caravan and yelled. All braced for devastation.

Traveler burst from his tent with his long sword in hand. The blade was engulfed by a transparent fire only perceptible by the heat distorting the air around it. Traveler was not alone. He ran at the creature at incredible speed. An animal followed him. It was the dog—three times its usual size. A bony exoskeleton covered its body. Its paws were eagle-like claws and its forehead was like a battering ram.

The larger ogre saw them and threw the smaller ogre at them. The dog rose on its hind legs as it ran, changing into a humanoid form. The dog caught the small ogre and threw it back. The ogres smashed into each other, but the larger one did not buckle in its stance.

"Pangolin! Kill the small one!" Traveler yelled with his own rage.

The larger ogre came at Traveler. It screamed as Traveler's firesword cut off two of its fingers. The dog returned to his previous beast form and rammed into the creature's shin, breaking bone. The large ogre screamed louder as it tumbled back, grabbing at the air. It crashed but got to its feet, then turned and managed to scurry away in terror. Traveler and the dog beast gave chase. Everyone watched as the ogre ripped up trees and threw them at the pursuers in its attempt to get away.

"Men!" Aereth yelled. "I want every projectile to hit the smaller one and kill it!"

The heavy weapons team moved into action.

The disoriented smaller ogre managed to stand. Pangolin was upon it, striking with full force at its Achilles tendon. The ogre snapped to alertness as it screamed with such intensity that men felt pain in their eardrums. Immediately, King Aereth's three heavy weapons teams attacked. The smaller ogre was struck with giant arrows again, but this time the arrows hit their mark, puncturing the ogre's leathery chest. One lodged in its neck and the ogre fell to the ground. Pangolin attacked again, his fury aimed at the creature's neck. When he was done, he had severed the creature's head from its body.

Pangolin ended his berserker rage attack. Covered in a blackish ooze that was the creature's blood, he walked to the closest men. "Bury that man and attend to the wounded," he said.

The men sheathed their swords and pushed the tree off their comrade. At least the man had not suffered; he had been killed instantly.

A horrific scream shattered the silence. It was the other ogre.

It was well over an hour later when they all watched Traveler and the dog walk back into camp. Traveler gripped his sword in one hand. The dog had returned to his regular form. Traveler saw the spot of the fallen man, now floating in a pool of blood from the ogre. He then saw where the men had buried him.

"You caught up to it," Pangolin said.

"It's dead, but I had to ensure that nothing could find the corpse. Instruct your men to do the same. Dig several feet down. Then we must burn it to ashes before covering it back up. Use all the men you need. Also, tell the men to do their best to stay out of the blood. Ogre blood is poisonous."

"Oh, now you tell me." Pangolin laughed, examining his armor. "We found a nearby source of water and I scrubbed my own clean as best I could while wearing it."

"Have Mr. Estus do a thorough cleaning tonight. As with many malevolent creatures of Faë-Land, ogre blood has been known to lessen magical properties."

"I knew you were about to say that."

Traveler returned to his tent. The camp still buzzed with what they had all seen—not one but two ogres from the magical lands, their guide and trailmaster's magical sword, and his powerful shape-shifting dog companion. Traveler and his dog had killed one ogre; the valiant efforts of Pangolin the Berserker and the teams of King Aereth had killed the other. Traveler entered his tent and forcibly flicked his sword. The transparent fire was gone.

Prince Reinborne stood at his tent. "Mr. Traveler, I am not sure what astonishes me more—two carnivorous giants, your magic sword, or your magic dog that can...change into other beasts and back into its normal form, or what we believe to be its normal form." The prince looked at Lady Aylen and King Aereth. "Did you know this about our guide and his dog?"

"We knew, Prince," Aereth answered.

"I saw the dog change before," Lady Aylen answered, "along with others."

"My dog is not magic, Prince. All of his species can do what he can do."

"Species?" the prince asked. "There are more?"

"That is a story for another time, Prince." Traveler noticed Hobbs. "Mr. Hobbs, tell Mr. Pangolin, as they dispose of the ogre, they are to also burn the corpse of the man we lost. No need to take any chances. Where ogres tread, foulness and disease tend to follow."

"Yes, sir."

"How many wounded?"

"The men are fine, sir."

"So we remain, Mr. Traveler?" King Aereth asked.

"We will not make it across the Bridge in time, sire, so we will have to set out tomorrow."

"Mr. Traveler, is this area frequented by ogres?" Gwyness asked nervously.

"No. Have any of you ever heard of an ogre on our lands? We are not in Faë-Land." They could see the anger in his eyes.

Pangolin and some of his men appeared. "Mr. Traveler, my men are saying there are not supposed to be ogres in Avalonia."

"Your men are correct, Mr. Pangolin."

"Yet we have a man dead here in Avalonia from one."

"Only the one man?"

Pangolin nodded. "Yes. Fear. He froze from the shock of the creature before him rather than reacting to its attack upon him."

"Sadly, it will not be the last time we lose men because they are paralyzed by fear of the evil before them, or by awe of the beauty before them."

"Beauty?" Lady Aylen asked.

"Yes, Princess. Fairies can kill too, and they have. Theirs are the lands we enter first when we cross into Faë-Land." He looked back to Pangolin. "Double the guards for tonight."

"What does this mean, Mr. Traveler?" Aereth asked. "We are all thinking it. We believed ourselves to be free of King Oughtred. Did he send those ogres?"

"Sire, there is no such thing as ogres. It is always one ogre. They are solitary and territorial creatures. They never hunt or live with another of their own kind—never. One ventures into another's territory, and it will kill the other and eat the corpse as it would with any other prey."

"The larger one did not seem to mind using the other as a living projectile to attack us," Pangolin noted.

"The creatures appeared just as we were about to head out," Aereth added. "It is as if we are being watched."

"Listen very carefully to me, all. Even if we did not face the murderous intent of the Four Kings of Xenhelm, we would be in constant danger on this journey. I have done my best to communicate that to you all, but I know the full impact of my words is lost on you, as I have been to those lands already."

"It is difficult to fear things that you do not know exist, Mr. Traveler, especially if you are given to bravery," Prince Reinborne said.

"Bravery has nothing to do with this, Prince. It is wisdom. We will fight most of them because we must. However, given the choice, I will avoid the dangers every time. Again, for every encounter we have with these dangers, men on our side will die. We buried another, and I will see to the wounded now as healer."

"No need, Mr. Traveler," the prince said. "I have healers in my camp. They will take that burden from you."

"Very good, Prince." Traveler looked to King Aereth again. "Yes, sire, the ogres were sent here, and it would appear they still possess the means to watch us. How, I do not know, but we will find out. Let me remind everyone: If we encounter the Kings' Caravan or any of their agents, no matter how seemingly benevolent, you are to attack and kill every one of them without hesitation."

"What?" the prince asked. He looked at their faces. "That is madness. We cannot make war on another king in that manner. It is not of the royal code. We would be making war upon the entire kingdom of Xenhelm; they are extremely powerful, with many allies throughout Avalonia."

"You did not tell him, then," Traveler said.

"Tell me what?" the prince asked. "You say they sent the ogres?"

"We will have a very long talk at the campfire tonight, Prince Reinborne." Aereth put a hand on the prince's shoulder. "When we finish speaking, you will be of the same mind, probably more so."

CHAPTER SIXTEEN

Titan's Bridge at Avalonia

Night had fallen after a day consumed with digging ground. The caravan was used to back-breaking work but never the burning and burying of the disgusting corpse of a giant cannibal. Many men remarked that, even dead, the beast emitted "a presence of malevolence."

It was one of the few times Traveler himself made rounds through the camp. The weaponsmaster was hard at work with the heavy weapons.

"Mr. Estus."

"Mr. Traveler."

"I see you are already doing what I came to suggest."

"Yes, our catapult attacks were very ineffective against the creatures. With this change in projectiles, all teams will be able to do the major damage they should. We can even set them afire if needed. My goal is for the teams to be able to kill any creature we encounter with one shot while you and Mr. Pangolin relax on the side."

Traveler chuckled. "Very good. We will stay an extra day for the men to rest. We need to be at our best when we start across the Bridge."

"Is it dangerous, Mr. Traveler?"

"It is both not dangerous and beyond dangerous at the same time. You will soon see for yourself."

All the men welcomed the additional day of rest. At dawn the next day, they set out. There were no advance scouts that day. Traveler led with Pangolin, his Cut-throats behind him, all on foot. The royals followed on horseback. The entire caravan followed with carts and wagons.

It did not take long for everyone to see that the land itself was changing. The green of plants, the trees, and the wooden areas became scarcer. The soil beneath their feet became thinner. By the time there was more light, they saw the entire landscape was solid, dark-gray rock. The elevation increased at a steady slope until they were upon a flat plateau that stretched for as far as the eye could see.

Hobbs realized that they had not seen much of Last Keep—the false one. Prince Reinborne and his men had, but they never did. Now, they would never see it or the real one. During the previous night meal, Traveler had told them that the next town they would reach would be in Faë-Land. Finally, they would see fae-folk. Hobbs smiled to himself, wondering what beings they would encounter first. Then there was the prospect of adding fae men to their caravan. He felt as giddy as Quillen was. For now, they had to get across the Bridge.

No one spoke. Everyone was too anxious. Though there were more lands to travel through, Titan's Bridge was thought of as the official end of the Lands of Man. They had not even passed beyond it but had already encountered and battled both magic and beasts from beyond their realm.

Traveler broke away from them with longer strides. No one had seen the dog. "He is sleeping," is what Traveler had told them. Traveler jogged ahead and then stopped. As they came upon him, they realized they were approaching a cliff. Pangolin and his men reached Traveler first.

"Shall we dismount?" Aereth asked.

The king, Lady Aylen, the prince, and Gwyness did so. They hadn't even reached the edge but were already overcome by the view. Their mouths hung open.

People spoke of Titan's Trail often, but none of the myths and tales matched the true magnitude of seeing it for first time with one's own eyes. The cliff dropped into a chasm so wide that it seemed an unfathomable depth. The sides of the chasm were barely visible in the far-off distance. Each side was lined with unclimbable mountains and a sheer sheet of rock. The bottom was beyond contemplating.

Then there was the Bridge. It was not a land bridge but a ridge, which made sense on sight, as no bridge could traverse the chasm without any underneath supports. However, the path surface was flat and smooth, as if polished, and over each side was the seemingly endless drop into the dark chasm. The Bridge was of the same dark-gray rock as the surrounding mountains, but it was only five miles wide. Such a distance would be considered a mammoth bridge anywhere else in the Lands of Man, but within the chasm, it looked like a mere string. Traveler had already told them it would take the whole day to cross.

"We get to the Bridge from there." Traveler pointed to the left. They saw the descending, winding path. "I wanted you all to see it before we started down. You can see why I wanted us to start early enough so that we would not be on it as the sun set. We should be able to pass without incident. However, as always, we must be prepared for anything."

"Should we not have your dog companion with us, Mr. Traveler?" the prince asked.

"My dog is always with us, Prince. Just because you cannot see him does not mean he is not here. He is—"

"Yes, Mr. Traveler. He is sleeping," Lady Aylen finished his sentence.

"The sooner we start, the sooner we finish."

Traveler walked past them, back to the caravan.

◆◆◆

Not one person was free of apprehension as they moved down the path to the start of Titan's Bridge. Everyone was thinking the same thing: If attacked here, there would be nowhere to go, except over the edge and into a seemingly bottomless chasm. Traveler was already on the Bridge, scouting ahead, looking through a telescope. Pangolin and the royals led the descending caravan to join him.

"Anything?" Pangolin asked.

Traveler put his telescope away into a pocket in his cloak. "All clear."

"Mr. Traveler, if I may suggest, could you walk at a more normal pace? I suspect the men's legs, and my own, are a bit shaky at the moment," King Aereth said.

"I can do that, sire. Here are my instructions: We move and do not stop until noon. Then we will continue on and briefly stop only two times, a couple of hours apart. We should reach the end well before dusk. I will stay several feet ahead of the caravan and continuously watch through my telescope. We will have the rear guard watch behind us at all times."

"I wish it were possible for us to march without any stops," Gwyness said softly.

"Only Mr. Pangolin could do that, and he does not need his armor to do so. The stops along the Bridge will not be long. We stop, drink water, and move. No noon meal today."

"None of the men, Mr. Traveler, I am certain, will likely complain," Lady Aylen added.

The caravan began across. They were not near the edge, but the mind made many conjure up all kinds of possibilities. Quillen looked at the mountains on either side, straining to see if there were any movements at the peaks. He feared an attack by some type of flying creature. He wished Traveler's dog were visible and walking with them. The night before, everyone could not stop talking about the excitement of seeing and crossing the Bridge. Now that they were there, they wished they were anywhere else.

What made their trek even more unnerving was the echoing of their marching. The sounds reverberated all around them. The creaking of the wooden wheels on their wagons and pull carts. The shuffling of their feet. The clanging of their weapons. The tapping of horses' hooves. It was not overwhelming or deafening but made many feel as if they were being followed—or worse, that something was underneath them.

Pangolin carried his axe-mace in his hands. It was not a light weapon, but he wanted to have it at the ready. The archers around him had their bows and arrows ready. The Cut-throats carried their swords.

The march seemed as if it would never end. If not for fear of being caught on the Bridge at nightfall, the distance would have been too much. Traveler raised his hand to stop the caravan and then walked back to them.

"Pass the word that we will wait for a few moments. Drink plenty of water."

"Is it noon, Mr. Traveler?" Lady Aylen asked.

"Yes. We have made it half the distance, Princess."

"It seems that we have been marching forever." Prince Reinborne was as sweaty as they all were, and was not in good spirits. One of his men handed him a canteen. Everyone wanted to get to the other side as quickly as possible. "Must we stop twice more along the way, Mr. Traveler? I believe the men would forego a stop if it meant reaching our destination sooner."

"I will see how the men look, Prince, when we are ready to stop again. In the meantime, think happy thoughts to relax yourself."

The prince grinned. "Happy thoughts? My only happy thought is of the other side of this Bridge. The Kings' Caravan passes across this every three years with one hundred thousand men?"

"I cannot speak of when they began, but I do not believe they have been across Titan's Bridge for many years."

"How do they get across, then?"

"Magic, of course, Prince. A means they have grown very accustomed to using."

Traveler left them to scout ahead. This time he was a mere dot in the distance.

"I really wish he would not move so far ahead of us," Aereth said.

"Our guide is fearless, sire, but not foolish." Lady Aylen drank from her canteen. "His dog is underneath his cloak or tunic somewhere, I wager. Sleeping, indeed."

Traveler walked back. He raised his hand and the caravan began moving forward again.

"Mr. Traveler, was this bridge truly created by the legendary Titan, the Maker of All Mountains, and his magic weapon, the Star Slayer?" Lady Aylen asked. "Wouldn't the actual construction of the Bridge disprove the myth?"

"No," Traveler answered. "The Star Slayer was said to be a celestial war-blade—not one sword but two, the blades a close but equal distance from each other and sharing the one grip."

They moved along at a steady pace. Quillen noticed a shadow at the top of one of the mountain ranges flanking the chasm. The sun was moving across the sky, which meant they were nearing the end. It also meant night would be following.

"Mr. Hobbs, do you think Mr. Traveler will allow us to continue on if the men wish it?"

"How would you determine that, Mr. Quillen?"

"I do not mind moving through the men and asking. We are all anxious to get off Titan's Bridge."

"Last night you were giddy at the prospect of being here."

"I was giddy at the prospect of seeing an ogre until it threw a tree at me."

Hobbs chuckled. "You are learning, lad. No need to ask the men. One of the kings has already suggested the same."

Traveler walked back to the moving caravan. "Continue on," he said as he stood still. The men moved by, and he looked at their faces. "Should we continue rather than stop?" he asked along the column. The men enthusiastically answered in the affirmative.

Traveler walked briskly to get to the head of the column.

"Are we continuing on, Mr. Traveler?" Aereth asked.

"We are, sire. It will take us another three hours to get to the end."

The news was welcome, but it meant they would all need to reach deep to persevere. All were tired from the long walk under the sun.

When Traveler left them later to scout ahead, he moved ahead a much greater distance than he had ever done before.

"Is something wrong?" the prince asked.

"We should be close," Lady Aylen answered.

They neared the end. Traveler's figure grew as they neared him. He stood to the side.

"We are here. Mr. Hobbs, when the last man steps off the Bridge, allow everyone to relax for a bit. Keep an eye on the sun, though."

"Yes, sir." Hobbs smiled.

As the columns passed, Traveler remained where he was. Men asked him if they had arrived. They all smiled or laughed when he told them "yes."

They had made it across Titan's Bridge with no incident.

◆◆◆

The laughter and good cheer returned. Hobbs had the tents for the leadership set up first. Then the fire-lighters did their work so that the cooks could do theirs. Pangolin had two-thirds of the fighters relax, while the others set up the guard perimeter.

Lady Aylen was sitting at the campfire with the prince when the dog appeared from Traveler's tent. The animal had obviously been sleeping. It yawned and shook each leg separately.

"Ah, look what we have here," she said. The animal snarled at her then returned to stretching its fore and hind legs. "I helped your master in his time of need, and you still do not like me." The dog gave her a final snarl, then trotted away.

The prince laughed. "I always remembered you to be exceptional in your ability to bond with animals of all sorts."

"All except for that one."

"Lady Aylen, since our times alone are rare, I did want you to know that I have always been fond of you."

"Yes, Prince. I know."

"Fontaare and Sirnegate have also always been strong allies."

"They have, Prince." She smiled.

"One day, we should—"

King Aereth joined them at the fire.

"We made it," Aereth said.

"For the first time, I feel that our journey has truly begun," Lady Aylen said.

"After that march, I would hope so," Aereth said. "As we sit here and reflect, there was no danger in its crossing. All the fear was from what our own minds conjured."

"I thought the march would never end," the prince said with a sigh. "A bridge that takes a day to cross. Not something I wish to repeat."

Traveler exited his tent, but not as a man ready to relax and settle in for the night. He was a man readying for battle. His real sword was strapped to his back, and he wore leather half-gloves.

"Mr. Traveler, will you not be joining us for the night meal?" Aereth asked.

"Not tonight, sire. I will be joining the night guard."

"I was hoping you could talk more about the journey ahead," the prince said.

"We can do so next time, Prince."

"Are you expecting trouble, Mr. Traveler?" Lady Aylen asked.

"None at all, but I believe the sight of my dog among the men will further calm them. Do instruct Mr. Hobbs that the camp will need more fires. It can get quite cold near the Bridge."

Traveler moved into the men of the caravan.

"It is getting cold," the prince remarked.

"I do hope Mr. Traveler was being truthful," Lady Aylen said. "Maybe we should have set the camp farther away from the chasm."

"Please, Lady Aylen. Say 'the Bridge,' not chasm. We do want a solid sleep free of our wild imaginations." Aereth laughed to himself.

◆◆◆

Traveler moved through the camp. The dog had joined him, and the sight of it did encourage the men.

"Anything wrong, Mr. Traveler?" a guard on the perimeter asked. Another guard stood nearby.

"Nothing at all, men. Continue as you are."

Traveler and the dog walked up the slope to where their caravan had left the Bridge. It was a full moon, so the colossal structure was well-illumination. Traveler pulled his hood over his head as he sat on the ground and grasped his knees. The dog lay down next to him.

Night came and went without incident. Pangolin stood at one of the campfires, drinking hot tea with some of the men. He thought he heard loud talking in the distance. Now he was sure. Two of the morning guards ran to him.

"What is it?" Pangolin saw the fear on their faces.

They led him to the Bridge. Pangolin stopped in his tracks. Though he was a berserker fearful of nothing, his mouth hung open. On Titan's

Bridge was an army that stretched as far as the eye could see, but their path was blocked by not one but two massive boulders. Traveler was on the other side of the boulders, inspecting them; he walked back off the Bridge to the ground so the army could see him with the dog at his side.

"I am sorry, sirs!" Traveler yelled. "The boulders cannot be moved. I do not know what to suggest."

The men looked to be marauders but wore shiny armor and bore weapons fit for only the best knights of a wealthy kingdom.

"It appears you will have to go back the way you came!"

Pangolin and his men were not alone watching the army on the bridge. The women and royals had joined them. Hundreds of men from the camp were gathering too.

The men of the army looked at one other, perplexed as to what to do. "How did the boulders get on the Bridge?" one of them asked.

"I do not know, sir!" Traveler answered. "They were not there last night. I fear there are dark forces all around this region. On our way to the Bridge yesterday, we saw a footprint that could only belong to a giant of at least one hundred feet. We thought demi-Titans did not exist. Sir, your army may be in great danger. I would start back immediately."

Traveler noticed the caravan audience and casually walked to them.

"Mr. Traveler, how large is that army?" Aereth asked.

"They told me ten thousand men, sire, but I know it to be at least five-fold that."

"What are their intentions?" the prince asked.

"They said they heard about us in Last Keep and were coming to join us."

"You do not believe them?" Aereth asked.

"For them to be here now on the Bridge, they would have had to travel on the Bridge by night," Lady Aylen noted.

Traveler smiled. "Yes. They came to kill us. They are not knights. They are marauders in knights' armor."

"Should we leave them where they are?" Pangolin asked Traveler. "Should we not ensure they are unable to follow?"

"They will go no farther. The boulders ensure that. Leave them there. They will eventually have to start back. Marauders are not completely without intelligence. The obvious simply takes them longer to understand. We should set out now."

Traveler walked past them to camp. The dog remained, watching the army. The royals looked at each other with nervousness but followed Traveler.

Hobbs was waiting when Traveler appeared. "Break camp, sir?"

"Immediately."

The caravan set out in half an hour. They were in the same formation, with Traveler at the head. The dog appeared and ran to join his master. The terrain was rocky and barren, with nothing in sight for miles.

"I wonder what manner of beast the dog became to place boulders of that size on the Bridge?" Lady Aylen asked. "I also do not think that army should have been left there."

"These occurrences disturb me greatly." Aereth's face had been pained ever since they had seen the army on the Bridge. "The sheer size of that army and traveling on Titan's Bridge by night. Madness."

"Mr. Traveler!" Lady Aylen called out.

Traveler turned, then walked back to them. "Yes, Princess."

"What are we going to do, Mr. Traveler?"

"Do?"

"Ogres. A marauder army on Titan's Bridge following after us. What waits for us ahead?"

"There is nothing for us to do until we come across the danger. That is all."

"You said, Mr. Traveler, that Oughtred may still watch us somehow," Aereth said. "Do you know how?"

"No, sire. However, the dog and I will find out tonight."

"Find out?" Aereth asked. "Tonight?"

"Yes, we will go and ask the marauder army. It will take them until nightfall to get back across the Bridge. I will ask them at that time."

The royals looked at each other again.

"Are you serious, Mr. Traveler?" the prince asked.

"We will set up camp early, at the threshold to the Mist Mires. We will remain there."

"Are we preparing for battle?" the prince asked.

"No, Prince. We are preparing for anything, as we should always do when we set up camp."

"Mr. Traveler, I cannot say I enjoy your missions."

"Sire, it cannot be helped."

"Mr. Traveler, you are the only one who knows how to get to the magical lands. You should not take this chance," Lady Aylen said.

"I will be careful, m'lady. We must continue on."

♦♦♦

No one in the camp saw when Traveler left. One moment he was in his tent, the next he was gone. High above the land, he was on the back of his dog—three times its normal size with the giant wings of an eagle, flying across the night sky.

♦♦♦

The marauder army ran the final leg of its march across Titan's Bridge. The lead man held a long torch that magically illuminated their way through the night. They were exhausted, but dawn was only about an hour away and they had arrived. Once off the Bridge and up the winding path to a plateau, they collapsed on the ground.

"You failed!"

The startled men rose to their feet. The lead man picked up the torch from the ground. It illuminated a man in a hooded cloak. "We did not fail. Our way was blocked."

"Blocked how?"

"Two boulders that could not be moved, and there was no way around them. We saw them, though."

"We did not send you to see them. My lord sent you to kill them! What should I tell him now?"

"You gave us magic to see our way through the night. Why not magic to remove any obstacles from our way?"

The wizard raised his hands, then lowered them. A new staff was in his hand. He threw it at the man. "You have what you asked for. Go do what you were instructed to do."

"We marched all night! We will rest and set out tomorrow."

"You will set out now! Otherwise, I will strip you of your weapons and armor and your skin from your bones."

The marauders looked at each other. Their leader glared at the sorcerer, but he gestured to his men, who reluctantly followed him back to the winding path to Titan's Bridge.

"If you succeed in your task by tomorrow, my lord will double your payment!"

The leader turned back and howled. He and his marauders had renewed energy. They ran back to the Bridge.

The sorcerer laughed. From nowhere, another staff appeared in his hand, and its tip began to glow. The air around it spiraled as the glow intensified and grew; the light became a portal. A shriek. From the portal tunnel came dozens of knights, followed by King Gervase the Fair on his hippogriff.

"M'lord, they are back on their trail," the sorcerer announced.

"My father has lost his patience. They should have completed their task yesterday."

"What are the king's instructions, m'lord?"

"Follow me back to the Caravan. We send out another army."

"What of them, m'lord?"

"Forget the marauders. They are no longer of any interest."

The portal re-opened and King Gervase turned his magical steed to step back through, with the sorcerer following.

Traveler and the dog watched from not far away in the darkness. He jumped on the back of his winged dog and they flew into the portal at tremendous speed. It closed.

◆◆◆

King Gervase's hippogriff galloped through the portal tunnel. His knights ran along in two columns while the sorcerer floated to the other side. The sorcerer emerged, his eyes yellow. The king and his knights waited.

"Wait here. I will summon the army," King Gervase said to the sorcerer.

Traveler leaped out of the portal and snatched the staff from the sorcerer. King Gervase jumped in his saddle, startled, and the hippogriff shrieked. Traveler knew he did not have enough strength with one hand holding the staff, but he struck with his sword hand anyway. He slashed and severed one of the hippogriff's front talons; the beast reared up, throwing the king.

The sorcerer's yell was of such fury that Traveler dropped the staff to the ground, grabbed his sword with both hands, turned, and swung. As the beheaded sorcerer fell to the ground, a mongoose unwrapped itself from Traveler's neck, jumped to the ground, and immediately changed into the dog. Traveler attacked the knights as the dog rushed into the approaching army. The dog dove and transformed into a worm-like creature, disappearing into the ground.

Traveler defeated fighter after fighter with superior swordsmanship—slashing and impaling. The hippogriff screamed as it flew away and disappeared into the sky. Traveler struck the king's armor but to no effect. The magical armor was too powerful.

"I will kill you, the one called Traveler, and feed your corpse to a nest of hippogriff cubs."

Traveler charged the king, knocking him to the ground. Then, in a wild melee, he struck at the king with all his might. None of his blows could even scratch the king's armor. Dozens of knights, weapons in hand, were almost upon Traveler, yelling battle cries.

"Now you die!" King Gervase cursed at him.

The ground shook and giant tentacles shot up from the soil. The knights were helpless against the attacking giant sand kraken. One man was crushed by a tentacle that smashed him into the ground. Another was crushed by a tentacle wrapping itself around his body and constricting. Most of the knights were swatted away—hundreds of feet into the air and to their deaths.

King Gervase got to his feet and ran to grab the staff on the ground. Traveler saw the space in the king's armor plating near the waist and thrust his sword.

"Mr. Traveler, did you truly believe that you were the first to see the 'weakness' of my armor? While I wear it, I am indestructible!"

A tentacle grabbed the king before he could grasp the staff. The sand kraken slammed the king repeatedly into the ground. They heard him laughing.

Traveler stood quietly and closed his eyes. The sand kraken stopped and began to change. The tentacle became the giant arm of a dog-headed ogre, growing to fifty feet, then more. It yelled and threw the screaming king so fast and so high in an arc toward the heavens.

The dog, in its new form, scooped up boulders in its hands and threw them at the camp in the distance. It was the Kings' Caravan. They were in Faë-Land.

Kings Wuldricar and Renfrey ran into their father's tent.

"Protect the king!" Wuldricar yelled at the sorcerers by King Oughtred's side.

They encircled around him and raised their hands. A force dome enveloped everyone in the tent. As it did, a boulder crashed down on the tent, then vanished. They watched as boulders no less than the size of a horse rained down on the camp. Men, horses, and livestock were crushed to death.

King Oughtred yelled with anger. He pointed his staff at the force dome barrier. It exploded out to cover the entire camp, knocking away all other falling boulders, then disappearing. However, the damage was done. The Caravan was virtually destroyed.

"M'lord." The knight who ran to King Oughtred was practically in tears. "Your griffin is dead."

King Oughtred trembled with anger.

"Where's Gervase?" Renfrey asked, looking around.

The king looked at the sorcerers. "Where is my son?"

The lead sorcerer touched his own forehead. "Oh no!" The man turned white.

Another group of knights ran in. "M'lord, the attackers escaped through a portal. He must have stolen the staff of King Gervase's sorcerer. The animal shape-shifter was with him."

◆◆◆

"Mr. Hobbs." Lady Aylen exited her tent. The camp was relaxed, as it often was in the morning. Men sat at campfires to eat their first meal of the day with their drink, having conversations and laughs.

"Yes, m'lady."

"Did you see Mr. Traveler set out last night?"

"No, I did not, m'lady. It was very late at night, and I had already turned in. He did check in with some of the night guards as he left."

"So here we wait. With no indication as to how long."

"I imagine, m'lady, that he will be back this morning so we can set out."

Lady Aylen looked into the distance at the journey to come. It was a wall of foreboding mist. "Mr. Traveler did say the mist was not a dangerous region, but it does not look so from here. Thank you, Hobbs. Continue your duties. Mr. Traveler leads us, but you ensure the camp runs properly."

"Thank you for saying so, m'lady."

Lady Aylen walked to the king's tent. Aereth and the prince sat at the campfire outside his tent, happily eating and talking.

"Lady Aylen, please join us," Aereth said.

The prince stood and gestured for her to take his seat.

"Thank you, Prince." She sat and smiled at him.

The prince sat and continued his meal. "The king and I were debating as to where we believed our next battle would come. The Mist Mires ahead, the Howling Mountains, my personal favorite, or the Stone Forest."

"Are those the choices, Prince? None of them sound particularly inviting," she responded. "And yesterday. Fifty thousand men, marauders, traveling over Titan's Bridge at night to ambush us from behind. It is quite astonishing. It is more than madness."

"We were discussing this all last night," the prince said. "What are we to do?"

"How is he observing us is my question?" Aereth asked. "We dealt with his spies, but his gaze remains upon us, tracking our progress."

"What does Mr. Traveler expect will happen when he reaches the marauder army on the Bridge?" the prince asked. "Does he expect them to volunteer answers to his questions?"

"I am sure his dog can be quite persuasive, Prince," Lady Aylen said.

"No doubt, Princess. Do you remember what Mr. Traveler said? His dog is not a unique animal, but a species. More of its kind are out there."

"We do not know all there is to know of our Mr. Traveler." Lady Aylen put her cup to her lips to drink, but her ears picked up a low hiss.

"Lady Aylen, is something wrong?" Aereth noticed her expression first.

Their campfire flickered as if a strong wind were acting upon it. The hiss grew louder as the fire expanded. The princess and the king stood from their seats. An image took form. *It was King Oughtred.*

"I curse you!" he yelled. "I curse all of you from where you stand to all of Pan-Earth. The Kings Elder, who have conspired against Xenhelm from before my birth, as did all the Lands of Man, I curse you.

"You have survived all my attempts to wipe you from this world. I thank you for setting my mind right, sending your Traveler and his other-worldly shape-shifter after me. They killed many of my men. You succeeded, Kings Elder. Yours is now the only caravan. Your Traveler and his dog have destroyed mine. You are the Caravan.

"But no matter. The Kings' Caravan will be reborn, and my ultimate purpose for it will be achieved. Until then, since you have taken one of my sons from me, I will task your son to do what so many others have failed to do."

"My son is dead, King Oughtred," King Aereth said.

"Yes, King Aereth. He is, and I will command him to kill you as I send my armies to reduce your kingdoms and all your allies to ashes, as if they never existed. Your petty sorcerers will not save them.

"Your foolish Traveler and his dog have stolen one of my staffs of magic light, but he is unaware of how to use it, unaware that I can control the portals at will. He carries in his hand the very means of his own destruction for he holds the gateway to my armies to spill out upon Avalonia.

"Good day, King Aereth. You will soon be reunited with your son."

The image of King Oughtred flickered away.

"Run!" Lady Aylen yelled.

The fire exploded.

♦♦♦

A portal opened above the plateau to Titan's Bridge. The flying giant dog broke through with Traveler on his back. The animal flew as fast as the winds of a hurricane.

The sorcerer pleaded with King Oughtred. "Please m'lord, we should not send the armies through without—"

"Silence!" King Oughtred yelled.

"M'lord," another sorcerer said. "It is simply that our seeing eye has gone dark, and we do not know why."

King Oughtred turned to his sons. "Ready the armies to march through the Light. No more will we rely on intermediaries to carry out my edict of death."

"M'lord!" Samac stepped forward from the audience of knights surrounding the kings. "May I lead the first attack?"

King Oughtred stared at him. King Wuldricar was not amused, and King Renfrey smiled.

"M'lord, let me lead them. If I am successful, where others have failed, allow my men and me to become full knights of Xenhelm."

"Are you certain? If you fail, your fate will truly be worse than death, for you, your men, and everyone you hold dear."

"King, for great rewards there are great risks. I know what I ask," Samac said with confidence.

"Lead the knights through the Light," King Oughtred commanded the sorcerers. "When the portal opens, have it engulf and render unconscious both man and shape-shifter. The army will march and make their bodies into corpses."

Traveler could see them—the marauder knights on the Bridge many miles away. He held the staff with his right hand as he gripped the mane of his dog with the other. He noticed the staff start to glow.

King Wuldricar waved the foot army through the portal of light. Samac led the first wave of silver knights in spiked armor, draped with the orange and white sashes of Xenhelm. Their swords were drawn. The second wave was armored archers—longbows and crossbows, with quivers on their backs that went from their shoulders to their thighs. The third wave of armored knights carried battle-axes, flanged or spiked maces, war hammers, morning stars, or pikes. The fourth wave was the armored horsemen with lances, spears, and swords.

They marched through the magic portal tunnel. As he stepped through, Samac thought to himself that the Traveler's swordsmanship was no match for his.

"No!" Samac was falling and quickly realized where he was—not on the ground but in the clouds high above Titan's Bridge. He heard the screams of the men; they were all falling to their deaths.

Pangolin stood at the perimeter of the camp with his Cut-throats, their necks craned to look at the sky. They had seen Traveler returning on his flying dog, only to watch them fly straight up as if heading into space. They saw the same atmospheric effect that they had witnessed when King Oughtred magically transported them away from outside Goodmound to the Grass Lands, but this phenomenon was much larger. A hole opened, and they saw the black rain fall. Horror gripped the berserker's face. It was not black rain; it was men, screaming men in armor, falling.

By then, everyone in the camp was on their feet, staring at the sky and watching the falling men. Pangolin also noticed the royals, who looked to be covered in soot. He could not ponder what had happened to them now. He heard the screams of the falling army too clearly.

The fate of Samac and the Xenhelm army was even worse. They fell to their deaths not upon Titan's Bridge but past it, into the chasm. Thousands of knights fell, endless screams into the darkness and the center of the world.

◆◆◆

They were the same battle elves that had hunted them before. However, it was not several or dozens but nearly a hundred of them racing through the portal tunnel on their war wolves. The first three jumped through the exit. They did not even have a chance to know what had happened to them; they were dead. Battle elves and war wolves instantly froze, the air ripped from their lungs, dead and drifting in the void of space above the world.

◆◆◆

A giant white creature sailed through space. It looked like an insectoid whale with six arm-like fins. A translucent film covered Traveler as they flew to the sun itself.

King Oughtred, followed by his two sons, stepped through a portal door and into New Xenhelm, in the heart of Faë-Land Major. The army of war wizards waited in formation—more than two hundred thousand soldiers.

"Open the Light! We march upon all the Lands of Man!"

Five sorcerers stepped ahead of the kings. One raised his magic staff. The circle of clouds appeared, then a light within its center. It grew, and the portal opened.

"Ahh!" the sorcerer screamed as he was instantly vaporized, and the sunburst engulfed them.

◆◆◆

Pangolin stood in shock, numb, silent, as did everyone else. The screams of the falling army were gone, but they were all still trying to grasp the enormity of what they had witnessed. Some men were scanning the sky for Traveler and the dog. They had flown up but had not reappeared.

"Telescope." Pangolin turned to one of his men, a hand outstretched.

"They have returned!" one of his men yelled, pointing.

Pangolin grabbed the telescope and scanned the Bridge. It was the marauder knights returning. The boulders were still in place, but the new army was running to them without slowing down.

"This is our task," Pangolin announced. He threw the telescope to his man and pulled his axe-mace from his back. "If they get past the boulders, attack—arrows, catapults, heavy crossbows. Go!"

The Cut-throats ran back toward the camp.

The marauders screamed as they attacked the boulder with their new magical maces and hammers. They easily shattered the first boulder to pieces, then raced to the next. "Destroy it and leave none of them alive!" one yelled as they shattered the final boulder.

The dust of the shattered first boulder was not yet gone when they heard the berserker's yell. Pangolin attacked the remaining boulder on the other side, striking with the full force of his weapon. The larger boulder shattered in an explosion of pieces, striking all within twenty feet. Now the marauders screamed as Pangolin knocked them off the Bridge and into the chasm.

Metal projectiles hit the marauder army from various distances, knocking men off the Bridge. From the sky, arrows rained down upon them and their flanks. The attack from the caravan was as relentless, as Pangolin jumped through the cloud of the boulder's dust and steadily cut through the men.

Titan's Bridge had been free of blood—until now. It was littered with bodies—those lucky enough not to be sent falling off its edge. Only the marauders at the front had the Xenhelm sorcerer's magical weapons, but Pangolin had dealt with all of them first. More than three-fourths of the marauder army was gone, and the remaining members fled. Pangolin was not about to let any escape; in his berserker rage, he ran after them until he too disappeared in the distance on the Bridge.

"Should we follow?" one of the Cut-throats asked.

"No need," another answered. "None of them will escape alive. The marauders are dead, and they will soon know it."

◆◆◆

Lady Aylen sat in her tent with a faraway look. With a damp cloth, Gwyness wiped the soot from her lady's face and neck. The maidservant wanted to speak but decided to allow her lady to have a moment of peace.

"Pangolin returns!" men called out.

Lady Aylen stood slowly. Gwyness also rose. "Horrible."

"M'lady, they came to kill us."

"They deserved their fate. I am not sorry for them, even those who fell to the bottom of the chasm. How much more of this? When will it end?"

"What is that in the distance?" Quillen's voice rang out.

Everyone came to see. Past the Mist Mires, very far away, they saw an orange glow. It seemed to illuminate the entire horizon with a greater intensity than the sun above.

"Is it a fire?" Quillen asked. "It seems to be growing fainter now."

"Traveler is back!" men called out.

Hobbs was checking on Pangolin when he heard the news. Pangolin sat on the ground and refused any attempts to wipe the blood from his armor. He also refused any food or water. Traveler approached the camp. Hobbs had never seen his master look so exhausted. In the trailmaster's arms was something wrapped in his cloak. As Traveler walked by without saying a word, Hobbs took a peek. It was the dog, but its body was smaller than that of a puppy.

Traveler walked past the royals to his tent. He was not seen for the rest of the day.

◆◆◆

"We must wake him," Lady Aylen said to Hobbs.

It was the next day. The sky had an overcast look, and the air was smoky. Everyone waited for Traveler to awaken. The leadership sat opposite Traveler's tent, outside the tent of King Aereth.

"Yes, m'lady."

No one else dared enter Traveler's tent but Hobbs. The dog would not allow it. Hobbs peeked in first, then stepped in. "Sir?"

He saw a form on the ground. It was Traveler's large woolly blanket. Something moved underneath.

"What is it, Hobbs?"

"Sir, everyone is waiting. They insist on speaking with you."

"Is the air smoky?"

"There was something in the distance yesterday—a large glow. The men said it seemed as if the whole horizon was on fire, but we saw no flames or smoke. The air smelled as if the very land were burning."

"Which direction was the glow? Was it the path to Faë-Land?"

"Yes it was, sir. Very far away."

"I will be out shortly."

"Yes, sir." Hobbs left the tent.

◆◆◆

Traveler emerged from his tent soon after. Hobbs handed him a warm cup of tea, Traveler's favorite morning drink.

"Thank you, Hobbs."

Traveler looked around. The entire camp seemed to have gathered.

"Who is to speak first?" he asked as he took a sip.

Everyone looked at each other. Their faces were as distressed as they had been the day before.

"Mr. Pangolin, you speak first, though I know I do not even need to ask."

"Every last marauder was killed on Titan's Bridge or sent over its edge to his death."

"Are there any signs they were ever on Titan's Bridge?"

"There is still blood there."

"Send a team of men and wash it down. Let us leave Titan's Bridge as pristine as it was before our battle. It is one thing to have the blood of honorable men upon it, but not the blood of their foul kind."

"I will see it done."

"Is it my turn?" Traveler asked. "Or do you want to tell your story next?"

"You should tell yours first, Mr. Traveler," Aereth answered. "I do not think you will like ours."

"That, sire, is exactly what I did not want to hear. It is simple. The dog and I flew to confront the marauder army when it reached the other side of the Bridge. However, on our way there, I decided it would be more advantageous to spy on them than to destroy them. I was correct. One of the Four Kings and their sorcerer was there to meet them. They came through one of their magical portals. We watched and listened. The sorcerer equipped the marauders to destroy the barrier of boulders the dog placed on the Bridge.

"I had planned to follow the marauders and kill them then, but as the Xenhelm King, his sorcerer, and his men walked back through their portal, I decided to do the unwise. I had no idea where the portal would lead. I had no idea if it would render me unconscious as it did the last time. However, I was angry. They were never going to let us be. We flew through the portal. It opened up at the camp of the Kings' Caravan—in Faë-Land."

"They have already reached Faë-Land." Lady Aylen was distressed, as was the king.

"Yes, but no matter. We destroyed many of them on the ground, and my dog dealt with one of the Four Kings. It seemed they all wore magical, indestructible armor, but I had my dog take the form of a giant creature, pick the king's foul body from the ground, and throw him as far as he was able, which for my dog is beyond what you can imagine."

"Into the stars above?" Aereth asked.

"I do not know, sire. Into the stars or beyond the farthest lands of Faë-Land. Who is to say where?

"Then, after I engaged in my own subterfuge to plant some magical spies of my own, we returned through the portal."

"Meaning?" Lady Aylen asked.

"It would seem that it did not matter. We flew back here to deal with the marauders on the Bridge, but King Oughtred engaged the power of the magical staff I stole. I knew what he was about to do, so we flew up past the clouds. The portal opened, and his advance army, all of them, fell to their deaths.

"And there is more. With King Oughtred, there is always more. He sent not dozens of battle elves on war wolves into our realm, but many more. I could not allow that; as I have said before, we do not ever want to fight elves. Our caravan is not yet ready. So we flew into the void of space for the next opening of the portal. They were all killed instantly."

"Into the void of the heavens?" the prince asked. "How? Your animal can fly off the world."

"My dog is not from this world, so yes, Prince, he can. But my wrath was not done. Though I wanted the magic staff for our own advantage, it was far too dangerous to keep, so I did one last thing."

"What?" Lady Aylen asked.

"I threw it into the sun. I did not know he would do what he did."

"He opened the portal again." Aereth looked at his colleagues. They looked sick. "The glow along the horizon."

Traveler had a slightly worried look.

"That was the sun? What could the rays of the sun do to our world?" Lady Aylen asked.

"It could have set the world on fire. Thankfully, the portal closed, so nothing happened."

"However, Mr. Traveler," Aereth said. "From the appearance of the sky and the taste in the air, the glow yesterday, something did happen."

"King Oughtred was about to pass through with his most formidable army. It was an army of war wizards. I saw them, but they did not see where the portal was. They opened it and allowed the power of the sun's fire to enter our world. There is no way for us to grasp the devastation. The fire of the sun is hotter than anything on this world, natural or magical. The Kings' Caravan is dead, and so are the Four Kings."

"There is one other thing," Aereth said with hesitation. Traveler looked at him. "Before you dispatched his armies to their deaths, he appeared here in the camp, a magical form in our campfire. He cursed and threatened us. He said he would send my son to murder us."

"Your dead son, sire?"

"Yes. My son is dead. Oughtred killed him, and I buried him myself. What could he mean?"

"Sire, it does not matter. They are dead themselves." Traveler turned his head to look at the Mist Mires in the distance. "It is over."

"But is it?" Aereth asked. "Does a curse survive the man?"

"King Oughtred the Wicked did say something that I agree with, sire, when he appeared in that form in the fire. And Mr. Traveler made it reality by making the treacherous Four Kings no more. We are the Caravan," Lady Aylen declared.

CHAPTER SEVENTEEN
Mist Mires

Most of the men of the caravan were not warriors. The horror of the former day weighed heavily on them as Hobbs walked through the camp, more to reassure the men than to oversee their nightly work. Even he could still hear the screams of all those men falling so high in the sky into the Titan's chasm. Those cries echoed deep within its darkness, almost never ceasing. Tonight would be a very difficult night for any to get a good night's rest, including himself.

Even Quillen, who would fall asleep right after his nightly scribblings, was wide awake, curled up under his blanket, staring at the campfire.

"So many dead, Mr. Hobbs," he said.

"Go to sleep, lad. Put the nightmares from your mind."

Even with Pangolin's warriors and the prince's new contingent, most of the men were no more than boys. The men whom Bard had left behind were not the Kings Elder's seasoned fighters but rather commoners with little, if any, battlefield experience. That was what Hobbs feared most. The men were dutiful and brave, but for their encounters to date against armies and monsters, if it had not been for the presence of Traveler, his dog, and Pangolin, most would have been slaughtered. The men were not so troubled by the living nightmares of recent as they were by those yet to come.

♦♦♦

The leadership gathered around the nightly campfire. In the minds of those in the caravan, the smoky air was replaced by a cloud of doom. Hobbs joined them as servants served the meals. Prince Reinborne had said little since the aftermath of the events; he appeared overwhelmed by it all.

"If I could suggest, sires," Hobbs said quietly. "We have again entered a state among the men that is worse than poor morale—fear."

"What do you suggest, Hobbs?" Traveler asked.

"I am not certain, sir. Some of the men remain quite disturbed by the sight of thousands of men falling to their deaths in Titan's chasm—if it did have that name. That is what the men are calling it. Now the thought of being hunted by the…undead…"

"Tell the men, Hobbs, that King Oughtred is dead. If he is, any spell he would have cast would be gone too," Traveler said.

"But is that true, Mr. Traveler?" Aereth asked.

"I am stating the most positive likelihood, sire. There is no reason for them or us to believe the worst."

"What if we have deserters?" the prince asked.

"Do you think that likely, Prince?" Aereth asked.

"In light of what your man Bard did, and he was a noble knight, the shock of this may be too much for the men," the prince answered.

"We did not give the men a chance to reconsider their decision back at Last Keep," Traveler reminded him.

"Because there was no need," Lady Aylen countered. "We joined with the prince and his men. We should not ask such a question now."

"We will allay the fears of the men," Traveler said. "I have no doubt. On a journey this long, the men's mood will be a steady up and down, fear and happiness, boredom and exhaustion. I have a new concern."

"Which is?" Lady Aylen asked.

"Sire, I will ask you one question and one question alone," Traveler said. "Do not answer immediately. Think on it before giving your answer."

King Aereth said, "You need not ask the question, Mr. Traveler. I know it already: If we were to encounter my dead son on this journey, would I have the courage to destroy him? The answer is yes. It is not him. He is gone, even if his corpse were to be used for evil deeds. He is gone. I know. I buried him with my own hands."

"We continue the journey."

"Do you truly believe King Oughtred to be dead?" Aereth asked.

"They said they wore invincible armor, but the portal was opened to the rays of the sun. I do not know what invincible means against such a force of the heavens. We cannot trouble ourselves any more with it. Let us set out in the morning to move through the Mist Mires."

"M'lord, the answers to our questions should come soon," the prince said. "If we encounter any other creatures, or marauder armies out of thin air, he is alive. If we see your late son, he is alive."

Aereth's eyes were teary. No one spoke for a while.

"We must all help Mr. Hobbs keep the order and morale of the camp," Traveler added. "The caravan is home." Hobbs nodded.

"I wish, Mr. Traveler, we could use your 'pocket' again," Gwyness lamented.

Traveler smiled.

"Why are you smiling, Mr. Traveler?" Lady Aylen asked.

"I was in Faë-Land, Princess."

"Did you have it with you? Mr. Traveler, please, we need some good news after all this," Lady Aylen said.

"I always have it with me. However, say nothing of it to the men. We have it if we need it. We should not have to use it. Let us make it through the Mist."

♦♦♦

Mr. Estus had done it again. He used chains to fashion a line that connected every last man into two columns as the caravan marched through the Mist Mires. Many held a torch to light the way, but the men did not know why. They could see nothing in the mist. Curiously, ahead of them all, Traveler walked—blindfolded.

The thick, moist mist enshrouded them completely. Neither the sky nor the sun was visible, though it was daytime.

"Mr. Traveler, I do not see how you can lead us through this with your eyes closed." Lady Aylen was annoyed.

"Princess, can you see through the mist?"

"No, Mr. Traveler."

"If you cannot see with your eyes, how could I with mine?"

"Then how are you seeing the way, Mr. Traveler?"

Traveler laughed. "You still do not understand, Lady Aylen. It is why so many have entered and never gotten through. You cannot pass through it with sight. You were not listening to my story before."

"I always listen, Mr. Traveler. It was created by magic to keep intruders out." Lady Aylen closed her eyes, then opened them. She jumped down from her horse.

"Princess?" Prince Reinborne said, concerned.

Lady Aylen walked forward with her eyes closed.

"Have you figured it out yet, Princess?" Traveler asked.

She opened her eyes. She could no longer see their trailmaster in the mist. Her eyes closed. "You feel your way through, Mr. Traveler?" She heard him chuckle.

"Lady Aylen, you should return to your horse."

"I am fine, Prince. I do not like to be beaten at anything. I am going to figure out Mr. Traveler's riddle."

As the march through the mist continued, many of the men swore they heard whispers around them. Pangolin himself almost grabbed his weapon from his back, so certain was he that someone was nearby.

"Stop the talking!" Pangolin yelled at them. He knew what they were thinking. "We are the only ones in the mist! Save your ghost stories of the undead for your nightly gossip around the campfire tonight!"

The ground was damp, almost muddy. Occasionally, they stepped into sloshing water. However, it was never that deep—at the most, up to their ankles. Within the Mist Mires, the passage of time was unclear.

Quillen was closest to Hobbs in the columns. He noticed the mist becoming thinner.

"I think we are there, Mr. Hobbs."

"How can you tell, lad?"

"The air. It is not so wet anymore."

"I think you are right, lad."

They had made it through the mist. The columns emerged from the wall of mist into an empty, barren land. The royals were on horseback, except for Lady Aylen—all waiting. The columns came through and wound around them to form up on the flanks of the Mist Mires. In the distance was a jagged, dark mountain range. Traveler waited on the path ahead.

"Did you solve the riddle, Princess?" he asked.

"It cannot be that simple."

"Why not?"

"Close your eyes and walk straight through until you get to the other side?"

"Are you asking me or stating it, Princess?"

"Stating it."

"Very good."

The royals laughed amongst themselves.

"So, Mr. Traveler, we did not need you for this part of the journey."

"You did not, Prince. And I am happy to turn my guide duties over to you."

"That will not be necessary, Mr. Traveler."

"Mr. Hobbs, set up camp here."

"Yes, sir." Hobbs stopped and turned with a smile.

"Is there something else, Mr. Hobbs?" Traveler asked.

"I do believe there is, sir."

CHAPTER EIGHTEEN
The Howling Mountains

The laughter and horseplay were back. Inside the pocket, the tents were scattered, and with the exception of a few, virtually all the guards were off duty. Prince Reinborne sat with Lady Aylen at the fire.

"I still cannot comprehend this," he said, looking up. "But there is a sky above us. There is a cloud covering us. The air, I feel a breeze, the ground, I can dig into the soil. Is this magical 'pocket' not real?"

"It is real, Prince. It is a hidden realm that we can access free of all others."

"I do not understand, but I am glad we have it. The men needed it most. At least they do not have to fear attacks from the living or otherwise."

"So true." Lady Aylen saw the dog first. "Well, what do we have here?"

The dog exited the tent, yawning. It was much tinier, almost a third of its normal size. It did not snarl at her this time but pranced away.

"He likes the pocket so much, he leaves his rest."

Pangolin took his seat at the entrance barrier into their pocket sanctuary. He watched outside; the path went straight to the Howling

Mountains. The dog reappeared, yawned, and sat in front of the entrance. Pangolin did not bother him. Traveler appeared with a small stool and sat.

"Mr. Traveler, did the dog come here because it knew you were on your way, or did you come because he was here?"

"He told me where he was going and that I had to follow, so here I am. As with many animal companions, they need to see or be near their masters at all times."

"When we leave the pocket tomorrow, does that mean we cannot use it until we get to Faë-Land?"

"That is how its magic works. If we had the right sorcerer, this would not be the case, but we do not."

"The spirits of the men are so lifted within it."

"Yes."

"Mr. Traveler, tell the truth about the Mist Mires," Lady Aylen said. "It could not simply have been to close one's eyes and walk forward. Even without clear vision, a person's natural instincts would be to move forward."

"That is the truth, but there is more. It makes you see shadows and shapes. It makes you hear whispers and strange sounds—all to make you move away from its exit. You experienced its full effect because you relied on me as the lead, and I was immune to its magic."

"What will we encounter in the Howling Mountains?" Pangolin asked Traveler.

"We should see nothing."

"The Stone Forest?"

"The same."

"What does your gut tell you about the fate of Oughtred? I will no longer refer to him as a king, because he was nothing more than a lowly commoner murderer that one would find in any wretched backroad town."

"I truly do not know."

"So much that should not be possible in this world is, in fact, possible. I care to believe he is dead, along with his evil sons."

"We do not know. We may never know until we cross into the magical lands. Maybe not even then."

"Whether alive or dead, one thing is certain. His army is no more, and neither is his Kings' Caravan."

"True, but if he were alive, he could simply remake them."

◆◆◆

King Aereth joined Lady Aylen and the prince at the campfire. Like all, within the safety of the pocket, he was relaxed and of good spirits.

"Ah, Gwyness," Lady Aylen said when her maidservant appeared. "A word." She stood. "Excuse us, gentlemen." They walked into the women's tent.

"Gwyness, will your amulet alert us?"

"It will, m'lady."

"How far away?" Lady Aylen asked.

"I do not know."

"You are supposed to know."

"Know? We both have no real experience with this."

"Gwyness, I do not want to see the king in anguish. He says he can vanquish his son, but I do not believe so. It could fall to you."

"Me? Mr. Traveler and Mr. Pangolin's weapons could destroy it too."

"Maybe, but we are not sure. Your weapons we are sure about," the princess said.

"Mr. Traveler said if King Oughtred is dead, any evil magic he cast would be gone."

"Dead or not, a spell could still survive. You know that. Gwyness, I rely on you. We have both trained all our lives."

"Yes. I hope it was enough."

"You must have faith in your abilities and your weapons."

♦♦♦

The valley through the Howling Mountains was extremely cold. Traveler had the caravan dress for near-winter weather, and they were thankful for his directions. The air got colder as they marched, then the winds began. The winds were fierce and freezing. One could not tell if it was the winds that howled or the mountains, but in either case, they were loud and haunting.

Traveler walked on point, but this time he carried a crossbow. He had his main sword strapped to his back, but no one had ever seen him carry any other weapon, let alone a crossbow. With the unnerving howls, the men wondered if he knew of some danger that they did not.

Quillen always paid close attention to the surroundings for his nightly journal writing. The mountains looked to be made of razor-sharp rock. Nothing could climb them, but he felt as if the caravan was being watched. The howling did not bother him as it did the men, but the feeling of something up there haunted him. He also noticed that Traveler had taken a crossbow. Why?

Ahead, the royals rode on horseback, followed by a contingent of knights and archers, then King Aereth's heavy weapons teams with their weapon carts. Quillen liked being in the first third of the caravan, where he was close enough to the action but not directly upon it should something occur.

Since Hobbs had dropped back to the center of caravan, Quillen felt justified in approaching the man next to him. "I feel as if something is watching us from the top of the mountains," Quillen said.

"We all do."

As with their march through the Mist Mires, they did not stop for the noon meal. Here, too, there was no indication of the time of day. An ominous overcast hung over the area.

Pangolin was the last man in the caravan. He had glanced back several times on the march; he was sure they were being followed but never saw a thing. Behind them was the empty, dark path through the mountains.

From the front, one of the men ran to him. "Mr. Pangolin, the caravan is almost through the Howling Mountains. Mr. Traveler will take us another few miles ahead, and we will set up camp."

"Any incidents?"

"None, sir."

"Good."

"We can see the Stone Forest ahead."

"Interesting." Pangolin noticed the man look past him. He quickly turned around. There was nothing. "What were you looking at?"

"I thought I saw something move."

"What?"

"It was nothing, Mr. Pangolin. It is this place. The men are hearing things that are not there, seeing things. It was nothing. Sorry."

Pangolin looked back at him. The man returned to the front of the column, but Pangolin hesitated before resuming his walk. He glanced back one more time.

CHAPTER NINETEEN
The Stone Forest

Prince Reinborne peered through the telescope for a moment, then passed it to King Aereth. All the royals stood at the edge of the camp, looking out. They were not alone; many of the men were doing the same.

"They look like man-made structures," the prince noted.

The Stone Forest was ten miles away but was already visible, as if it were a shining beacon. While the area of the Howling Mountains was covered by a perpetual overcast, the sunlight was unimpeded past it.

"We need to get closer, Prince," Aereth said. "Then we will be able to see its actual form. What I do not understand is its purpose. Mr. Traveler said these regions were meant to keep people out of the magical lands."

"What was the purpose of the Howling Mountains, sire?" Lady Aylen asked. "Howling, frigid winds are not exactly impenetrable."

"Let us not forget that our guide decided to carry a crossbow for this part of the journey," Aereth noted.

"But was it for where we have been or for the Stone Forest?" she asked.

As Traveler walked through the camp, he nodded and greeted the men.

"Is the dog still sleeping, sir?" a man asked.

Traveler smiled. "He likes to sleep after a good battle. Are we not the same?"

The man laughed. "Yes, sir, we are. However, I do not need an excuse."

The trailmaster finally made his way to the rear of the camp. He noticed Pangolin approaching and smiled.

"Your smile says you were expecting me," Pangolin said. "It means I am becoming predictable."

"Predictable in a good way."

"Do I need to double the guards?"

"No, I do not believe that is necessary."

"I never got a chance to ask if you are as accomplished an archer as you are a swordsman."

"Hardly, which is why I grabbed the crossbow rather than the longbow. I want the ability to shoot a projectile quickly should I need to do so."

"Mr. Traveler, on the walk through these mountains, I felt certain we were being followed or, at the very least, watched. Are we, Mr. Traveler?"

"This entire region, Mr. Pangolin, is meant to fool your senses. There is nothing here. There used to be, in the past, but not anymore."

"What was here before?"

"The paranoia you felt was from the winds. It used to be much worse and made you mistake shadows on the mountains for actual people. The power has diminished over the centuries."

"Magic?"

"What you are feeling, and probably most of the men, is that residual magic. In the past, the Howling Mountains drove people mad and made them run back the way they had come. The name signified not that the mountains howled but that any who entered its domain would run away howling mad."

Pangolin looked up at the mountains. "Was it that way when you previously came through the Trail, when you first went to Faë-Land?"

"Yes, and the caravan I served as healer did run away."

"This power naturally diminished?"

"No. I suspect it has been diminished by magical means. Likely the Kings' Caravan, but I am not certain. However, if it was them, it is not unwise to assume they would have added something malevolent to replace it."

Pangolin nodded. "I do hope you killed that devil, King Oughtred."

♦♦♦

Traveler cautiously moved through the forest of stone. He knelt and picked up something from the ground—a petrified beetle. He squeezed it between his fingers, and it crumbled. As he stood, Traveler grabbed his crossbow from the ground.

"There is Mr. Traveler," Lady Aylen remarked.

They watched their guide and trailmaster approach from the distance. The entire caravan had been waiting nearly an hour for him.

"We were beginning to worry, Mr. Traveler," Aereth said.

"I wanted to be thorough in my scouting, sire."

"I wished you had not gone alone," the prince said with a frown.

"I am never alone, Prince."

Reinborne smirked. "I suppose that is true."

"What did you find, Mr. Traveler?" Lady Aylen asked.

"What I expected," he answered. "Nothing. Let us move through, then we can relax."

"Relax, Mr. Traveler?"

"Yes, Princess. What we have all been waiting for—the final land before we leave the Lands of Man behind."

Lady Aylen smiled. "Thank the Fates. Why do you not seem more pleased, Mr. Traveler?"

"I am pleased, but I leave the grand expressions of emotion to you and the men." Traveler turned to Hobbs, who had joined the front column. "Mr. Hobbs, set up camp as usual when we arrive. Mr. Estus will be busy with his own tasks to get the camp ready for the journey across the Mirage Plains. Make sure no one goes past the perimeter of the camp for any reason. The magic of the Howling Mountains was to repel trespassers, though its power is mostly gone. The magic of the Mirage Plains is to attract. If anyone runs into the realms of the Plains, we will likely not see them again. They will not be harmed, but they may emerge here, a hundred miles away, or any place in between, now, tomorrow, or months from now."

"Mr. Traveler, are you leaving us again?" Lady Aylen asked.

"I am, Princess. This leg of the journey will be led by you and the royals of our Titan's Caravan."

"Are we in danger, Mr. Traveler?" Aereth asked.

"No, sire, not that I am aware of, but I wish to ensure that there is no danger for us to encounter."

The royals did not like his answer—the prince especially so.

"I really wish you would not go, Mr. Traveler," Aereth said. "We are close to the first major crossroads of our journey. We should meet it together, as one. I believe it to be important. If the past is any indication, your instincts are telling you that something is wrong. I wish you would confide in us. You said so yourself: This is a long journey. We should be able to speak of such things."

"I echo the king," the prince said. "We should stay together. What are you hiding?"

"I am not hiding a thing, Prince. As a royal, you should know that leaders do not speak of everything they must deal with. Men follow steady leaders, not those ravaged by the burden of that leadership."

"Do not presume to tell me about your understanding of royal leadership. You are nothing but a commoner, no matter how capable."

"Then I shall leave to do my scouting, and Prince Reinborne the Royal Leader can lead you all through the Stone Forest." Traveler abruptly left them.

King Aereth gave the prince a look. "Prince, there is no cause to agitate our guide and trailmaster," the king said. "He has ably gotten us this far, and I have full confidence in his ability to get us to Atlantea."

"Yes, sire. We should pass through this Stone Forest and be done with it."

♦♦♦

The caravan marched through the Stone Forest.

"Mr. Hobbs." Pangolin came alongside Hobbs. "What happened between the royals and Mr. Traveler?"

"It was Prince Reinborne."

"Let me be blunt. The prince is interested only in Lady Aylen, not in the men or the safety of this caravan."

"Mr. Pangolin, it will sort itself out."

"Sort it out now. Even if Mr. Traveler did not have his magic sword or his dog, I would follow him and so would the men. The prince is nothing."

"Sir, you speak as if you have ill will toward the prince."

"We lost Bard and his men, and the next day we came across him."

"Mr. Pangolin, what are you suggesting? King Aereth has known the prince all his life."

"All I am saying is the prince brings nothing to the caravan. Let him take his men and be on his way. We cannot have any conflict within the caravan now. We have come too far, and we are about to cross into the magical lands. Conflicts on the march lead to men getting killed. You should sort it out, or I will."

The berserker left Hobbs to return to his post at the rear of the caravan.

"What is happening, Mr. Hobbs?" Quillen asked.

"Nothing, Mr. Quillen."

The horses stepped onto the petrified ground of the Stone Forest. It was strange—hearing the knocking of the hooves, then the marching of the men. Everything around was petrified—the grass, the shrubs, the weeds at their feet, the trees that hung over their heads. Lady Aylen noticed what looked to be "stone" insects on the ground.

"How long will it take to get through this so-called forest?" Gwyness asked.

"We do not know. Maybe if Mr. Traveler were here, we could ask him."

The echoing of hooves and marching on the stone surface of the Forest unnerved everyone; it was worse than when they had been on Titan's Bridge. It became an incessant clamoring that prevented them from hearing anything else. The stone trees went on and on; despite the hours, they could not see the end of the forest. The hot sun beating down on them made matters worse. Irritation grew within the ranks. Mr. Traveler had instructed them to return their winter clothes to the storage carts and wagons and to dress light, but they were still sweltering.

"We must stop," Aereth said. "We have too many men in armor. They must rest." He stopped his horse. The others did the same, except for the prince.

The prince brought his horse to a stop and asked, "What if we are attacked?"

"Prince, what of it? If the men are attacked in this heat and in their condition, they would be of little use to us or themselves. We must stop."

"Oh no." Lady Aylen nervously watched an approaching Pangolin as he marched up to them with more than a dozen of his Cut-throats.

"In Mr. Traveler's absence, who is leading the caravan? Is it you?" Pangolin asked.

"You will address me as Prince or m'lord."

"I will address you as neither, but you are welcome to come down from your horse and teach me some manners."

"Mr. Pangolin, you will return to your post," King Aereth commanded.

"We have men who are suffering from exhaustion because you did not have the courtesy to think of them from your lofty mounts. Mr. Traveler always thought of the men. Without them, there is no caravan!"

Hobbs held up his hands. "Mr. Pangolin, please return to your post. This is not the way to handle this. I told you I would sort it out."

"You heard him, and you heard the king!" the prince yelled. "Go back to your post, where you belong!"

Hobbs turned to him. "Prince, please do not speak. I am trying to resolve this matter."

"Do not speak? I am the heir to the Fontaare Kingdom, and I will speak whenever and to whomever I choose. This caravan is being led and commanded by royals."

Pangolin looked at Hobbs. "I am taking command of my men. You can do whatever you wish. We will move ahead and wait for Mr. Traveler."

"How dare you!" the prince yelled.

"Prince Reinborne!" King Aereth yelled back. "Now I direct you not to speak." It was the first time any had seen him angry. He turned to the berserker. "Please, Mr. Pangolin, let us move through the Forest, set up camp, and speak there—calmly. That seems to be the most sensible thing to do."

"Sire, it does. We will continue on." Pangolin shot the prince a dirty look, then led his men back to the rear.

"We rest and then move from this place," Aereth directed.

The royals dismounted. As men got water from the wagons, many looked down the path. The Stone Forest continued for as far as the eye could see.

"When does this cursed Forest end?" the prince asked.

No one answered him.

They were supposed to rest for only a moment, but Hobbs knew they had been sitting for close to an hour. Like many of the men, he felt they were being roasted alive under the sun. Lady Aylen stood from her seat and looked down the path. "We need to get out of this place."

"Yes, we must." King Aereth rose from his seat, too, though he was still weary.

"Maybe this Stone Forest does possess an element of magic. We march until we drop from exhaustion. Even now, we cannot see the end of it. We have marched all day and nothing. The sun above is not even setting."

They looked up at the sky.

"You are right," the prince noted as he stood.

"Mr. Hobbs, get the men to their feet," Aereth directed. "We set out again."

♦♦♦

Gwyness gripped the saddle of her horse to catch herself; she was lightheaded.

"We must stop again," Lady Aylen called out. "King Aereth, you must be correct. This land has magic. Remember what Mr. Traveler told us before. The Lands Between were created to keep people from getting into Faë-Land. That is what is happening to us now."

She stopped her horse, and the royals did the same. The caravan stopped its march as the princess got off her horse. She, too, was about to fall over from heat exhaustion.

"It is a puzzle," she said, "like the Mist Mires. There, you had to close your eyes and walk straight to get through. Maybe to defeat the Howling

Mountains, you had to cover your ears, like the stories of ships besieged by sirens. There is a puzzle here too. Solve it and we get through. I am convinced there is no end to the Stone Forest. You march until you collapse and turn back, or until you die."

"Where is our guide? He should be here!" the prince yelled.

Lady Aylen ignored him. "We can solve this on our own. We must."

The king also dismounted and stared down the path. The Stone Forest went on forever.

"What do we know already?" he asked. "Mist Mires, deceiver of the eyes. Howling Mountains, former enchanter of the ears. Stone Forest and Mirage Plains left," he mused.

"What sense is being deceived now?" Lady Aylen asked.

"We are being roasted under a sun that never moves from its spot in the sky above us," Aereth said as he looked up.

"The sun is not real," she said.

"Then maybe the heat from it is not real," Aereth said.

"M'lady!" Gwyness yelled.

Lady Aylen bolted away. "I will not be tricked and kept from getting out of this place!"

She heard people calling after her but ignored them. As she ran, the air around her cooled. She stopped and laughed.

"She is gone!" the prince yelled.

They had all seen the princess run down the path, stop, and then vanish. The prince ran down the path.

"Prince, do not follow!" Aereth yelled.

He ran back to them. "Where is she?"

An expression of puzzlement came over King Aereth's face. "She laughed."

"What? She laughed? What does that mean, sire?"

"We are already out of the Stone Forest!"

It was a vast green field. There were no trees, but in the distance, Lady Aylen saw a bluish barrier that went straight to the heavens. She knew what it was: the threshold into the Mirage Plains.

"Beautiful, is it not?"

She turned to see King Aereth walking up to her.

"It is, sire," Lady Aylen said with a smile. "Who do we wager will—" Maiden Gwyness appeared. "Who do we wager will appear next?"

Before the king could answer, Pangolin appeared, then, in a moment, all his warriors began to appear. The berserker led them to the royals. Quillen, Hobbs, the knights, Prince Reinborne, then the rest of the men appeared on the plains.

Hobbs instinctively carried out the task of identifying all the caravan leaders to get a count of the men.

"Lady Aylen, you solved the puzzle of the Stone Forest."

"Thank you, sire."

"Mr. Traveler!" a man called out.

Traveler approached from the direction of the Mirage Plains, the dog at his side.

"Mr. Traveler. Where did you come from?" the princess asked.

"I was wondering when you would come through," he said.

"Pardon me," Lady Aylen asked. "You mean you purposely left us in there?"

"No, but I had a task to complete and thought you would have been waiting for me by the time I returned rather than still being within the realm of the Stone Forest. Who solved it first? You, sire, the princess, or Mr. Pangolin? I knew the answer would come to one of you based on the qualities of the previous regions we passed through."

"You were testing us, then, Mr. Traveler?" Aereth asked.

"No, sire, but it was a good exercise for you all, nonetheless."

"One escapes the Stone Forest, under its baking sun, by running through as if neither sun nor heat are there. And, yes, Mr. Traveler, I solved the puzzle," Lady Aylen said.

"It is that kind of reasoning from all that will aid us in the magical lands. Mr. Hobbs!"

"Good to have you back, sir," the steward said, smiling. "I will have the camp set up within the quarter hour."

"Good."

Hobbs went about his duties to direct the men.

"What now, Mr. Traveler?" Lady Aylen asked.

"We will plan our course across the Mirage Plains. However, before that, we need to address the structure of the caravan."

"What does that mean, Mr. Traveler?" Prince Reinborne asked.

"Yes, what does that mean, indeed, Prince?"

"We are at the threshold of the magical lands. There is no need to make any changes to the structure of the caravan. We are here."

"Prince, separate your men from the camp. You will be allowed to follow, but no longer as part of the main caravan. Also, your camp will be separate from ours. When we set out, you will form up at the rear and follow. You can keep up with us, or not."

"Mr. Traveler, there is no reason to behave in such a punitive way. People handle adversity differently. If I offended you, I apologize."

"Prince, it has nothing to do with me. It has to do with the men, your party and ours. When we lost Mr. Bard, which I am sure you have heard of by now, I was not concerned by the loss of manpower, but the effect on morale. In light of the dangers we have faced and will face, we must be especially cautious about those who join the caravan. A caravan can be a fragile thing, and its morale is essential to keeping it stable. Ultimately, it is the caravan that will see us through.

"I made it a point, and promised our steward, to fully scrutinize any newcomers to the caravan. This was to avoid any repeat of the situation with Mr. Bard suddenly leaving because there were clear signs of trouble. So, Prince, I have been watching you. I have observed that you do not command the respect of your own men; therefore, you have lost your standing within the caravan. We need them, but we do not need you. I do not care about your relationship with the Kings Elder or the alliance of your kingdoms. It is only because of that relationship that I allow you to stay here at all.

"You are quite preoccupied by status—commoners versus nobles and royals. That is a dismissive and dangerous trait to have on a journey such as this. I am preoccupied by value and respect. You offer no value to this caravan whatsoever. And you do not have the respect of the men. Every man and woman in this caravan must have the respect of the men. Every member of the leadership must be able to take on any task for the good of the caravan, no matter how menial. Even the king has helped with basic chores. You can follow, but you are no longer welcome within the camp of Titan's Caravan."

"Do you really want to cut your caravan in half, Mr. Traveler?" the prince asked, holding his anger at bay.

Traveler ignored his question. "We make camp here for a day. Inform me of your decision by tomorrow morning. Tell me if you wish to follow—or return to Avalonia, which I recommend. That is all, Prince. You can go."

CHAPTER TWENTY
Mirage Plains

What should have been glee at the reality of being at the very threshold of the magical lands was instead filled with uncertainty and concern. Again, the men spoke in hushed tones amongst themselves.

"What does this mean?" one man asked.

"We have lost half the caravan again," said another.

Prince Reinborne had moved his five thousand men to a separate camp, which flew the Fontaare flags high from multiple poles.

Traveler watched their movements from his tent.

The king approached him with a downcast expression. "Thank you for your words, Mr. Traveler. The words stung, but you were correct nonetheless."

"It is not necessarily a loss, sire. This is how it will be in the magical lands too. There will be parties and individuals whom we will take into our main camp, and there will be others who will have the privilege of falling in behind the lead of our caravan."

"Yes, of course. I hope my standing has not fallen in the eyes of the men."

"Not at all, sire."

"Does anything else trouble you?" King Aereth asked.

"No, sire."

"It would seem that we are not as strong a party after the Stone Forest as we were before."

"None of you should be troubled, sire. We have a good size already, and there will be plenty of opportunities to grow. What's most important is the ability of the men in our caravan, not the number of men."

"So, if our caravan was indeed halved, it would not be a concern?"

"Not at all, sire. My experience on long journeys such as ours is the complement of a caravan grows and shrinks as it travels. There is nothing unusual here."

"And we still have to take on our fae members."

"Yes, indeed, sire."

"That should lift the men's spirits, especially Mr. Quillen's."

"Hopefully, sire, you will not stay melancholy over losing your colleague, the prince."

"Prince Reinborne has been a loyal ally and friend to our kingdoms since he could walk. We will never regret our support. I do regret and apologize for his behavior with the men. That is unfortunate and unacceptable. Your decision is a just and wise one."

"Sire, always remember that the most important commodity on this caravan is not me, my dog, my sword, Mr. Pangolin and his magical armor, or you. It is the men."

"Certainly, that is the truest thing that can be said."

Hobbs appeared, having made his rounds. "Sir, sire, I will ready our nightly meal and meeting."

"Very good, Hobbs."

"Mr. Hobbs, ensure the men know that I am sorry for any role I may have played in the prince feeling that he could behave the way he did towards them," the king said.

"Sire, the prince is the only one to blame for his behavior. And I did so already," Hobbs said, smiling.

"Are we meeting here, sire?" Lady Aylen came from her tent, accompanied by Gwyness.

"No, m'lady," Hobbs answered. "I am preparing the night meal for our meeting shortly."

"There is no hurry at all, Mr. Hobbs. We can surely converse here until then."

Hobbs nodded and dashed off.

"Well, Mr. Traveler, tell us more about the intriguing prospect of acquiring men for the caravan from within the magical lands," Lady Aylen prompted.

"Before we discuss that, may I?" Aereth interjected. "Mr. Traveler, can you give us an account of where you went when you left us and what transpired? We emerged from the Stone Forest, and you were already through, meaning you either passed by us without being seen or you came from the Mirage Plains themselves."

"I had to gather information, sire."

"From where?"

"Faë-Land."

"Mr. Traveler, were you and the dog disappearing into other lands again without us?" Lady Aylen asked.

◆◆◆

The Fontaare camp had three times as many guards as the Traveler camp. Sentries were stationed directly around the camp, more in a perimeter that encircled the camp ten feet out, and roving guards patrolled the area beyond that. In the plains between the Stone Forest and the Mirage Plains, the sky changed from day to night every hour. The guards spent most of their time looking up at the transitions.

A Fontaare guard marched around the camp's outer perimeter. He stopped, seeing something in the distance, not from the Stone Forest or the Mirage Plains barriers but from the same open plains between them. The figure looked like that of a woman.

◆◆◆

Hobbs sat at the campfire, relaxing with his pipe. "What are the scribblings for tonight, Mr. Quillen?"

The young man sat at a nearby fire. Most of the men around them were already sleeping.

"We are in a realm that changes from day to night to day by the hour, Mr. Hobbs." Quillen smiled. "I cannot wait until we get into the real magical lands."

"Are you sure, Mr. Quillen? You have not enjoyed the few creatures we have encountered already."

"True, Mr. Hobbs, but I will get over my fears. I must. How else can I become the world expert on such creatures? I must face them, record their descriptions, peculiarities, and habits—"

"And live."

Quillen laughed. "Yes, Mr. Hobbs. That is a given, but I undoubtedly will."

"Ah, the certainty of youth. I remember it well."

One of the guards approached Hobbs. The steward removed his pipe from his mouth as the man bent down.

"Mr. Hobbs, we may have a situation."

Hobbs jumped to his feet and took the guard away from the men. Quillen watched intently.

"What situation?"

"Some of us believe that the Fontaare camp is about to depart, Mr. Hobbs."

"How do you know?"

"They have a few tents erect, but all else is packed up. From what we can see, they are waiting. We think they plan to march on soon."

"March where?"

"Into the Mirage Plains."

"Let me see for myself." Hobbs looked at Quillen, who he knew would try to follow. "Remain here, Mr. Quillen, and continue with your writings."

The guard led the way. They arrived at the perimeter, where two other knights were watching. Pangolin and another warrior were also there.

"Mr. Pangolin."

"Mr. Hobbs. What is our prince up to?"

"I cannot fathom him rushing off into the Mirage Plains unaccompanied. They will get lost."

"Let us wait and see. It will be daytime again soon enough."

♦♦♦

"Mister Estus, come quick," one of the camp musicians called. Estus had just found the perfect spot for his night's sleep.

"You must be joking."

"Mister Estus." It was another one of the Brothers Brimm.

They were calling out but in hushed voices. He grudgingly got up. The weapon wagons had many guards on continuous duty. "No sleep for you it would seem, Mr. Estus," one of them said.

"Maybe they plan to sing you to sleep," another said.

He ignored their joking and walked to where the musicians waited. It was not the outer perimeter, but he could see fine despite the sky darkening with night.

"A woman, Mr. Estus," one of the musicians said.

Estus watched the woman reach the Fontaare camp, meet with two guards, speak for a bit, and follow the guards into their camp. "What is happening?"

"Should we tell Mr. Hobbs or Mr. Pangolin?" a musician asked.

"Tell them what?"

"What do we do?"

"They are under our auspices, so we will march in there and find out."

"Mr. Estus, we cannot do that."

Estus was already walking to the Fontaare camp, the Brothers Brimm following.

The woman was led directly to Prince Reinborne's tent. She was thin and very tall, wearing a shiny silver dress and a band across her forehead. An ancient being but far from elderly. Her silver hair was braided elaborately, indicative of a royal.

Prince Reinborne stood, flanked by his biggest knights. The woman walked to him slowly, as if her legs were longer than they appeared.

"Good day. How may I address you?" the prince asked.

"I am the noble representative of the Kingdom of Magica within Faë-Land. Do I speak with the leader of this caravan?"

"You do," Prince Reinborne answered.

"The caravan of the elder human king, the elfess, the berserker with the weapon and armor of magic, the bearer of a star-sword, and the animal shape-shifter?"

"Yes, you do. We are Titan's Caravan."

"Titan's Caravan? Amusing. I have given your man a gemstone to carry you across the Mirage Plains. It will guide you through our lands and to Atlantea, which is what I am told is your destination."

"It is."

"I observe that you have done as instructed."

"Yes, we are prepared to depart. The other camp of commoners has decided to remain behind."

"Move quickly, as the gemstone's magic is temporary."

"We are grateful for your aid, mistress."

"It is what we do. We did the same for the Xenhelm Caravan twenty years ago. We do it for you now. Move quickly before the next setting of this realm's sun."

◆◆◆

Estus hurried through the camp, waking some men with the sound of his feet. He saw Traveler at his tent and ran faster. "Mr. Traveler, I must tell you."

"Mr. Estus, tell me what?"

Before the forge could answer, a man yelled from the perimeter. "Mr. Traveler!" Others called out his name too.

Traveler dashed to them. The commotion alerted the women and the king, who emerged from their respective tents and followed. At the perimeter, they saw the Fontaare party running into the magical barrier to the Mirage Plains. Traveler turned to see Estus stop next to him, breathing hard.

"Mr. Estus, speak."

"Some of the men saw a noble woman appear and walk into the Fontaare camp."

"What woman?" Lady Aylen asked.

"Mr. Estus, continue," Traveler said.

"We snuck into their camp. No guards were posted. The woman may have been an elf or fairy; she seemed to glow. Prince Reinborne pretended to be the leader of our caravan."

"Undoubtedly, she assumed so because of their royal flags flying," Traveler surmised.

"The woman gave them a magic gemstone she said would guide them through the Mirage Plains and all the way to Atlantea. She said she had done the same for Xenhelm. She said she was from the Kingdom of Magica."

"Magica, Mr. Traveler?" Aereth asked.

"It is the first city one reaches after leaving Faë-Land Minor on Titan's Trail, sire. However, the fact that she said she was of their kingdom means nothing. Many fae claim to be from there when they speak to humans. What else, Mr. Estus? What did the woman look like?"

"She was very tall. Her dress was white. She had a golden band on her head. Very long braided hair, like a princess, down her back to her ankles."

"A fae noble. What else, Mr. Estus?"

"Are we going to do anything, Mr. Traveler?" Aereth asked as they watched the last of the Fontaare party disappear through the magical barrier to the Mirage Plains.

"Do what, sire? We do not need a magical gemstone to get to Atlantea. We know the way already."

"You know the way, Mr. Traveler," Lady Aylen corrected.

"Mr. Estus, anything else of value?"

"I am not sure."

"Think, Mr. Estus. Even something small could be of immense value to us."

"Yes, Mr. Traveler. She knew us. She referred to you and the dog, Mr. Pangolin. The king. She also said the 'elfess.' What is an elfess, Mr. Traveler?"

"I will tell you later. Anything more, Mr. Estus?"

"I—I cannot think of anything more, Mr. Traveler."

The magical barrier to the Mirage Plains turned bright red.

"I told you that I cursed you! I told you that you would never leave the Lands of Man! I live, but you die! No more intermediaries. I destroy you and your caravan with my own hand!"

The voice that echoed from the magical barrier was that of King Oughtred. The red of the barrier diminished and returned to its lightning-blue color. Every man in the camp was awake and on his feet, watching in fear.

"What happened?" Lady Aylen asked.

"Mr. Estus, I want you to go to your weapon wagons and do the same as before. Long chains to bind the horses and to connect each man of the caravan together. Mr. Hobbs, get the men ready to march immediately."

"But, Mr. Traveler, what just happened?" Aereth asked.

"Prince Reinborne and his men have taken the wrath of Oughtred's curse upon themselves. We are not waiting another moment. We must move now."

◆◆◆

As the camp hastily packed up, Traveler appeared with his sword in hand. They had seen Traveler's magic blade engulfed in an almost translucent blaze; this time it was more intense.

"Keep up and stay together!" he yelled, then bolted through the magical barrier and into the Mirage Plains with his dog at his side.

The royals galloped forward, horses chained from saddle to saddle. Immediately following were Pangolin and his Cut-throats, each holding a long chain with their free hand, their weapons in the other. The men held one long chain from the first man to the last in their column. Into the magical barrier they went.

It was a strange experience none would be quite able to explain. It was similar to being submerged in water—very dim, all the sights with a wavering quality. The sights ahead changed from wooded area to dense forest to riverbanks. It appeared as if they were running straight forward, then downward, then upward, winding around. Pathways appeared above them where the sky should be, then at their sides. Suddenly they were through; they emerged into another large, open green field, this one in a wooded area with massive trees towering above them and a mountain in the far distance.

One of the last men through turned and screamed.

Everyone turned and immediately saw them. Other men screamed or jumped. Levitating in the air were the bloodied bodies of what had to be the five-thousand-strong Fontaare party. "The prince's final gift to his men—their needless deaths."

The dog made a snapping sound; Traveler saw the woman first, appearing from nowhere.

"That is the woman, Mr. Traveler!" Estus yelled.

The very tall, thin woman in the luminescent silver dress, wearing a band across her forehead, stood before them. "You!" she cried.

Pangolin acted instinctively, flinging a dagger from his side into her neck. The fae woman's eyes widened in shock. She grabbed the growing wound on her neck but made no sound. She disappeared into thin air.

All the levitating bodies tumbled to the ground.

◆◆◆

They ran from the wall of falling bodies. Then the land itself opened up and swallowed the corpses, and no trace of them remained. Fearful that they, too, would be absorbed, the men quickly backed away from the barrier wall of the Mirage Plains.

"What was she?" Pangolin asked their guide.

"A fae sorceress," Traveler answered.

"Did I kill her?"

"You did. She should have resisted the temptation to see her evil complicity."

"So the prince took the brunt of Oughtred's evil spell," Aereth said sadly. "So many poor men. Needless deaths."

"Their bodies will forever be a part of the magical earth of this region."

"We all would have died had we gone first," Lady Aylen said.

"No, Princess, we would not have. We would have been immune from the spell, and so would the prince and the men of Fontaare had they remained part of our caravan. His own pettiness became his death sentence."

"How would we have been immune, Mr. Traveler?" Lady Aylen asked.

"I acquired a bit of magical protection for us all. But it does not matter now. Put it all from your minds. Mr. Hobbs!"

Their steward moved quickly to him. "Yes, sir?"

"Set up camp there," Traveler said as he pointed to an area nearby. "When that is done, the leadership will meet here. Give the men a chance to recover from the shock of the prince and the Fontaare party."

"Yes, sir."

"Assure them that they are safe here."

"Yes, sir. I will see to it."

Hobbs oversaw the set-up of the camp. He realized it was the first time he had done so in the new realm. He looked up at the sky. It was the same sun of their world, but here it looked different—magical.

"We have arrived, finally," Traveler declared to the gathered leadership. They stood together apart from the camp under one of the giant trees. "The Lands of Man are behind us. Think of it no more. Look around us now."

They all did so. Beyond the shimmering lightning-blue magic wall of the Mirage Plains, the sight was breathtaking. They saw the towering, green, moss-covered trees, larger than any they had ever seen. As the earth continued from the magical barrier, it became lush green grass into the distance. The sky was a perfect blue, filled with massive, billowing white clouds that looked solid enough to walk upon. The sun shone with a strange rainbow-like hue. Finally, on the horizon was a large, solitary mountain. Now they could see another threshold, another forested area, around it.

"We are in Faë-Land," Traveler said.

"At last," Lady Faylen said, smiling wide.

"There is much for the dog and me to do in preparation. I leave you here."

The leadership looked at each other in surprise.

"Leave us here, Mr. Traveler?" the king asked.

"Where are you going, Mr. Traveler?" Lady Aylen asked. "What of this fae evil sorceress? Are others in wait for us?"

"You are safe, as even now, you are under the magical protection of this realm. It absorbs the dead and prevents evil acts of magic. The corpses are gone, and the fae sorceress could not have harmed us. Though the reverse was not true for her.

"I said to you that the Lands Between was meant to keep humans from the magical lands, but it was also created by the fae empires out of compassion for our lands. The Mirage Plains is our common name for the barrier, but the fae have a more sinister name for it because it is also intended to keep them from our lands. Without it, fairies would have overrun our lands eons ago—or goblins, orcs, or other evil fae races would have conquered us, or worse, the ghostly or soulless creatures of the Necropolis. As a boy, I always wondered why more fae had not reached our lands. This is why, and there would be no Lands of Man, even with our sorcerers and armies, without it."

"But where are you going, Mr. Traveler?" Lady Aylen asked. "Why?"

"What shall I have the men do, sir?" Hobbs asked.

"Enjoy the brief respite. However, that is not the reason you must stay here. All of you must get acclimated to the realm, so you will stay here until you do. You will experience many magical effects, but do not panic. It will all pass, and none will harm you in any way. The changes must occur for a time, then you will be yourselves again."

"Mr. Traveler, I don't understand what you just told us," the princess said. "And I am certain that I speak for all of us."

Traveler smiled. "You will see, Princess. All you need to remember is to stay within the circle, remain calm as the effects of being in the magical lands for the first time come upon you, and get plenty of sleep."

Lady Aylen was about to ask for all of them, but Traveler simply pointed. They saw a white line in the earth, encircling the area where the entire caravan stood.

"When I return, we will make our way through the lands of the fae. We will seek out the fae members we need for our main party, add allies to the general caravan, and finally set out through Titan's Trail for Atlantea. Then, our journey will truly begin. Treasure for us, and fantastic beasts for Mr. Quillen to sketch in his book. I will see you all in a week—a fae week, which in this realm may be a week or three."

The dog transformed into a giant white hawk with multi-colored wings like a peacock. Colored plumed feathers sprouted from its head, and its eyes were the brightest blue any had ever seen. This was the true fauna, flora, and lands of this place. Not merely a giant hawk, but so much more. Traveler mounted the hawk and both flew high into the sky, then disappeared into the clouds.

The Fabled Quest Chronicles continues in Book Two: ***In the Shadow of the Kings***.

THANK YOU FOR READING!

Dear Reader,

I hope you enjoyed **Through Titan's Trail**.

Can You Write Me a Review?

If you enjoyed **Through Titan's Trail (Fabled Quest Chronicles, Book 1)**, I'd greatly appreciate an honest review on one or more of the following sites:

amazon **BARNES & NOBLE BOOKSELLERS** **kobo**

goodreads **iBooks**

Reviews are the best way for readers to discover good books. My writer's motto is simple: "Readers Rule!" Thanks so much.

Always writing,

Austin Dragon

CONTINUE THE ADVENTURE

Get Your Next *Fabled Quest Chronicles* Books!

♦*Through Titan's Trail* (Fabled Quest Chronicles, Book 1)
♦*In the Shadow of the Kings* (Fabled Quest Chronicles, Book 2)
♦*Comes the War Wizards' Wrath* (Fabled Quest Chronicles, Book 3)

♦*Fabled Quest Chronicles Box Set* (Books 1-3)

Also by Austin Dragon

See all my books in fantasy, science fiction, and horror: http://www.austindragon.com/books

Want to know when the next *Fabled Quest* novels come out? Sign up to my VIP Readers' Club! Click **HERE** to get started: http://www.austindragon.com/be_a_vip

ABOUT THE AUTHOR

Austin Dragon is the author of the new epic fantasy adventure *Fabled Quest Chronicles*, the *After Eden* Series, including the *After Eden: Tek-Fall* mini-series, the classic *Sleepy Hollow Horrors*, and the cyberpunk detective series, *Liquid Cool*. He is a native New Yorker, but has called Los Angeles, California home for the last twenty years. Words to describe him, in no particular order: U.S. Army, English teacher, one-time resident of Paris, political junkie, movie buff, Fortune 500 corporate recruiter, renaissance man, dreamer.

He is currently working on new books and series in science fiction, fantasy, and classic horror!

Connect with Austin on social media at:

Website and blog: http://www.austindragon.com

Twitter: https://twitter.com/Austin_Dragon

Pinterest: http://www.pinterest.com/austindragon

Google+: https://google.com/+AustinDragonAuthor

Goodreads: https://www.goodreads.com/ADragon

Other books by Austin Dragon

See all my books at: http://www.austindragon.com/books

AUSTIN DRAGON